COURTING
TROUBLE

KATIE
ROSE

BANTAM BOOKS

New York Toronto London
Sydney Auckland

COURTING TROUBLE
A Bantam FanFare Book / April 2000

IBSN 0-553-58139-2

Published simultaneously in the United States and Canada

Bantam Books are published by Bantam Books, a division of Random House,
Inc. Its trademark, consisting of the words "Bantam Books" and the portrayal
of a rooster, is Registered in U.S. Patent and Trademark Office and in other
countries. Marca Registrada. Bantam Books, 1540 Broadway, New York,
New York 10036.

PRINTED IN THE UNITED STATES OF AMERICA

OPM   10 9 8 7 6 5 4 3 2 1

AFTER-HOURS MISCHIEF

"I did promise not to seduce you while you were working here," Charles said. "But, Winifred, it's after hours."

He kissed her, a soft brushing of his lips . . . a kiss meant to question as much as it did to seduce. Winifred sighed, unable to resist its potency. She had waited too long, wondered too long, wanted for far too long. Sliding her hands inside his coat, she felt the crispness of his shirt beneath her fingers, the smooth satin of his vest, and the firmness of his hard muscled body.

Feeling her response, Charles turned her in his arms, determined to fully enjoy his plunder. He'd meant to simply stake his claim, to move their relationship to the next level, but somehow things had gotten quickly out of hand. Winifred was surrendering, every inch of her body pressed against his. The buttons of her prim dress were hard against his chest, while her soft breasts teased him alluringly. A hot, throbbing arousal pounded within him as he realized his little student was more than ready for the next lesson. . . .

BANTAM BOOKS BY KATIE ROSE

A HINT OF MISCHIEF

A CASE FOR ROMANCE

COURTING TROUBLE

In dedication to Elizabeth Cady Stanton, Susan B. Anthony, Myra Bradwell, Lavinia Goodell, and all other incendiary females who fought for our equality. Well done, ladies.

Special thanks to Stephanie Kip, Linda Cajio, Marlene Murdock, and Judy Spagnola for their help, talent, and support.

"A gentleman should never lower the intellectual standard of his conversation in addressing ladies. Pay them the compliment of seeming to consider them capable of an equal understanding with gentleman. You will, no doubt, be somewhat surprised to find in how many cases the supposition will be grounded in fact, and in the few instances where it is not, the ladies will be pleased rather than offended at the delicate compliment you pay them. When you 'come down' to commonplace or small talk with an intelligent lady, one of two things is the consequence: she either recognizes the condescension and despises you, or else she accepts it as the highest intellectual effort of which you are capable and rates you accordingly."

—OUR DEPORTMENT (1882)

COURTING
TROUBLE

⌐ *New York,* 1874

MISS APPLETON, while I agree that your application is perfect, your essay well written, and your desire noble, I'm afraid we cannot accept you at this time. Unfortunately, our enrollment is complete, and we have already exceeded our allotment of *females*. I wish you every success in your endeavors."

Mr. Grimsby, the dean of the college, settled back into his chair with a smirk. Although the woman before him was comely, with burnished gold hair, hazel eyes, and elegant features, he could not allow himself to be influenced by her looks. He had to stop this nonsense and put these new women in their place. What earthly benefit was it to be male if women had all the same advantages? Patting the belly that peeked through his vest, he did not see the sparkle of determination that came into the young woman's eyes.

"Mr. Grimsby." Winifred Appleton placed her hand over his to still the impatient tapping of his pencil. "I know your college is exemplary. The academics are renowned, and the law school unmatched. It is for that reason I wish to attend. I think my credentials speak for themselves. There is no doubt that I can do the work. I have already researched quite a few cases, documented here before you. I have excellent references. And unlike many of your male students, I can pay full tuition immediately. Given that, I fail to understand your hesitation. I am only one more person."

The dean of the prestigious school turned an interesting shade of purple. He stared at the elegant hand covering his and noted the simple but expensive emerald ring she wore, then raised his eyes to the woman sitting before him. His stern gaze softened to a grandfatherly expression.

"Miss Appleton, your ambition is noble. I know that times are changing, and the suffragettes are determined that women should go to college, vote, even wear pants, for God's sake! It is all unseemly, to say the least. But surely you do not think to ever pass the bar or practice law? The entire notion is ridiculous! Now, be a good girl and go home, find yourself a nice husband, and have children. You will soon be so busy, you will forget this nonsense."

He smiled indulgently, convinced he had given her good advice, so he was astonished to feel her surprisingly strong hand tighten on his.

"Sir, I understand these ideas are new," Winifred gritted, "but women need other women to be their voice in the courtroom. Do you realize that today in some states, women cannot hold property, have no rights, and are legally considered little more than chattel? Good heavens, those of us who are born female are looked on as children, indulged, and smiled at, but we are never treated as equals. Our options are limited, our choices in life are but one. As a result, women are often wed to men well beneath them, men who indulge in alcohol, abuse them, stray, then leave them saddled

with children and debts. When I practiced spiritualism, I heard their stories quite often. Do you not see
that this must change? Until women have a voice and
legal protection, these injustices will continue!"

Passion lit her elegant face, making her beauty
even more remarkable. There was fire in her voice,
directness in her speech, and courage in her conviction.
Mr. Grimsby was momentarily fascinated. Shaking off
her spell, he sank back into his seat, clearly angered by
her words.

"Miss Appleton, had you been born a man, I have
no doubt you would have been an excellent attorney.
But this is preposterous! No court will allow you to
practice, nor will you have clients. No man will take
you seriously, no jury listen to your arguments. The
whole idea is ludicrous."

"But not impossible," Winifred said, warming to
her cause. "Myra Bradwell passed the bar exam. So
did Lavinia Goodell and Belva Lockwood. You see, Mr.
Grimsby, it is not so silly. Women can and are doing it."

"But they will not do it here." The dean rose, his
grandfatherly expression gone. Male supremacy and
order were being threatened, and he didn't like it one
bit. "As long as I am in residence, it will never happen
here. I find your argument faulty and unmannerly,
Miss Appleton. Most of the women you cited did not
pass the bar on their own. They apprenticed under
their husbands or other male sponsors and got their
license only with a man's help. So you see, women are
not capable of the same intellectual demands as men. I
am afraid this interview is at an end. Good day to
you."

Winifred opened her mouth to protest, but as if
on cue, a clerk stepped in and held the door open,

indicating for her to leave. Having no choice, Winifred picked up her papers, her painstakingly written essay, her thought-provoking research, and her perfect application and put them into her valise. With as much dignity as she could muster, she brushed past the clerk into the hallowed halls of the all-male sanctum.

Curious students stared at her, but Winifred ignored them and walked swiftly toward her carriage. Her driver, waiting in the shade, hopped up to the door and held it open, taking the case from her as he had done many times before. Seeing the expression on his mistress's face, he sighed in sympathy.

"Shot down again, miss?"

"Yes, Egbert, they rejected me." Winifred climbed into the carriage with a firm smile. Once the sting of tears might have burned her eyes, but not today. Today she would not cry.

It was so unfair. Settling back into her seat, she recalled the dozens of interviews just like this one that had taken place over the past few months. She had started with the major schools—Harvard, Yale, Princeton—then gradually worked her way down to this smaller, eastern college. While she hadn't thought achieving her goal would come without effort, she hadn't anticipated this kind of resistance.

Yet nothing would deter her. From the time she was little, Winifred had always wanted to be a lawyer. While other girls had discussed dresses and hair ribbons, she had pored over every legal text she could find. It was painfully clear to Winifred that without female legal representation, women would never achieve real equality. Her mother laughed and called her a bluestocking, and her father smiled indulgently, certain she would outgrow her odd obsession. But her ambition only increased with time.

When her parents died in a carriage accident, leaving Winifred and her two sisters orphaned, she thought her dream was over. Thankfully, their Aunt Eve gave them a home, and in an effort to stave off poverty, her sister Jennifer came up with the idea of becoming spiritualists. So Jennifer, Winifred, and Penelope became fortune-tellers, amassing more than enough money for Penelope's debut and Winifred's college fund. Jennifer herself met a man, Gabriel Forester, and was happily married.

So now Winifred had the money, but no school would take her seriously. Her nose wrinkled as she thought of Mr. Grimsby. While most of the other colleges had been less openly negative, they all saw her ambition as an enormous waste of time and money. Winifred knew she could get through law school. What if the Mr. Grimsbys of the world never gave her a chance?

The more she thought about it, the angrier she got. By the time the carriage finally pulled up in front of her house, she was in a fine froth indeed.

"Winnie, is that you?" Aunt Eve called out. The windows rattled in their panes as she heard the door slam below. Rushing downstairs, Aunt Eve stood on the threshold, not at all surprised to see her niece toss aside one glove before wrenching the other from her hand. Removing her cloak, she hurled it at the unsuspecting rack, seeming not at all concerned when it slumped to the floor. Pacing the carpet, she muttered to herself while the parrot squawked in a curious echo.

"How could he speak to me like that? Of all the nerve . . . 'exceeded our allotment of females'. . . ."

"Winifred," the elderly lady ventured cautiously, "I take it things didn't go well at the school?"

Her niece stopped pacing and glared. "Not only did the dean reject me, but he declared my ambition to practice law 'foolish and a waste of time.' "

"He didn't actually say that, did he?" Eve asked, appalled.

"It was worse than that," Winifred admitted. "He advised me to wed and forget all this nonsense. Men! They think the only thing we are good for is marriage and children. As if we are nothing more than brood mares!"

"Not all men feel that way about women," Aunt Eve said. "There are enlightened gentlemen in the world."

"Ha!" Winifred replied. "*I* will never get married. It is a trap designed to hobble our sex, to hold us down and suppress us. Did you know that only idiots, married women, and children are unable to make a will in many states? The good Mr. Grimsbys in the world are determined to keep women in their place. Well, they cannot stop a high tide from flooding! Change will come, whether they like it or not!"

Aunt Eve gazed worriedly at her niece. Of the three girls, Winifred had always been the odd one, her nose buried in a law book, her mind extraordinary for a young girl. Not even the death of her parents had ruffled her cool composure or swayed her determination. Now at twenty, Winifred had blossomed into a stunning young woman. Although she was certainly capable of taking on the world, how many more disappointments would she have to suffer?

A knock on the door startled them both. Eve peeped out the lace curtains.

"It's that nice Mr. Howe!" she exclaimed, relieved. "He must have come for tea."

Winifred groaned. "Charles is here?"

"Now dear, Charles cannot help the fact that he is a man," Eve responded. "He seems very taken with you, though. This is his third visit this month, I think. Now do sit down and have some tea while I get the door. You have wrapped the carpet around your feet with your pacing."

Looking down at the floor, Winifred saw that her aunt was right. Shaking the brightly colored Persian rug from her boots, she lowered herself into a seat before their guest strode into the room.

"Mrs. Appleton! How wonderful to see you! Miss Winifred."

Charles bowed to Aunt Eve, then inclined his head toward her. He was dressed impeccably in a charcoal-gray suit and paisley vest that showed off his broad shoulders and trim waist. Carrying his top hat in his hand, his jet-black curls framed a face that could only be called devastatingly handsome. Yet for all their warmth, the sparkle in his black eyes couldn't hide the fierce gleam of intelligence that had made him one of the city's most promising prosecutors.

Frustrated beyond words, Winifred set down her teacup and stared into the fire as if it interested her. The last thing she needed right now was to entertain Charles Howe. He was far too perceptive, too dangerously distracting. He would learn in an instant that something was wrong, and he was the last person she wanted to know about her latest humiliation. Winifred ignored him as her aunt bustled to make him comfortable.

"Do take a chair, Mr. Howe, and I will fetch the tea right away. Your timing is perfect! Winifred just came home." Eve hurried toward the kitchen, casting a sharp glance toward her niece.

A log snapped in the fire, then fell into the

sizzling ashes. Winifred looked as if the embers held tremendous importance for her.

Finally, Charles broke the silence. "I take it things did not go well today?" His voice was properly sympathetic, yet for some reason it only served to outrage her.

Winifred responded more brittlely than she intended. "No, they didn't. I was rejected again."

Charles studied the beautiful woman before him. Although she tried to appear righteously indignant, he could see the disappointment in her hazel eyes. Her gaze into the fire was so fiercely determined that he almost smiled. He could just imagine the interview with the proper dean. The man was lucky to have escaped alive.

"Will you tell me what happened?" he asked.

"There is no need." She waved her hand dismissingly. Finally, she looked his way. "The dean made it quite clear that he thought my ambition ridiculous. I know it won't come as any surprise to you, Charles. You did warn me. Go ahead and say 'I told you so.' I wouldn't blame you in the least."

"Winifred, you cannot honestly think I'd be happy about this?" he said sharply. "I, of all people, know exactly how it feels to want to be a lawyer."

"I'm sorry," she said softly. "You are a good friend, and I have no right to take it out on you. I'm just so frustrated and disappointed! I will find a way to succeed, mark my words. Somehow I will become a lawyer, even if I have to petition the dean of every school from here to the Pacific!"

Charles rose to stand beside her, admiring the fire in her eyes and the passion in her words. She was Joan of Arc, Morgan le Fay, and Helen of Troy all rolled into one beautiful woman. Something constricted inside him, and in spite of his own good sense, he lifted her face toward his.

"Winifred," he said softly, "there is another way. You can become an apprentice."

"And who would agree to that?" she asked tartly. "If the schools won't take me seriously, what lawyer would?"

"I would," Charles said simply. Her gaze widened, and he nodded. "If you are determined, I will take you under my wing and teach you the law."

The words came out almost before he had formed them. Why was he doing this? he wondered. Winifred was the last woman he should be involved with. She was notorious, a spiritualist, a suffragette, a woman who would cause him nothing but endless trouble. And her ambition, while noble, could only result in her heartache.

Yet Winifred was more than capable—he'd seen some of her work firsthand. He'd spent many a pleasant evening with her arguing legal issues. But dabbling in legalities wasn't the same as practicing law. The *practice* of law involved endless paperwork, terrible hours, and tedious research. As his apprentice, Winifred would learn what she was really undertaking. Charles figured that after a few months of legal drudgery, she would forget her ambition and confess that it wasn't what she wanted after all.

"Oh, Charles! How can I thank you?" Winifred flung herself into his arms. Charles felt his body react immediately to her nearness as her lavender scent filled his nostrils and the silkiness of her hair teased his face. Groaning, he was amazed that this slip of a girl should have such an effect on him. It didn't escape his notice that as his apprentice, Winifred would be working closely with him every day, and he would have endless opportunities to win her. When she finally gave up this nonsense about becoming an attorney, she would be his for the asking.

"We'll talk about that later," Charles said hoarsely. "Yes, we will definitely discuss that in the near future."

CHAPTER I

STATE ATTORNEY'S OFFICE HIRES LEGAL SIREN!

It has been reported that the state attorney's office has hired a female, one Winifred Appleton, as an apprentice law clerk. Miss Appleton, an ardent devotee of the law, has offered to work for the office in exchange for instruction to pass the bar examination. The Supreme Court recently heard the case of another female attorney, Myra Bradwell, who had been barred from practice. The Court found that "The right of females to pursue any lawful employment for a livelihood was not 'one of the privileges and immunities of women as citizens.'"

"The paramount destiny and mission of women are to fulfill the noble and benign offices of wife and mother," Justice Samuel Miller wrote. "This is the law of the Creator. And the rules of civil society must be adapted to the general constitution of things."

In spite of this, Miss Appleton appears determined to forge ahead. Much like the willful Miss Anthony and the controversial Mrs. Woodhull, Miss

Appleton, with the help of the state attorney, seems to blithely disregard the Court's ruling. When questioned about her ambition, Miss Appleton said, "I must do what I was destined to do."

One might speculate why the state's office would encourage Miss Appleton. Could the office seek to generate publicity, which could then further the political career of the state attorney? Or perhaps there is a more personal motivation, for even this reporter was struck by Miss Appleton's beauty and elegance, the fire flashing in her eyes, and the moderate tone of her speech. . . .

Beneath the story ran a much smaller piece about a woman who had been arrested and accused of attempting to murder her husband by arsenic poisoning.

WINIFRED APPLETON STRODE into the state attorney's offices bright and early, ignoring the newsboy at the curb who shouted the screaming headlines. Dressed in a simple navy-blue suit and white shirt that on another woman might have appeared unfeminine, she looked professional and beautiful, her classical features only enhanced by the severity of her costume. Her valise clutched tightly in her hand, she stood inside the hall of the imposing building, trying to quell the butterflies in her stomach.

It was really happening. Her dream was coming true. A thrill raced up her spine as the attorneys bustled past her, the clerks rushed around with reams of paper, and the secretaries organized endless piles of files and notations. The office had a life of its own, and Winifred was about to become part of it.

Everything would be different now. She would work hard, study, learn everything she possibly could, and pass the bar examination. She would then take her own place in these hallowed halls and, as an equal partner to her male brethren, contribute in the fight to help other women with their legal battles.

It would work. Tears misted her eyes, and she hugged her valise to herself in glee. She had waited so many years for this moment, she could hardly believe it was happening. But it was. And she had one man to thank for it.

Charles Howe. Winifred smiled softly at the thought of the handsome attorney. She would do everything she could to repay him for his kindness, and she would prove to him that she could be an asset, not just his beneficiary. They would work together, side by side, day in and day out. He would show her the ropes, and she would help him with his workload.

Her smile dimmed as that thought led to other, more troubling ones. Charles, she silently admitted, was one of the most compelling men she had ever known. He had a way of looking at her that sent shudders of awareness right down to her high-buttoned boots. Once he had kissed her, and she had been shocked at the physical reaction that flamed through her. Even their legal discourse aroused her on every level, making her corset feel far too tight and her thin chemise unwelcomely warm. If he had this effect on her now, what would happen when she was working closely with him?

Squeezing her eyes shut, Winifred refused to entertain the thought. Charles was a colleague, nothing more, and any romantic overtones would only destroy that fragile relationship. Freshly determined, she walked up to his office and knocked on the door. It would all work out—she just knew it would.

"COME IN!" Charles called out, adjusting his tie before the polished silver coffeepot on his desk.

The newspaper lay before him, but he ignored the raucous headline. A broad smile crept over his face as he thought of his new legal assistant. Although he had reviewed his impulsive offer in the cold light of reason, he had to admit, it was a brilliant idea. He would have the maddening Winifred Appleton all to himself. What a golden opportunity for seduction! He could just see her now, those wonderful hazel eyes darkening with desire, her breathless rebuttals transformed into something else entirely, and her full, soft mouth parted for his kiss. . . . The possibilities were too many to count, and he intended to make the most of every one of them.

The object of his thoughts stepped into the room, looking utterly adorable in her neat blue suit. Winifred smiled uncertainly at him, holding her valise tightly against her. He rose and closed the door, then turned to her. Taking a step back, her questioning gaze settled on him.

"Good morning, Mr. Howe. I'm ready to start. What would you like me to do first?"

Her voice was as starched and formal as her linen collar. Charles frowned. This was not at all the way he had expected her to behave. He was even more disgruntled when she set the valise on the floor and faced him directly with a no-nonsense, businesslike air.

"Miss Appleton, would you like to join me for coffee? I thought we could discuss your duties in a more casual way." He gestured to a sofa. A tray had been set out on the table before it, along with two cups, sugar, sweet rolls, and a single rose in a porcelain vase.

"I . . . already breakfasted," Winifred said stiffly. "But please help yourself if you haven't eaten yet. I can take notes while you do."

She bent over to retrieve her book, and he received a wonderful view of her round backside. Trying desperately not to react, he picked up the coffeepot and retreated to the couch. After pouring a cup of the pungent brew, he patted the sofa, indicating that she should join him.

Winifred's eyes measured the close distance that would result if she accepted his silent offer and sat on the couch. Instead, she dragged his chair around his desk to a polite distance from the sofa. Picking up her book, she sat on the chair, then eyed him like a schoolmarm waiting on a particularly annoying pupil.

"I thought we could begin with my regular duties," she said, opening the brand-new book to the first page. "I am certain that you will occasionally need assistance with particular cases, but I assume there are chores that will need to be done daily. Let us start with those."

Her eyes held all the warmth of a New York winter. Charles stared at her for a long moment, sipping his coffee, wondering what in God's name she was thinking. This was not an auspicious beginning.

"Miss Appleton," he began, "you and I have enjoyed a very friendly relationship in the past few months. That doesn't have to change just because we are now working together. You can safely sit beside me, I assure you. You and I have shared more than a seat together."

To his delight, her face reddened, and she bit her lip. Unwillingly, his thoughts went back to a night a few months ago at the Rutherfords' ball. Winifred had been dressed like a goddess in gold, her hair artfully swept up, her earrings lighting up a face that needed no artifice. She had stood out among the other girls like a lily in a field of cornflowers, and Charles had been completely bewitched by her. That was when he had kissed her, and the memory of that moment was seared onto his brain.

Was she thinking of the same thing? Unconsciously, she moistened her lips. Charles watched in fascination as she drew herself up, inhaled, then squared off to face him directly.

"I'm glad you brought that up," Winifred said briskly. "Our relationship, I mean. I am certain you will agree that in order for our association to be mutually beneficial, it cannot be complicated by romance. Such a situation would be disastrous and would ultimately result in my withdrawal as your apprentice."

"I see," Charles said.

"Furthermore, I do not blame you for thinking I desired your . . . attentions in the past, for I certainly did nothing to discourage them. In fact, one might even think I did the opposite."

"Yes, one might," he agreed.

She shot him a sideways glance. "You are not making this easy for me."

"I didn't intend to." He put down the coffee cup and rose to stand beside her. Before she could react, he reached for her hand and pulled her into an upright position. Her notebook fell to the floor.

"My book—"

"Forget the damned book," he growled. It was all he could do not to pull her into his arms and experience those liberties all over again. Thankfully, the surging pulse in her wrist told him that in spite of her words, her feelings for him were alive and well. Forcing himself to stay in control, he spoke slowly. "Winifred, we need to talk about this. I am no schoolboy to be dismissed that easily."

"Mr. Howe—" She began stiffly.

"Charles."

"Charles." She took a deep breath, then closed her eyes, as if struggling within herself. "You know my views on all this. We have been seeing each other informally, I know, but now that we are working together, I assume things will change. I did not suppose you meant *this* when you offered me the apprenticeship—"

"Of course I didn't!" he said, appalled that she would even suggest such a thing.

"Then you must respect my wishes," she said. "I want nothing more than a friendship or a working association. You are a good friend, Charles, and I don't wish to change that. As a lawyer, you must agree that logic and emotion do not mix. I am sure you understand." She gave him a meaningful look, as if she had put together an argument so compelling that he couldn't possibly object.

He understood all right—much more than she would ever know. What did he want from her? He wasn't sure. She would certainly not be the best choice of wife for him, for as one of the Appleton sisters, Winifred was notorious. His family had made it clear that they did not approve of her and that many other women would be more acceptable. In spite of all that, he had not been able to put her from his mind, and he'd be damned if he'd give up on her now.

A smile came to his face, and he searched hers, looking deeply into those magical hazel eyes. "I think I do understand. You claim you are not interested in pursuing a more personal relationship with me. What if I prove otherwise?"

"What?" Winifred stared at him in confusion.

Charles grinned. "You might as well learn this now, Winifred, for you surely will in a courtroom one day. There is liability, and then there is personal responsibility."

"I do not know what you mean," she whispered, stepping back as he moved closer.

"I think you do." Charles's voice was like silk. "But I will give you a case. If a lady gives a gentleman reason to think his . . . advances are not unwelcome, then he cannot be held responsible for making them." At her continued confusion, he lifted her chin and gazed deeply into her eyes. "All you have to do is to refuse me. I will never force you anywhere you do not wish to go. The choice is always yours."

Winifred drew in a breath. "So . . ."

"So that means that while I will play fair, I *will* continue to play. Miss Appleton, it is no secret that I find you extremely desirable. I cannot hide what I feel, or pretend it does not exist because of our situation. Nor am I convinced that you find my attention completely unwelcome. However, I will respect your wishes. I will do nothing to embarrass you or make you feel uncomfortable working here. But you are on my turf, as they say, and I will not hesitate to take advantage of that."

"I see." Winifred bit her bottom lip, looking a little less sure of herself.

Charles fought to keep from tasting those lips, remembering how delicious they had been the night of the ball. Yet he had no desire to frighten her away, if she even could be frightened. He released her, then stepped back and picked up her book. He handed it to her.

"All right, let's get started with your schedule." He was all business now. "I had thought to have you work with one of the clerks, to assist in researching some of the cases he has on hand. In addition, you could help the secretary, Crocker, with some of his duties. You passed his desk on the way in. He will show you around. Is that agreeable to you?"

"Yes, of course," Winifred said, disconcerted by his manner.

"Legal work is not glamorous. I know you have considerable experience reading briefs and developing arguments, but you will not do that here initially. Most of the work assigned to our clerks is very boring but necessary. You will not be seeing the inside of a courtroom for a long time. I cannot afford you special treatment just because of our . . . association."

"I understand," she said quickly.

"Good. I shall want to work directly with you later, to assist you in your studies and to give you some special assignments. I warn you, Miss Appleton, that I can be a strict taskmaster. Does that concern you?"

"No. I mean, yes." The teasing note in his voice only seemed to confuse her more. Rising, she picked up her valise. "Did you . . . need anything else?"

"Of course, but I did give you my word, did I not?" As she continued to look flustered, he decided to call a truce. "I have a meeting scheduled this morning in the conference room. Would you mind bringing the texts I requested from the secretary?"

"Not at all," she replied.

"Good." He smiled, then turned away, opening the door and holding it for her. She looked at him in confusion, as if unsure what to do next. "Why, Miss Appleton, have you changed your mind already? The coffee is still hot."

"No, thank you," Winifred said quickly, then brushed past him into the hallway.

Charles closed the door, chuckling softly to himself. Winifred Appleton was obviously quite used to getting her own way.

But unfortunately for her, so was he.

"FOLLOW ME, MISS APPLETON. I'll show you to your office."

Winifred walked behind Miles Witherspoon, the young, ambitious clerk whom Charles had assigned to work with her. The man clearly resented having to deal with her at all. Still, as she followed him out of the office, Miles was the least of her concerns.

She had not expected the conversation with Charles to go the way it had, and she felt like a courtroom novice who had been firmly thrashed by an experienced prosecutor.

He was a good lawyer, Winifred thought, forced to admire his tactics. She had thought her argument noble and well thought out, but somehow he had managed to turn the tables on her.

Or had he? Winifred thought long and hard. In spite of her reaction, she had to admit that the hidden, feminine side of her was secretly pleased that he didn't cave in to her demands. Worse, part of her was exhilarated by what she saw as the ultimate male-female challenge. If Charles was no schoolboy to be led around by a leash, she was no mawkish miss, inclined to swoon at the slightest male attention.

Determination rose anew within her. It was really quite simple. All she had to do was keep her head, and she would win the war. Charles really had put the power into her hands. He had promised that nothing would happen unless she wanted it to.

Yet as she marched down the hall, an emotion nagged within her as she remembered that kiss at the Rutherfords' ball.

Would she be able to keep it from happening again?

CHAPTER 2

HERE WE ARE." Miles paused at a dimly lit corner of the library. A small desk took up one third of the space, and a smoky gaslight fumed ominously on the table. "I am certain you will be very comfortable here."

Winifred knew he didn't mean that, but she refused to complain. The last thing she wanted was to gain a reputation as a prima donna. "Thank you," she said sweetly. "You are so kind. How can I help?"

He fumbled with a sheaf of paperwork before answering. "Here. Copy these documents, then give them back to the secretary. When you finish, I suggest you assist with the filing. You might also want to help out here in the library. Our cleaning woman has not come in this week, and it is a disaster."

With a smug smirk, he sauntered out of the room, pleased to have put this female upstart in her place. Winifred's heart sank as his words penetrated.

Copying and cleaning. She had spent most of her life studying the law, and they saw her only as a foolish woman. Discouraged, Winifred put aside the files and walked to the next table. There she picked up a mountain of books, trying hard not to listen to the voice inside her.

How could they treat her this way? Didn't they realize things would never change if they didn't give her a chance? She put the books away furiously as the indignity of it all struck her. Didn't they see what was going on in the world? Didn't they know that Susan B. Anthony, by voting in the Rochester election, was demonstrating that women were people, too? Even though the Supreme Court had found against Miss Anthony, surely they understood that it was simply a matter of time before everything changed?

That thought made Winifred even more outraged. Picking up a duster, she began furiously cleaning the first wall of books. Feathers shot out, wafting silently to the floor. They had to realize the injustice of it all. Men spent years fighting for freedom! More feathers fell. Yet if the Constitution did not protect women, then what good was the law? How could all men be created equal if fifty percent of the population wasn't even included in the sum?

There were now but three feathers left on the duster. The rest were scattered at her feet like autumn leaves, leaving a brown trail between the towering bookcases.

Stifling her chagrin, she cleaned up the feathers and tossed the useless duster into the trash bin. She then returned to the table to fetch the next pile of books. As she began to put them away, she realized that the library was in very poor order. Like many law libraries, it had grown over time, but it had never been organized to allow for the new additions. Winifred stared thoughtfully at the jumble of books. Retrieving her notebook, she diagrammed the shelves, noting the way the books were distributed.

It was completely haphazard. Winifred recalled the neat system employed by her friend Bernard Goodman, a lawyer who had generously given her the use of his own library. The old gentleman would fall over into a faint if he saw the way the state's legal library was kept.

Determination sparked within her, and she removed all the books from the first shelf, then the second. By the time she was finished, Charles would be able to lay his hands on whatever he needed at a moment's notice. The thought of pleasing him sent a little shiver of anticipation through her. He would be proud of her.

She would see to it.

"YOU HAVE GOT to get rid of her!" James Meyers cried, pounding the table like a judge in court.

"We cannot have a woman working here!" Edgar Whitcomb protested. "It has never been done! Women belong at home, not in a law office!"

"Have you seen the *Times*? It won't be long before the *Sun* or *Harper's* gets hold of this. I can just see the Nast cartoon. The office will be a laughingstock!" Miles Witherspoon pushed a copy of the newspaper, with its glaring headline, before Charles.

Charles gazed at the reddened faces around him, then calmly pushed back the paper. The lawyers and clerks gathered around his desk, all of them indignant that a woman was working in their office.

Sighing, Charles helped himself to a glass of water. He had expected some resistance and had, in fact, spent the last few days in court to avoid a confrontation, but this overwhelming protest surprised even him. And it wasn't just the older ones who appeared outraged. The younger men, whom he would have thought more open-minded, were, if anything, even more furious than their elders. But he understood their attitude. Male dominance was the unquestioned order of the day, and none of them took kindly to seeing it threatened.

"Gentlemen, calm down and take a seat. This is not as serious as it seems." The men, still grumbling, reluctantly accepted chairs. The room gradually quieted, and they gazed at him warily.

"Thank you. Miss Appleton is a friend and has offered to help out in the office. As you know, the city's budget has been under increased scrutiny, and we don't have the same funds as we did last year to hire help. Miss Appleton will do the filing, copying, and researching—all of the things we do not like to do and do not have the time to do. Unlike most of our clerks, she has considerable background in research and writing briefs. She can be of tremendous assistance and will not cost us a dime. What is wrong with that?"

Whitcomb thrust out his chin, his bushy whiskers twitching with a scowl. "It is unseemly, that is what! Next thing you know, the office will be crawling with petticoats. These new women have to be stopped! Those scourges, Mrs. Stanton and Miss Anthony, are getting them all fired up. My own wife went to hear them speak, and she has been spouting suffragette nonsense ever since!"

"They want to vote, to run for office, to become involved in politics and business!" Meyers said in outrage. "There is even a woman in the papers who tried to murder her own husband! I never heard such nonsense! In my day, women knew their place. Like delicate flowers, they were seen and not heard. A soft voice, a pretty face—these are the things that are desirable in women, not these masculine ideas!"

"Besides the vote, they want to control marriage!" Drew McAlister added. His red nose became even redder. "Why, Mrs. Stanton wants to enable a woman to get a divorce if her husband drinks! Can you imagine? A man takes a glass of whiskey and comes home to an empty house!"

Charles rolled his eyes. McAlister took more than an occasional drink, so it was no wonder he worried about his wife leaving. But none of that had anything to do with Winifred. As the men continued muttering, acting as if Winifred were less than womanly simply because she was ambitious, his own outrage increased.

A glimmer of understanding came to him as he realized what Winifred must have encountered in trying to get accepted into law school. She must have faced multiple Whitcombs and McAlisters, all of them appalled at her goals, all of them certain they knew what was best for her. A sour taste came into his mouth as he saw that he hadn't been much better. He still thought Winifred would ultimately quit, but it annoyed him considerably that his male brethren were discussing her in such a manner.

"Gentlemen, once more let us be reasonable about this," Charles said sternly. "I do not think you have considered the ramifications of dismissing her. Are you all willing to do your own filing and copying? Our secretary cannot continue to support us all."

The silence that followed was pregnant. None of them wanted to go back to doing the grunt work, as they had done in the first days of their apprenticeships. Meyers thrust out his lip and scowled openly.

"Can you not get a male student to help out? I am sure there are candidates available." He looked at his colleagues, who nodded, satisfied.

"Not at our price," Charles said flatly. "We just do not have the money to pay someone a decent wage.

And the only way to attract a male student is to spend time teaching him the law. Are any of you willing to give up countless nights and weekends reviewing your old law books with a young lawyer? You all know what is involved in passing the bar. The only reason any student in his right mind would agree to such a thing is if there were something tangible in it for him."

Whitcomb groaned. Here was another unappealing prospect. The other lawyers studied the hardwood floor.

"I thought so. I don't mind spending my own time with Miss Appleton, since we are friends and she is attractive." At this, Charles earned a few smug male smiles. That was something they could understand. "But I don't have room in my schedule for the intense tutoring that a law student would require. If any of you have that kind of time, see me after this meeting. You obviously are not getting your share of cases."

The lawyers exchanged furtive glances. None of them wanted any more files plopped on their desk.

"But what about the newspapers?" McAlister pointed to the *Sun*, unwilling to give up that easily. "We will be a laughingstock."

"Maybe," Charles said with a smile. "But consider this. Our funding comes from the voters. While none of them are female, women have influence. Having them on our side will only help our office. Miss Anthony and Mrs. Stanton, both tigers, are very good at vocalizing their support. More than one recent election has been swayed by their involvement."

The attorneys nodded reluctantly. While none of them would publicly admit it, they all went home to women who read the papers, heard speeches, organized clubs, and shared gossip over the backyard fence. More than one man's life had been made hell by a wife whose viewpoint was not respected. Even after the curtain closed behind a man standing in an election booth, he had to consider his wife's wishes.

"So you see, we stand only to benefit here," Charles continued, sensing that he was winning them over. "Miss Appleton will take much of the busywork off your shoulders, allowing you to focus on your casework. I would also recommend that you consider utilizing her research skills. She has had several years of experience and can provide assistance."

Before another man could comment, Jared Marton appeared at the door. He appeared surprised to observe the gathering. "Good afternoon. I didn't know we were having a meeting."

"We're not," Charles said. "This was an informal session, and we were just finishing."

"I just wanted to tell you about the library," Marton said, sounding impressed. "Someone has straightened it up beautifully. Everything was put away in the right order for once, and I found all the texts I needed quickly. Have we hired someone new?"

Charles glanced at Miles Witherspoon. The clerk shrugged his shoulders, then sheepishly admitted, "Miss Appleton has been working in the library. She must have done it."

"There you have it." Charles gazed at the men triumphantly. "Miss Appleton has already proven her worth. Now if there is nothing else, this meeting is adjourned. I have a lot of work to do."

As the men filed out, Charles hid a smile. The notorious Winifred Appleton had already made her presence felt.

"MISS APPLETON, could I speak to you a moment?"
Charles entered the library holding a dozen roses

behind his back. Winifred was buried behind a stack
of books. One of the shelves above her head was
empty, and she struggled to put several four-inch-
thick volumes into the vacant space. Charles put the
flowers aside and took the books from her, placing
them away easily.

"Mr. Howe," she said, "I haven't seen you recently.
Have you been away?"

"Just to court," Charles said, observing her with
considerable pleasure. "Did you miss me?"

"I—just wondered where you were," she stammered. "Did you wish to see me about something, Mr.
Howe?"

The starched formality was back in her voice.
Charles smiled. "Yes. I brought you these." He handed
her the roses, sunny golden blooms that filled the air
with scent.

Winifred gazed at him doubtfully, not moving to
take them. "They are beautiful," she admitted. "But
you should not have done this."

"Why? Is yellow not for friendship?" The warmth
in his eyes had returned, along with a gleam she was
beginning to recognize.

"Charles—I mean, Mr. Howe—we've discussed
this," she said primly. "I wish to be treated as any
other employee. I highly doubt that you give flowers
to your apprentices."

He did not appear at all dismayed by her little
speech. Instead, the gleam grew brighter. "As the
boss, it is my responsibility to reward exceptional
work, and I will not take no for an answer." He firmly
pressed the flowers into her hand, ignoring her gasp as
a thorn found her finger. Before she could say anything else, he glanced around in admiration. "I had
heard you did a good job here in the library. Actually
you have done a fantastic one."

He gazed at the library shelves. He could tell exactly which ones she had finished. The six shelves beside him were neat, the books were in good order, and their spines were all facing out. Small tabs of paper with numbers written on them had been glued to the spines, and the duster had been used to full advantage.

Looking ridiculously pleased at his compliment, she glanced toward the table. "I am starting a card catalog that will correspond to these numbers," she said proudly. "Soon you will be able to find any book within a few minutes."

"You have done a great job," Charles said in admiration. "My applause, Miss Appleton."

Winifred smiled, unconsciously burying her nose in the flowers. "I am just glad to make a contribution. I finished most of the copying this morning, then the filing. I thought I would keep busy with this until Mr. Witherspoon comes back with more work."

"I see." He suddenly noticed her dingy desk. "Is this where you have been working?"

"Yes." She nodded. "Mr. Witherspoon suggested I do the copying here. It is perfectly adequate, even if the lighting is poor."

He walked across the library to a suite of offices. Taking out a key, he unlocked the door and held it wide open. "Take this one. Chambers is on leave and will not be returning until spring."

"But—" She put the roses down and peeked inside. The office was comfortable and functional. A green leather chair stood in one corner, shelves lined the wall, and a polished oak desk graced the center of the room. There was an oil lamp on the table, and a gas chandelier hung overhead. Charles turned it up, and the room burst into brilliant light.

"This is beautiful," she said, gazing at the office in awe. "But I could not possibly—"

"Why not? It isn't being used. Besides, without enough light, you will damage your eyesight. Didn't your mother ever tell you that?"

The teasing quality was back in his voice. Winifred swallowed hard. "Thank you," she said awkwardly. Suddenly she realized how close she was standing to him. Taking a step backward, her bustle hit the door, preventing her escape.

"You are welcome." He took a step forward, closing the distance between them. "That is twice you owe me. I think I like having you in my debt."

There was something alarming about his voice. Winifred took a deep breath, but that proved her undoing, for the scent of his cologne, lime water mingled with male, filled her head, making it difficult to think. Remembering her resolve, she tried to compose herself, but when his hand gently touched her cheek, his thumb softly brushing the fullness of her lip, she was undone. She closed her eyes in anticipation, waiting for his kiss. . . .

It never came. Her eyes flew open after an embarrassingly long pause, and she saw Charles watching her with an odd smile.

"Why, Miss Appleton, are you tempting me to forget my promise?"

Mortification filled her, as she realized that he had never intended to kiss her!

"No, I never! I don't know what you mean—"

He laughed, then chucked her affectionately under the chin.

"Good night, Winifred. I am looking forward very much to continuing our . . . working relationship."

He turned on his heel and left. His manner was less of a cocky assurance than of cool determination. As his footsteps receded, Winifred sighed in relief.

Picking up his flowers, she stared thoughtfully at the gorgeous blooms. It had been her first test, and she had failed miserably.

"It will not happen again," she said to the empty room.

CHAPTER 3

THE NEW YORK SUN did little to warm the cobbles of the street. Rag pickers furtively sorted through the trash, while construction workers, numb from the cold, huddled over a blazing barrel. Houses were shrouded against the morning chill with rich velvet draperies, while servants struggled to light fires and bring in wood. Horse-drawn carts moved slowly through town, as if it were painful for the animals to put one foot ahead of the other on the wet stones. Spring had arrived, but in New York, one would never know it.

Winifred hurried toward the office, wanting to arrive before everyone else, particularly the reporters who had camped outside. She had been an apprentice for just a few short weeks, yet it seemed as if she had been there forever. It didn't escape her notice that the other lawyers were not happy with her presence, so she was committed to making a good impression. She wanted to be the first to arrive and the last to leave, and to take on all the work they didn't want without complaint.

In addition, she had to send a clear message to

Charles that she meant business. He needed that message: every morning when she came into her office, another bouquet awaited her. Sometimes it was violets, sometimes daisies—always innocent friendship flowers. But her protests were met with upraised brows and bold reminders that he was in charge here and sought only to reward her hard work. Any further remonstrances only brought amusement and teasing on his part, embarrassment on hers. She soon stopped mentioning them at all, deliberately leaving the blossoms each night for the cleaning woman. Yet even this didn't discourage him.

Winifred quickly learned when Charles was in court and how to avoid him on the days he wasn't. He was persistent in asking her out for lunch or dinner, but seeing him in the office was tempting enough; she couldn't risk seeing him outside of it as well. He was no schoolboy, and she was just beginning to taste the weapons in his arsenal. She sensed that he was watching her with infinite patience, like an expert chess player, waiting for the right moment to make his move. The thought was as unnerving as it was exciting.

The office workers dashed into the warm buildings, their coats huddled tightly about them. Clutching her own cloak, she had started for the stairs when she suddenly found herself besieged by more than a dozen derby-hatted reporters.

"Miss Appleton! Is it true you are clerking for the prosecutor's office?"

"What contribution do you think to make?"

"Are you a suffragette?"

"Do you really think to ever practice law?"

Apparently, the reporters had learned of her early morning hours and thought to outwit her.

Winifred tried to push past them, but they circled her like hawks.

"No comment," she said firmly. "I am simply here to help the prosecutor's office. Now will you move and let me pass?"

It was a mistake. Having gotten that much, the reporters pushed even closer.

"Can you explain that, Miss A.?"

"Is it true you are a spiritualist and were once incarcerated?"

"Do you favor free love, and are you truly Mr. Howe's mistress?"

Shocked, Winifred held up her skirts, intent on getting inside even if she had to physically shove her way in. She heard a shuffling, then a soft *plop!* followed by gasps of astonishment from the men around her. To her horror, something slimy was dripping down her face. Wiping it quickly, her stomach tightened in revulsion as yellow yolk congealed on her glove.

"Someone threw an egg at her! It was that rogue across the street! Catch him, mates! Maybe we can get a quote from him!"

The reporters rushed after the furtive figure, but not before another egg landed at her feet. Disgusted, Winifred rushed quickly inside. Breathing heavily, she slammed the door closed behind her.

The sticky egg felt cold as it dripped down her cheek onto her collar. Peering into a hall mirror, she took her ruined glove and attempted to scrape the awful stuff from her face.

"Good morning, Miss Appleton," Charles's voice boomed behind her.

Winifred froze, her heart sinking. No! Charles could not see her like this! Frantically she tried to clean up the mess, but the goo only smeared more as she tried to clean it.

"Miss Appleton?" Charles stood behind her, searching for her reflection in the glass. "Are you all right?"

"Yes." Turning toward him, she shrugged. "Someone objected to my presence. One would think eggs too costly to waste in such a manner."

Her words were joking, but Charles was appalled by the remnants of yolk still plastered on her cheek. "Who did this to you?"

His outrage surprised her, as did the fury glittering in his black eyes. He looked as if he would rout the hoodlum himself and beat him to a pulp.

"It doesn't matter, Charles," she said quickly. "I'm sure whoever it was is gone. The reporters went looking for him to try and get the story—"

"What!" The light in his eyes blazed out of control, and his jaw tightened furiously. "They didn't help you, but went after him, so they could write about it in the paper! By God, I will see them in jail first! Gallagher! Where the hell is that guard?"

"Right here, sir." A burly policeman ambled up from the hallway, a cup of coffee in one hand and a sweet roll in the other. "Did you need something?"

"Yes." Charles took a step closer to the man and said through gritted teeth. "Get rid of those reporters on the steps, and make sure they do not return. Someone assaulted Miss Appleton. Find the man. I want to press charges. If I come in tomorrow and those wretches are back, I am holding you personally responsible!"

The officer jumped, nearly spilling his coffee. He opened his mouth to explain. Charles did not wait for his reply but grabbed Winifred's hand and began dragging her down the hall.

"Mr. Howe, this is ridiculous. I am fine," she protested, but he ignored her. Taking her into his office, he whipped out his handkerchief and dipped it in water. Pushing her hands aside, he insisted on cleaning her himself. Feeling humiliated, she stood like a little girl while he scrubbed her face.

"There." He examined her face and was satisfied. "I think I got it all. I cannot believe someone would do such a thing." His eyes narrowed. "Winifred, perhaps we should reconsider your working here. You should not be subject to assault."

Panic welled up inside her. He was considering terminating her! "It was just an egg! I am not at all hurt. Really, Charles, there is no sense getting into a tizzy over this."

"What if it had been a rock or a physical attack?" Charles's eyes blazed. "There are a lot of people against women stepping out of their roles as wives and mothers. Tensions in the city are running high, particularly with the suffragettes agitating. Things could escalate."

"I am sure it was just a prank, nothing more," Winifred said smoothly, surprised at the passion in his voice. "I think this incident was only for the benefit of the reporters. Usually I miss them, since I arrive early, but they must have figured out my schedule. Now that they are gone, there is no reason for anyone to bother me. Please, Charles, let us just forget the whole thing. I am certain it won't happen again."

"I am not so sure." He gazed into her hazel eyes as if considering the matter deeply. "I do not suppose I can convince you to give up because of one egg, but if it happens again, we will discuss it. I certainly do not want you walking to work anymore. If you cannot take your carriage, then I will supply cab fare. I will not be moved on this, Winifred. Otherwise everything else is off."

She nodded, relieved that he had relented about her position. "Yes, Charles," she said, laying a hand on his shoulder. "I will be more careful."

He looked down at the slender white hand resting on his dark coat. Something changed in his expression, and he reached up and gently touched the cheek that he'd just scrubbed. The warmth of his fingers soothed the chafed skin, and he was looking at her with such genuine concern and kindness that her throat tightened.

"You know, you look beautiful," he said honestly, "in spite of the egg."

His voice betrayed a kind of emotion that appeared to mystify even him. He seemed to be fighting some internal battle—and to be rapidly losing it. Winifred started to respond, but there was a discreet knock at the door. Quickly she withdrew from his embrace and self-consciously smoothed her hair. The secretary entered, carrying a coffee tray.

"Your morning coffee, Mr. Howe. Would you like the paper?" The little man held up the *Times*.

"No, thanks, Crocker. Just leave it by my desk."

His voice held a note of frustration as the secretary carefully placed his paper. Excusing herself, Winifred quickly took her leave. As she closed the door behind her, her heart was pounding, and she felt as if she'd had a narrow escape. Charles Howe was becoming entirely too much of a distraction.

CHARLES TOSSED his paperwork onto the desk, unable to concentrate. Picking up his coffee, he walked toward the window and gazed down into the street below.

The reporters were gone. At least the guard had been effective in removing them. His fingers tightened on the cup as he thought of someone pelting Winifred with an egg. Yet instead of intimidating her, as they intended, they had only strengthened her resolve.

A begrudging smile curved his lips. He was forced to admire her—the way she held her head high with dignity, even as she tried to remove the egg from her face. Something inside him broke at that, and within a few short moments, a surprising range of emotions flooded him: fury, that someone would do this to her; protectiveness; and an overwhelming need to kiss her, love her, take her into his arms, and erase all the ugliness.

Winifred Appleton was an enchantress. It would take every ounce of his willpower to remain firm and refrain from physically seducing her. If he yielded to temptation, she would accuse him of not respecting her ambition and ideals. Besides, he had promised her that he would not make her uncomfortable working here, and he intended to keep that promise.

Yet the egg incident only strengthened his resolve to see her abandon her crazy ambition. Some of the suffragettes were openly ridiculed, showered with vegetables, arrested, fined, and imprisoned. Even Miss Anthony had found herself behind bars when she attempted to vote. While most protesters stopped short of inflicting actual harm, the line had become very thin indeed.

Somehow he had to make Winifred see that this path was not for her. He realized that he shouldn't make her apprenticeship too attractive, for then she would never give up. She had settled in nicely over the last few weeks and was getting entirely too comfortable. And he had done nothing to discourage her; if anything, he had done quite the opposite. Maybe he had gone about this all wrong. Winifred, as a young

law apprentice, was convinced that she had been sent
to rescue the downtrodden masses from the inequities
of the legal system. He had to expose her to the realities of the law, and show her that the downtrodden, far
from being noble beings in need of help, were often the
dregs of the earth. Wife beaters, thieves, drunkards,
and murderers—these were the ranks that filled their
docket. It was time Winifred knew about that.

"CRIMINAL JUSTICE, crime statistics, the county
trust . . ."

Fighting a yawn, Winifred dutifully copied each
folder, trying hard to stay awake. Yet she could not
stop her mind from wandering. The tender scene she
had shared with Charles yesterday morning, the way
he had rushed to her defense like a knight in shining
armor, and the look in his eyes filled with emotion . . . Winifred shook off these thoughts in
alarm. What on earth was the matter with her? She
would never finish her work if she kept daydreaming.
More than that, she sensed something below the
surface, something that could cause tremendous
complications if she let it. . . . She quickly returned
to copying, forcing herself to concentrate.

In the next file, something caught her attention. It
was a fairly recent complaint. Miles must have picked
it up by accident, Winifred mused, for this wasn't one
of the older ones to be copied. She was about to put it
aside when she noticed that the complaint was filed
against a woman who had reportedly tried to kill her
husband. Interested, Winifred began reading it.

The woman, a Mrs. Black, had been jailed because
her husband believed that she had tried to murder
him. She had given him a cup of tea to drink, and

shortly afterward, he had become violently ill. The tea had been sent out for testing. The results had not yet been returned. More than likely, nothing would be found, and the case would never go to trial. And yet . . .

Putting the copying aside, she headed for the research books. It couldn't hurt just to take a peek and see if there had ever been a case like this one. As she cracked the books, keen excitement rose within her. This was her milieu, her element. It was like detective work, looking for the clues that would solve the mystery. Excited, she surrounded herself with books and began making copious notes. She would prove to Charles that she could do it, and in the process, she would prove the same thing to herself.

A short time later, as she was just finishing her research, Miles entered her office and dumped another armload of work onto her desk.

"Miss Appleton," he said smugly, "Mr. Howe asked if you could bring the coffee into the two o'clock meeting, since Mr. Crocker is out. What are you doing?" He lifted up a sheet of her notes and tried to decipher it.

"Nothing," Winifred said defensively, fighting the impulse to snatch the sheet back from him. "There was a complaint here that I thought I would research. Nothing important."

"Did you?" Witherspoon looked at her as if she had lost her mind. "Miss Appleton, I thought your orders were very clear. We have a lot of copying that needs to be done. If you cannot follow instructions, I am afraid I will have to report that to Mr. Howe."

"But it is just a simple complaint! It will probably never even go to court—"

"Then our lawyers will not have any trouble with

it, will they? I will take this with me. The coffee, Miss Appleton. Try not to forget."

He walked off, carrying her work with him. Winifred scowled, fighting the urge to dump the files on his head. Picking up the coffeepot, she carried it down to the kitchen and washed it in the sink, then put it on the gas stove to boil. As she assembled the cups, she tried hard not to feel resentful.

But she also felt a rush of pleasure. She had found several other poisoning cases that could help. Although her accomplishment would go unnoticed, she knew that she had succeeded in one of her personal aims.

When the coffee was ready, she put the pot on the tray and carried the assemblage into the conference room. The rumble of voices fell to an awkward hush as she entered and deposited the tray on the side table. Charles gave her a brief smile, then addressed the group of men.

"Good afternoon, everyone. Let us get started. Marton, why don't you go over the caseload?"

Winifred placed the coffeepot in the center of the table, then set the cups where they could easily be reached. She was about to leave when Charles stopped her.

"Miss Appleton, would you mind taking notes during the meeting? Our secretary is out today." He handed her a notebook.

"Not at all," Winifred replied, accepting the book and taking a seat. A few disgruntled noises came from the lawyers. The elderly Whitcomb played with his mustache, thoughtfully twirling it while he gazed in her direction, the younger Marton sent her a flirty smile, Witherspoon scowled at her, and Charles acted as if nothing at all unusual were happening.

Jared Marton flipped open a file. As he was about to read the cases, he paused and looked at Charles questioningly.

"Are you sure you want me to go through this?" Jared asked. "We have some sordid reports here. I am not sure this conversation is meant for mixed company." He looked uneasily at Winifred.

"Go on, read it," Charles said cheerfully. "I am sure Miss Appleton would not want us to act differently in her presence, would you?"

"Of course not." She bristled. "I have read law cases for years, and I am quite familiar with detailed descriptions of crimes. Please proceed."

Jared cleared his voice doubtfully. "We have the Lipset case scheduled to go to trial this week. That was the one where Mrs. Lipset's husband was missing, and she was mailed his . . ."

"Yes?" Charles said encouragingly.

"She was mailed a box containing his ear, packed in salt. The crime was carried out by the Bowery gang, no doubt. But the evidence against them is, as always, circumstantial. It is very doubtful that we will get a conviction."

At the description of the macabre crime, there were a few glances at Winifred, but she continued to take the notes calmly.

Charles frowned. If Winifred was upset, she certainly didn't show it. He glared at Jared impatiently. "What else do we have?"

"Mary Sullavin, arrested again for prostitution. The Blessington burglary. The Merrick murder. . . ."

"What about the Battery murder? Is that not on the calendar this week?"

Jared looked appalled. "Are you certain you want to discuss that?"

"Go on," Charles said flatly. "The case goes to court this week. We have to discuss it."

Jared hesitated, then began to read. " 'Rufus Woods has been brought up on charges before, but we have never had one stick. The police call him Slip for that reason. His last victim was found near the docks. It was a particularly ghastly murder.' "

"Go on," Charles said.

Jared cleared his throat. " 'The victim, a forty-five-year-old male, was found lying in the gutter with his throat cut from ear to ear. Apparently, he had been there for several hours, for he was as white as a sheet, most of the blood having drained from him. Rats had eaten a good part of his face before anyone arrived, and it was difficult to make a positive identification. . . . Even a hardened policeman threw his guts up when he saw him.' "

A few of the men coughed, looking directly at Winifred, all of them expecting some display of female repugnance. Such matters were discussed only in male company, since women, far too sensitive for such graphic conversation, had to be protected from the harsh realities of life. But Winifred only scribbled her notes, intent on what she was doing. The sound of the pencil scratching was the only noise in the room. As the men looked at each other in bewilderment, she finished, lifted her face, and waited for them to continue. Suddenly, a thud drew everyone's attention to the opposite end of the table.

Edgar Whitcomb had fallen to the floor.

"He fainted!" Winifred said, astonished, seeing the empty chair and the man's boots sticking out from beneath the table.

"Quick, get a glass of water!" Charles rushed to Whitcomb's side, while Jared opened the window. Winifred reached for the pitcher, then brought it to where Whitcomb was sprawled across the rug. The elderly man looked as if he were sleeping, his eyes fluttering, his skin deadly pale.

Drew McAlister shook his head, withdrawing a flask from his jacket. "Squeamish," he muttered, helping himself to a drink instead of providing it for the victim. "He never could take a discussion that involved blood."

Charles glared at McAlister, then slapped Whitcomb's wrists in an attempt to get the blood flowing. Winifred handed Charles the pitcher of water, which he immediately dumped into the older man's face. Whitcomb sputtered, then sat up like a corpse coming back to life.

"What happened?"

"Jared's details were a little too thorough for some of us," Charles said, grabbing McAlister's flask and offering it to the older attorney. "Have a drink and pull yourself together. We have the rest of the cases to review."

Whitcomb looked sheepishly at Winifred, but he obediently tossed back a large quantity of McAlister's whiskey. Then he got to his feet and took his chair with dignity, as if nothing at all had happened.

Charles hid a groan. So much for discouraging Winifred. Of everyone present, she appeared the least disturbed. "What else is on the roster?"

"The usual robberies, assaults, and burglaries. . . . We also have the Black case, the woman who is locked up for trying to poison her husband. I am sure it will never go to trial. These things always blow over. By tomorrow, she and her husband will be desperately in love again."

There were a few snickers around the table as the men exchanged knowing glances. Winifred felt her fingers tighten on her pencil. It was the complaint that she had read in her office. Obviously, the woman would find no sympathy in the prosecutor's office.

"We won't know that until the case goes to trial," Charles said pragmatically. "Still, it cannot hurt to get a start on it. Marton, why don't you and McAlister go and talk to the police? See if they have really got anything."

"Right," Jared said. "I saw the complaint. I have been meaning to research it, to see if we have any records of another case like it, but my calendar is too full."

"I have already taken care of that." Miles Witherspoon rose and placed a file before Jared Marton. "I took the liberty of researching the case myself."

Winifred's mouth dropped. Miles stared at her, as if challenging her to expose him. A thousand emotions swept through her at once. She could protest and claim she did the work, but would any of them believe her? Or would they defend Miles as one of their own? If so, she would earn the man's animosity forever.

Winifred bit her tongue. Charles read the document, his brows lifted in surprise. Slowly, his smile grew, and he looked at the clerk with genuine appreciation.

"This is wonderful, Witherspoon, exactly what we needed. Thank you. You have saved Marton quite a bit of trouble."

Miles preened, while the other lawyers congratulated him. "By the way, Miles, where did you find these citations?"

The clerk's face changed from white to red, and he talked in a queer stutter.

"I—I—"

"In the *Law Review*," Winifred said quickly. "I moved the books, but Mr. Witherspoon was able to find the right text. Several poisoning cases were cited, including one where a woman was the accused. I believe it was *State v. Decker*."

Her words seemed to hang in the air for a moment. The lawyers appeared as astonished as if the coffeepot had just spoken. Charles's smile grew broader. "That is exactly what we needed. Well done, *Miles*."

The attorneys went on to discuss the implications of the case. Charles sent Winifred an approving look.

He knew she had done the work and was letting her know it. Filled with gratitude, she saw that he was looking at her with pride and something else— something that made her collar seem suddenly too tight and her corset too warm.

"That is it for today. Miss Appleton, would you mind staying after for a moment?"

Winifred gathered her belongings but paused until everyone was gone except Charles.

"Miss Appleton," he began sternly, "did you research that case?"

"I—" Winifred stammered. "I picked it up accidentally. I am terribly sorry, I did not mean to cause a problem."

"Actually," he said slowly, "you prevented one. Marton could not get to the case, and if it does go to court, we will need that research. Your work appears to be some of the best in this office. I congratulate you."

His words held an odd tone, as if he were both happy and unhappy with his findings. Winifred swallowed hard. "How did you know—"

"Witherspoon could not find a precedent if it was handed to him on a silver platter," Charles said bluntly. "I do not like you covering up for him, though. Don't ever do that again."

"Yes, sir." Winifred started to leave when Charles stopped her.

"Miss Appleton, there is another case that needs the same kind of research you did today. Do you think you could handle it, between the copying?"

"Why, yes!"

"Good. You will find it on your desk first thing in the morning." He smiled, then once again was all business. "Take care of it right away. Nice work, Winifred." He winked at her, then brushed past her and returned to his office.

CHARLES RETURNED to his office deep in thought. His strategy had failed. None of the cases, not even the most sordid, appeared to have moved Winifred at all. And everyone present knew it was she who had done the research on the Black case.

Still, he wasn't discouraged. Winifred wouldn't last—he was certain of it. A part of him regretted it, since she had the instincts and daring to be a damned good attorney. But she wouldn't last.

His frown deepened when he recalled holding her in his arms yesterday morning. No woman had ever been able to draw him from himself the way she did. He would have to be very careful not to fall completely under her spell. In the next moment, he found himself wondering if she would consent to a late supper. She had become adroit at avoiding him—a fact that merely encouraged him. He had discovered that she worked late on her studies in the library. He would corner her there tonight and would not allow her to refuse him. He knew just the place—quiet and romantic, with excellent food and piano music.

Rifling through the cards on his desk, he muttered an oath when he saw the last one. Charles Howe Senior had apparently stopped by while he was in the meeting. The back of the card had a succinct but meaningful message:

Dinner tonight at 8:00.

Evidently, his parents had seen the papers.

CHAPTER 4

P ASS THE BUTTER, please, Charles."

Charles perked up, his mind somewhere else completely. Having dinner at his parents' house was never the most interesting of occupations, but tonight he found it even more tedious than usual. His sister was absent, having gone on a tour of the Continent, yet his parents had invited a friend of hers, Elizabeth Billings, as a guest. Charles had escorted Elizabeth a few times, and his parents wholeheartedly approved of her—and were clearly making their wishes felt.

Having captured Charles's attention, Elizabeth gave him a flirtatious sideways look, then dropped her eyes demurely to the butter dish. The silver-plated vessel was actually closer to her than to him, but she peered at him helplessly. Groaning inwardly, he reached for the dish and handed it to her.

"Why, thank you, Charles," Elizabeth said. "You are always so gallant and attentive! I cannot remember when I have enjoyed a meal more."

Charles smiled politely. He hadn't been the least attentive all evening. Although he had tried to get Winifred out of his mind, she constantly crept back in. A smoldering passion lay just beneath her cool exterior—he was certain of it. How enjoyable would that passion be when taken to the next level? He couldn't wait to find out. As if knowing what distracted him, his father coughed, while his mother smiled fondly at the young Billings girl.

"That is so sweet of you to say, Elizabeth," Charlotte Howe remarked, patting her lips with her napkin. "I am sure Charles thinks so, too. Do you not, Charles?"

"Of course," Charles said, then glanced across the table once more. Elizabeth Billings was quite a pretty girl, and he knew he should be more appreciative of her company. Superbly dressed in a pink-striped taffeta gown with a lace ribbon at her throat, she appeared quite fashionable. The color was very appealing with her brunette hair and rose-blushed cheeks, and she looked soft, sweet, and delectable, like a Christmas peppermint—and about as complicated.

"So what are your plans this fall, Miss Billings?" Charles's father questioned. "I understand from your father that you performed some charity work for the local orphanage last year. Quite noble of you, I do say."

"Thank you," Elizabeth said shyly. "Mother, Jane, and I have been helping the orphanage for a year now. We take up collections of clothes and other things our acquaintances do not need anymore. Then we bring them to the orphanage. I like to think that we brighten the children's day somewhat."

"I am certain that you do." Charles's father said. "Now charity work is a wonderful occupation for a woman. A gentlewoman can make a contribution, without taking away from her primary role in life. These modern women today just do not know their place. Unsexed they are, wanting to be involved in everything from politics to the workforce."

Charles knew exactly what his father was getting at. Although the older man had a heart condition which caused most of his family to walk on eggshells around him, Charles was infuriated by his indirect criticism of Winifred. He opened his mouth to reply when his mother stood up abruptly. "I think it is time we had dessert. Gentlemen, would you like to go to the study with your cigars and brandy? We could join you later."

Charlotte Howe smiled graciously, indicating the parlor. Her husband got immediately to his feet, and after a moment, Charles did as well. There was no sense in involving Elizabeth or Charlotte in this; nor did Charles wish to make them uncomfortable. But he could not resist defending Winifred.

"I think women should make up their own minds about what they want to do, and not be forced into a role for which they may not be suited," Charles said hotly. "Charity work is very noble, but what is wrong with women having choices?"

He surprised himself. A few weeks ago, he would have agreed with his father's opinion. Now he saw his father's face darken with displeasure, even as he held open the door to the library. Elizabeth stared at him in astonishment, as did his mother. Charles smiled. The effect Winifred was having on him was apparently very unpopular.

"YOU SIMPLY CANNOT let that woman stay in the state's attorney's office! The men at the club are appalled, and my contacts in the Senate are openly displeased. . . . Charles, are you listening to me?"

Charles suddenly became aware that his father had

stopped speaking. His mind had wandered back to Winifred again. She had looked so appealing that afternoon, her eyes sparkling as the attorneys discussed their cases. Even while conducting the meeting, he had envisioned peeling that stiff linen collar from her, placing kisses on every inch of skin that he bared. Downing the rest of his drink, he scowled, clearing the pleasurable thoughts from his mind.

"Yes, I heard you. But I don't care what anyone says, I have no intention of dismissing Winifred. We need the help around the office, and she is a real asset. She assisted one of the junior attorneys with a case today and found the proper precedent for him. With our workload and lack of help, I would be a fool to get rid of her."

"You would be a damned fool to keep her! The newspapers will not stop, nor will the gossip. Winifred Appleton is the discussion in every drawing room, and speculation about your relationship with her is rampant."

When Charles did not react, his father shrewdly changed his tack. "You know, your exploits as the state's attorney have garnered you favorable press. In fact, your reputation can only do you good, particularly now, with the Tweed corruption exposed. The citizens are tired of graft and dirty politics. It's time for a breath of fresh air."

"What has that got to do with me?" Charles asked impatiently.

"I'm getting to that." His father baited the hook, then dangled it before him. "There is growing support for someone like you in the next gubernatorial election. Someone with a spotless reputation. Someone who is willing to roll up his sleeves and take action, who is known as a champion of justice, and who doesn't know the meaning of the word *graft*. In short, those in power are not opposed to considering you."

"Me?" Charles asked, incredulous. "For governor?"

"Yes. Morality swings like a pendulum, Charles, but a campaign doesn't happen overnight. It takes years of work, of meeting the right people, getting the right press, and laying the groundwork. It is something I want you to consider. It involves Miss Appleton, since any stain on your reputation would weaken your chances and jeopardize everything."

"Bah!" Charles threw up his hands in outrage. "I should have known you were getting to this. I have no desire to become a political figure. My work as the people's attorney is all I ever wanted. Winifred's apprenticeship in my office could hardly stop my career."

"Not yet," his father said shrewdly. "But there is bound to be speculation. Marriage would help you tremendously, I would think, particularly to someone like Elizabeth Billings. Her good name and reputation could only help your political career."

Charles gazed at his father in disbelief. "Are you suggesting that I marry Elizabeth simply to gain advancement?"

"No, of course not." His father looked deeply offended. "I am simply stating the obvious. Marriage, in your case, involves more than just personal satisfaction. And Elizabeth Billings would be a good political wife. It is something for you to consider, Charles. That's all."

Charles rose from his seat.

"Are you going?" his father asked. "We have not had dessert yet. I believe your mother ordered your favorite, apple pie."

"I haven't much appetite," Charles said. "Give

Elizabeth my best. As the state's attorney, I have work to do."

He strode out the door, missing his father's scowl.

"EXCUSE ME, Miss Appleton."

Winifred glanced up from her work to see Edgar Whitcomb standing at her desk. Shifting his weight from one foot to the other, he looked extremely uncomfortable. She waited patiently for him to speak.

"I could not help but admire your remarks during our meeting the other day," he said, squeezing out each word as if it pained him. "And I noticed the work you did on the Black complaint, as well as the research you provided Mr. Howe. You seem to have an uncommon grasp of the law."

"Thank you," Winifred said uncertainly.

"Not that I think women are not capable," he continued quickly, patting his shiny vest. "It is just that I agree with the Court's ruling, that women were destined by nature to bear children and maintain hearth and home."

"I see," she said politely, trying not to show her impatience.

"But still . . ." The elderly man tugged on his curled mustache, as if trying to figure out just how to say what was on his mind. "That is, one can make exceptions—"

"Mr. Whitcomb, did you need my help with something?" She sweetly cut through his stalling.

At her offer, the man quickly thrust a large envelope toward her. "Would you be so kind as to look through that case and see if there is a legal angle that comes to you? Nothing too difficult, of course. Would do it myself, except my caseload is overwhelming this week."

"Of course," she replied, placing the envelope on top of the papers she had piled on her desk.

The man sagged with relief. Putting on his polished hat, he was about to leave when he turned and gave her a conspiratorial wink. "You will not tell anyone about this, will you?"

"No," she said, a smile curving her lips, "it will be our secret."

"Good. Very good. Not that there is any reason you should not help. I just would not want anyone to get the wrong idea, if you know what I mean."

"I think I know exactly what you mean," she replied. "Good morning, Mr. Whitcomb."

The door closed, and Winifred chuckled softly to herself. The old guard was finally beginning to come around. Not that she had any complaints, for she much preferred this kind of work to dusting the library or filing. Still, it amused her that the old gent would rather be caught dead than accepting advice from her.

She was about to return to her work, when another knock sounded on the door. This time Drew McAlister stepped in, giving her a brisk nod. Winifred put aside her pencil and waited patiently.

"Miss Appleton," he began, pausing in front of her desk. "I had a chance to review some of the work you have done. I thought your research was . . . very well thought out for a woman."

"Thank you." She tried not to bristle.

"I can tell you have done quite a bit of reading before you ever came here. Either that, or you have had excellent tutoring. I know Mr. Howe has been helping you, and frankly, I am amazed." He waited for her comment, and when none was forthcoming, he pretended to study his walking stick thoroughly.

"Mr. McAlister, I am sure you did not stop by just to discuss my work," Winifred said softly.

"Yes. I mean, no. Of course not," the man said, pacing the room once more. When he finally stopped, he stared at her uneasily, as if unsure of how to approach her. "What I mean to say is—"

Winifred took pity on the man. "Mr. McAlister, could you possibly have something you would like me to research?"

"As a matter of fact, I do." With that, he deposited another fat envelope onto her desk. "One of Tweed's associates is up on charges. It would not do at all for him to slip out of the rope, yet I feel some of the evidence is lacking. If you could just pinpoint, maybe make some notes . . ."

"I would be happy to." She smiled.

The man flushed in gratitude, then suddenly seemed to remember the time. "I really have to run. I will look for the work tomorrow. By the way—"

"I would not think of mentioning it to a soul," Winifred finished the sentence for him.

The man flushed again, then quickly dashed out, closing the door behind him.

This time Winifred really laughed. Fingering the envelopes, she saw that between the two cases, she easily had a week's work. More importantly, the attorneys' stealthy actions indicated that she had taken a step toward acceptance, a real step. And the education she would earn was priceless.

She had one man to thank for it all, Winifred thought. Charles Howe. He had done the unthinkable and given her a chance. The press had continued its relentless coverage of her presence in the state's attorney's office, and he had to be getting a lot of grief for hiring her. Still, he never let on that she caused him any inconvenience, and he only seemed proud of her achievements. There weren't many men who would put themselves in such a position, especially for a woman. Charles, Winifred realized, truly was a man among men.

And in addition to being a good friend, he was rapidly becoming something more. He continued to send the flowers and occasionally added little gifts, such as bonbons or poetry. Winifred refused to acknowledge them, finding herself in a verbal quagmire whenever she did, but his thoughtfulness was having an effect on her. A sexual tension ignited between them at every encounter, and her fantasies lately were becoming more and more explicit. She had trouble sleeping, tossing and turning all night, dreaming of his kiss, of him touching her, arousing her, teaching her far more than the law. . . .

Shaking her head, she forced herself to return to her copying, but her sensual ruminations still intruded. Legal work, which had always fascinated her, proved pale in comparison to thoughts of Charles. Good Lord, something must really be wrong with her! They had to remain friends, she reminded herself. Anything else would jeopardize what she had worked so hard to achieve. . . . Grimacing, she dug her pencil into the paper.

A few hours later, she had done a good amount of the research. Although the hour was very late, she had promised herself she would get to her studies that night; and she planned to do exactly that. Picking up her books, she buried herself in the study of torts, writing out answers to the essay questions in the dim light.

"You look beautiful when you are working."

Winifred jumped, then breathed a sigh of relief as Charles stepped into the room.

"I did not hear you come in. How long were you standing there?" she asked.

"Long enough," he said, delighted with her disconcerted manner. "What are you doing here so late? Looks like you have been busy."

"Thanks to you," Winifred said quickly, indicating the paperwork. "I have become quite an underground success."

"I thought that might happen." Charles chuckled, eyeing the bulging envelopes from the other attorneys. Looking past them, he saw the pages where she had been writing, and the books open at her elbow. "More legal work?"

"These are my essays. The ones you recommended I try," Winifred said. He picked up one of her papers, and she held her breath as he read the first few sentences. As she waited for his reaction, she felt extremely vulnerable.

A few minutes later, he looked up at her and smiled in surprised approval. "Winifred, this is good."

"Really?" Her heart beat faster. "Are you certain?"

"Yes, quite certain. There are a few little changes needed, a few places where you could expand, but otherwise, it is good. The writing is crisp, the references clear. It is excellent. Do you mind?" he asked, picking up her pencil.

"Mind? Charles, I would be so grateful! But you really shouldn't—you have done so much."

"Miss Appleton, I do not do anything without expecting a reward, and I am anxiously anticipating this one." Before she could respond, he indicated her work. "This paragraph is really well thought out. I think you need to expand on the ideas here, though." He stepped behind her, then reached lower to show her his notes. Winifred turned, and their faces were barely three inches apart.

"I think . . ." she breathed, deeply affected by his nearness, "your grasp of the legal concepts here is quite . . . seductive. I mean, impressive." Her mouth dropped at her own gaffe, and a heated rush spread through her skin.

"I see," Charles said a moment later, his eyes twinkling. "Well then, you will find this even more enthralling. Rewrite the third paragraph. It does not do you justice."

"Charles!" she looked up at him, exasperated. "You are teasing me, aren't you?"

"Yes, I admit it." He put down the paper and sat once more on her desk, laughing freely. "Don't look so horrified, Winifred. What is wrong with that? You could use a good teasing. You are entirely too serious."

"Is that so?" she said frostily.

"Yes, that is so. And I am certainly the one to do it, if I choose to," he said, earning another indignant look. Unable to resist, he softly touched her cheek with a gentle caress. "Do not worry,"—laughter was apparent in his voice—"I have a lot of teasing in mind for you."

A wave of hot anticipation shot through her. How did this man, with a few caresses and comments, make her feel like a complete idiot? She rose and faced him squarely.

"Mr. Howe—"

"Charles," he said softly, turning so that she stood within his grasp.

"What are you doing?" Alarm filled her, mixed with pleasurable anticipation, as he took her into his embrace. She tried to sound indignant, but somehow it didn't come out that way at all.

"I did promise not to seduce you while you were working here," he said, his voice a husky promise. "But Winifred, it is after hours now."

She inhaled an excited breath. Before she could launch into a dozen reasons why their relationship had to remain platonic, he was kissing her, a soft brushing of his lips.

It was softly compelling, a kiss meant to question as much as to seduce. Winifred sighed. She had waited too long, wondered too long, wanted for far too long. Sliding her hands inside his coat, she felt the crispness of his shirt beneath her fingers, the smooth satin of his vest, and the firmness of his hard, muscled body.

She leaned closer into his embrace, hearing his groan, feeling his hot, hard desire for her. Never would she have guessed it was so pleasurable to be kissed like this. The kiss they had shared at the Rutherfords' ball had been different, startling them both, but this one was even more potent in its tenderness.

Feeling her response, Charles turned her in his arms, determined to fully enjoy his plunder. He had meant simply to stake his claim, to move their relationship to the next level, but somehow things had already gotten out of hand. Winifred was surrendering—every inch of her body was pressed against his. The buttons of her prim dress were hard against his chest, while her soft breasts teased him alluringly. A hot, throbbing arousal pounded within him as he realized his student was more than ready for the next lesson. . . .

When he raised his head, he saw her dreamy expression, the confused wonder in her hazel eyes, and slight flush of her cheeks. "We really should not," she tried. "Someone might come in."

"You know, you are absolutely right." With that he disengaged, smiling at the disappointed look on her face. Instead of walking out, however, he simply reached inside a Greek urn that stood on top of the barrister cases and retrieved a shiny gold key. Locking the door securely, he turned to her with a wicked grin. "I am glad Chambers is so organized."

"You know that is not what I meant," she said reprovingly.

"Do you want me to stop?" he asked softly, taking her once more into the warmth of his embrace. "If you really do, I will."

"I do not think . . ." Winifred protested, but he was placing scorching kisses on her neck. Her fingers dug into his jacket, even as she tried to resist him. "It's not a good idea—"

"Most things worthwhile in life are not." Charles kissed her once more, this time deepening the kiss, slipping his hands through the prim knot on the back of her neck, and releasing her carefully constructed bun. Golden hair spilled out onto her shoulders, and hairpins tinkled to the floor. The smell of her, the scent of that wonderful hair, went straight to his head, as did the feel of her, all soft, warm, willing woman. . . .

Any last hope of restraint was gone. "Winifred . . . my sweet Winifred . . ." He cupped her breast through the stiff fabric of her dress and felt the nipple harden beneath his fingers. As he stroked her through the coarse cotton, her eyes flew open.

"Oh, Charles!" was all she could say as he lightly touched the fully aroused tip of her breast, then her fingers dug deeper into his back as he kissed her once more. His tongue took full possession of her mouth, plunging inside to taste her sweetness, even as the warmth of his hand cupped her. When he finally eased from her, she clung to him, her beautiful hazel eyes filled with longing. "Charles, that feels so wonderful. . . . I don't know what to think. . . ."

"I know," he said softly, though his voice was pained. "If I don't stop now, I won't be able to. As it is, I will have a wretched time walking back out into that hall."

Perplexed, her eyes traveled downward, then flew back up, mortified. He chuckled, touched her cheek softly, and gave her one more admiring look before resignedly kissing her forehead.

"I much prefer you looking like this, all disheveled, with your hair loose and full. Too bad I have a meeting tonight. Is your carriage outside, or do you need a ride?"

"No, Egbert is waiting. Do you have to leave?" she asked softly.

He nodded regretfully. "Unfortunately, yes. Besides, Miss Appleton, I think you have had enough lessons for one day. We have to leave something to study later."

He kissed her once more, hard on the lips, and then with a warm smile and wink, he unlocked the door and tossed her the key. A moment later he was gone.

CHAPTER 5

"CHARLES, ARE YOU TRYING to murder that thing?"

He glanced up through a haze of sweat and saw his friend Gabriel leaning against the ropes of the makeshift ring. Wiping the perspiration from his brow, he removed his gloves and tossed them aside. As he straightened and shook out his arms, his muscles hurt but the burning ache actually felt good, especially compared to the painful arousal that Winifred had left him with.

"Just getting some exercise," Charles replied casually. "I was too keyed up tonight to go home and sleep."

"I can tell," Gabriel said sarcastically, indicating the punching bag. "I thought you were going to pulverize that bag. I half-expected it to fly across the room."

Charles leaned down and picked up the robe hanging on the ropes. "It's been a frustrating month."

"So I heard," Gabriel replied. At Charles's sharp glance, he grinned. "I'm married to Winifred's sister Jennifer. Remember?"

Charles nodded. "I do recall that."

"Then why the workout?" Gabriel's smirk grew deeper. "As if I couldn't guess. Winifred is terribly attractive, and having her around all day—"

"Stop it," Charles said, cutting his friend off quickly. "Let's just say I find my association with her to be a challenge."

Gabriel threw back his head and laughed, and Charles scowled as he climbed out of the ropes. "Charles"—Gabriel flung his arm around him—"there is but one cure for getting involved with an Appleton. Either marry her, or drink a lot of whiskey."

Charles smiled. He *was* getting involved with Winifred—perhaps too involved. She was a decent woman, and he knew he couldn't just toy with her without eventually courting her. Marriage? The thought wasn't as troubling as it might have been. She fascinated him. And, having her in his office, so damned close and tempting . . . his blood pounded at the thought of that kiss, her eyes closing, the soft whimper in the back of her throat. . . .

"Whiskey," he decided quickly. "Fast."

WINIFRED PUT the last stack of books away in a daze, her mind still reeling from her encounter with Charles. It was late, and she knew she should go home. But she could not face Aunt Eve and her sister just yet. The feelings roiling inside her were too new, too raw, to share with anyone, and she was not at all certain she could successfully conceal them.

Closing her eyes, she tried to make sense of what was happening to her. She was supposed to be clerking, working as Charles's apprentice—not falling apart like a giddy schoolgirl! Yet the memory of his kiss, his intimate touch, the way he held her, threw her into giddy turmoil. Alone, she could admit the truth: she hadn't wanted him to stop. She had wanted him to make love to her, to take her to the next level, to teach her much more than the law. . . .

She felt as if there was a fever in her blood, an illness that defied all common sense. She had been unable to concentrate for weeks, had not been sleeping or eating right. When Charles kissed her, she had actually felt woozy. Maybe there was something physically wrong with her. It had been a long time since she had seen a doctor, but perhaps it wasn't a bad idea.

As she put the last volume away, a discreet black book sandwiched between two others caught her attention.

Doctor Spatterfore's Medical Book for Women. Frowning, she withdrew the volume, wondering how it got here, in the law library. She recalled something about Spatterfore—he was a radical who had written for *Woodhull and Claflin's Weekly*, an advocate of modern thinking. Flipping through the pages, she found chapters on pregnancy, menstruation, female complaints . . . her finger paused at the chapter on female sexuality.

"Men are catabolic in nature. They are concerned basically with fertilization, and thus are encouraged to expend energy. Women, by contrast, as the weaker sex, are anabolic. They must conserve energy, and are thus considered receptacles for a man's pleasure. It is the female then, who controls sexual advances, and is held responsible for the morality of the culture, who can say 'yea or nay' to the consummation of intercourse."

Winifred's nose wrinkled thoughtfully. Receptacles? What on earth did that mean? She read on.

"However, it must be said that with the study of evolutionary theories, there is a distinct possibility that women, as well as men, are endowed with mating instincts which compel them toward completion of the sex act. These instincts may be subtle, or may cause physical symptoms such as rapid pulse and breathing, distraction, lack of concentration, night sweats, and fantasies. Many believe that these feelings are associated with the seasons, much as they are in the animal kingdom, spring being a particular time for female sensitivity. The only cure appears to be the sex act itself, which temporarily purges the body of impurities and rids the mind of toxins."

Her hand was shaking as she slammed the book shut. So that was what was wrong with her! Mating instincts! The symptoms the doctor listed could not have been more like the ones she was experiencing if she had recited them herself.

Relief sped through her. She could finally put a name and a cause to her condition. Good Lord, why didn't anyone inform women about this, tell them that these feelings were normal, healthy, and indeed, good for the species? Instead of watercolors and needlepoint, why weren't women taught anything useful, especially about their own bodies? Surely she was not the only female who thought she was losing her mind when the only thing she could concentrate on was a man.

Yet her thoughts wandered back to that last sentence. *The only cure appears to be the sex act itself.* That she could believe. Her little experience in lovemaking, rather than sating her, only left her wanting more. Was this the way of it, then, and why lovers would take any risk to be together? Or perhaps, once the act itself had taken place, one felt satisfied?

That notion made some logical sense, and a solution began to suggest itself in Winifred's mind. What if she were to become Charles's mistress, at least for one night? Excitement pulsed through her as she tasted the thought. Their romantic interest was becoming entirely too distracting from her work. Surely, if they experienced the ultimate in a physical relationship, they could both put it from their minds and concentrate once more!

Before she could congratulate herself on her brilliance, a sobering thought came to her. There could be consequences to her plan. Even as sheltered as Winifred was, she knew how women became pregnant, and that the very act she was contemplating could have such a result. Her nose wrinkled, and she opened the book once more to read the section on female fertility:

"The female fertile cycle is a three-day period occurring approximately fourteen days before the onset of menses. If a woman forgoes sexual intercourse during the fertile period, she may safely indulge during the off cycle without pregnancy occurring. Conversely, if a woman desires pregnancy, conception is most likely to occur during the fertile period. Thus any woman can control the size of her family and number of children by adhering to a few simple rules."

That was it! Winifred knew most married women must practice something like this. They spoke of it in hushed whispers that died when she or another young woman entered the room, and now, she finally knew the particulars. A burden seemed to lift from her as she anticipated her fantasy coming true, without the worry of complications. Charles Howe was the one man in the world who could truly make her happy. And if she could enjoy only that for a time, she would take it.

A FEW DAYS LATER, she had an opportunity to approach him.

"Yes, Winifred? Come in." Charles gestured to a

chair before his desk while trying to clear the oak tabletop of paper. She entered and took a seat, waiting patiently for him to finish. He expertly placed one document on top of another, handing some to Mr. Crocker, tossing others into a cardboard bin. When the secretary was nearly buried under the stack of papers, Charles turned to her expectantly.

"You wanted to see me? I'm afraid this is not a very good time—"

"I need to talk to you, Charles," she said loudly. "Alone."

Charles nodded toward Crocker, and the little man exited, closing the door behind him.

"What is it? Are you out of work already? I have a few other cases you can take a look at—"

"No, nothing like that." She smiled softly, then took a deep breath. "I—"

There was a loud knock on the door. Charles swore beneath his breath, then yelled, "Come in!"

Jared Marton entered, clutching a handful of briefs.

"There you are," Jared said. "I heard you had come back from court. I have a few cases to review with you—hello, Winifred."

Jared's tone changed from brisk to warm. Charles could not help the irritation that arose in him at the handsome lawyer's attentions to Winifred. He scowled in the man's direction.

"Mr. Marton, Miss Appleton and I are in a meeting. I will be happy to go over your cases later."

"All right," Jared said, flashing Winifred a smile. At Charles's continued scowl, he withdrew quickly, closing the door behind him.

"Charles," Winifred began again, "I mean, Mr. Howe, the reason I asked to see you—"

There was another knock, followed by Miles

Witherspoon's entrance. The clerk placed another stack of papers on Charles's desk, along with a pile of mail. After a prolonged silence, he finally took the hint and departed.

"One would think this was the train station instead of my office," Charles grumbled. He turned once more to Winifred. "Please continue."

Winifred had just started to reply when the door burst open once more. This time two of the attorneys entered, loudly arguing over some legal semantics. Charles rose impatiently and held open the door.

"Gentlemen, I am speaking with Miss Appleton," he said firmly. "Would you mind taking your disagreements elsewhere?"

The two men glanced at Winifred in surprise, then shrugged. One of them spoke. "Sorry, we didn't realize—"

"A closed door around here apparently means absolutely nothing," Charles said sarcastically.

The two lawyers reluctantly took their leave. This time when they had exited, Charles bolted the door, then returned to his desk. Shaking his head, he absently picked up another stack of papers.

"I am sorry, Winifred. Now you were saying?"

"Charles, I have decided I want to be your mistress."

"What?"

The papers he had picked up fell to the floor. Winifred scrambled to her feet, attempting to retrieve the scattered documents. Charles grabbed her hand and held it tightly, preventing her from bending over.

"Charles, your work!" she exclaimed.

"Don't worry about that. I will pick up the damned papers later. I am far more interested in this conversation. What did you just say?"

"I have given this a lot of thought," Winifred said

quickly. "It is the most logical decision for both of us. This solution is the best for everyone involved."

"Go on." Charles released her, then fumbled to sit down on the front of his desk like a blind man. This had to be some kind of wile, he thought, an Appleton ploy to trick him into Lord knew what. Still, like a starving man being offered a feast, he was helpless to do anything except go where this led. His pulse pounded at her innocent words, and his breathing quickened. Could she really mean what she said? Could Winifred Appleton really boldly proposition him in his own office, intending to let him—

"So I think this is the only answer," Winifred continued. "The . . . passion between us is interfering with our work, and I presume the only way to subdue it is to experience it to the fullest."

"I see," Charles said. Understanding dawned as he finally grasped her reasoning. His seduction had been effective, all right, so much so that she wanted to experience it all in an effort to put him from her mind! Only Winifred could have possibly come up with such an idea, he marveled.

She was offering him the chance of a lifetime—an opportunity to make love to her. He would have to be a fool not to consider it. He stared at her once more. She had lowered her face again, and he felt a moment's sympathy for her, knowing what it had cost her to make this daring proposal. Lifting her chin with his fingers, he gazed deeply into her eyes.

Her expression made his breath stop. Along with shyness and embarrassment, he saw confused desire smoldering there, and a need that was as urgent as his own. His mouth went dry, and it was all he could do not to pull her into his arms right then and there.

"Winnie," he said hoarsely, "what makes you so

sure that once we have . . . consummated this relationship, the passion between us would die?"

"It always does," Winifred said, surprised at his question. "One does not see married couples acting entranced with each other over time. And even the most ardent lovers eventually become disenchanted."

"I see," he replied, knowing all too well what she meant. Unfortunately, Winifred's observations about married couples were correct. He, too, knew few of them who rushed home into each other's arms. His own parents maintained a cordial relationship, yet so formal that it was hard to believe they had ever experienced the kind of desire he felt for Winifred. But between some married couples, he knew, such passion did exist.

Winifred didn't know what she was asking, Charles was certain of that. But what were her motives?

"Winnie, this is not because of the apprenticeship, is it?" he questioned. "I would not want you to enter into something like this because you felt indebted to me."

"Of course not!" Winifred said, thunderstruck. "I am clerking for you in exchange for your help in preparing for the bar examination. I certainly feel I am contributing more than my share to your office," she bristled.

"Yes, you are," Charles said softly. "But Winnie, I am not convinced you have thought this all the way through. Someone here has to have some sense. There are many possible repercussions, physically, emotionally—I am not certain you understand what you are proposing."

"I most certainly do." She gave him a penetrating look. "Charles, I am determined to do this, but I sense you are not entirely committed to carrying it through.

I find this peculiar, given that you have done everything in your power to seduce me since I have been here. But if you have had second thoughts, then I will proceed with someone else, if necessary. Perhaps Mr. Marton will stand in for you, if you feel compromised."

Charles swore under his breath. Winifred knew unerringly how to skewer him, and it was all he could do not to turn her over his knee. Yet in all fairness, she was perfectly correct. It was he that had seduced her—too successfully, it seemed. As she gazed at him with all the directness of a hardened trial lawyer, her hazel eyes brimming with eagerness, he realized he could not resist her, no matter what his resolutions or his common sense told him. He was as trapped as she. Chuckling, he shook his head in defeat.

"All right, then. Where and when do you want to commence with this?"

Winifred breathed a sigh of relief. "I don't know about such things," she confessed. "I had hoped you—"

"Would figure it out, since I have been so successful so far," Charles said in amusement. "The best I have managed is stolen kisses in the library. I will have to give this some thought. One does not have an assignation without a careful plan. My home is out of the question. There are too many servants, and reporters have been following me there. I do not think you would want your name in print in that sort of context."

"Goodness, no!" Winifred said, appalled.

Charles smiled. "I suppose a hotel would be safer, but many of the more elite establishments frown on such doings. What I'd have to do is register us under an assumed name, as husband and wife. Would that trouble you unduly?"

"No." She shook her head, clearly perplexed at how complicated this was.

"All right. When did you want to . . . proceed?"

Winifred gazed at him uncertainly. "Why I think . . . the sooner the better."

Charles laughed quietly. When Winifred glanced at him questioningly, he shook his head. "How did I ever get so lucky to know a woman like you?" She started to say something, but he reached for her and kissed her hard, leaving her speechless. When he finally released her, they were both belatedly aware of someone knocking at the door.

"Go away!" They cried out in unison. The knocking stopped, and after a moment, they heard footsteps disappear into the hall.

"Yes, the hotel would be a much better place to continue this discussion," Charles said, reluctantly releasing Winifred. She felt so good in his arms, all soft and trembling. The self-assured lawyer was gone, and in her place was an innocent temptress. "Tonight then, at about seven-thirty? Would that give you enough time?"

"That is perfect. My aunt is out this evening. I won't have to explain my absence," she said, smiling warmly at him, as if relieved that the first difficult step was over. There was something incredibly naïve about her, something that totally belied her brazenness in offering to become his mistress. She acted as if that kiss had been her first. When she rose and exited, closing the door softly behind her, Charles had to shake his head in wonder.

He had just been given a tremendous gift. Winifred Appleton, his legal siren, would be his for a night.

CHAPTER 6

THE HOTEL WAS a beautiful structure on the corner of fashionable Fifth Avenue and Twenty-third Street, opposite Madison Square. Yet as the carriage pulled up to the curb and Winifred saw the glowing gaslights surrounding the lofty building, an uneasiness mounted within her. She drew her cloak tightly about her shoulders, glancing furtively into the street. There was no one passing by, no one to look upon her and notice her. Swiftly, she stepped up to the door, nodded to the doorman, and entered the lobby.

The scene took her breath away. Gold chandeliers glimmered overhead, with crystals dripping from their branches like icicles from a tree limb. The ceiling was a dome, and angels cavorted in the center, while elegantly carved plaster lined the walls like icing decorating a cake. Marble columns arose at the doorway, leading into the dining hall, while gilt-edged portraits stared down at her from the walls.

Awestruck and uneasy, particularly when the doorman eyed her questioningly, she strode toward the lobby as if she were perfectly familiar with everything there. She was well aware that ladies did not loiter in such areas; nor could they take a seat and read the evening paper as the gentlemen did. Yet Charles was nowhere to be seen. Not knowing what else to do, she simply stood near the wall behind an Indian rubber plant, pretending to be intimately involved with studying the portraits. Surely Charles didn't mean for her to sign the register herself, or to ask for a key? That would create all sorts of speculation! Yet why wasn't he here? Could he have possibly changed his mind?

"Miss, may I offer you assistance?" the doorman asked, approaching her.

He knew. Winifred was certain the man had figured out that she was here on an intrigue. Was it only her imagination, or was he looking at her with disapproval and disgust? Heat rose to her face, and she was about to respond when a voice sounded directly behind her.

"Sir, I assure you that my wife is well provided for. Hello, dear. Sorry I am late."

Relief sped through her as Charles stepped forward, offering his arm. As awkward as it was to be referred to as his wife, Winifred noticed that the doorman grew immediately respectful. Taking Charles's arm, she glanced coolly at the hotel employee.

"Thank you for your concern, sir," she said softly. Glancing at Charles, she managed a wan smile. "Darling, do you think we might go to our room? I suddenly have a headache."

"By all means." Charles nodded solicitously. "This way. I reserved your favorite suite."

The doorman, hearing her remark, hurried to the passenger elevator. "If you please, sir," he said quickly, aware that he might have offended them, "the vertical railroad would be faster. Allow me."

He opened the door, indicating that Charles and

Winifred should enter. Joining them inside the brass contraption, he physically closed the collapsing caged doors, then stared discreetly at the ceiling.

Within moments, Winifred's stomach jolted as the floor began to rise. Thankfully, Charles held her hand tightly as her stomach did flip-flops, and the tiny room ascended. The lobby disappeared, then a solid wall enclosed them inside as the elevator climbed the floors. When they finally reached the fourth, the contraption magically stopped, and the doorman held open the caged gate.

"Thank you," Charles said quickly, pressing a coin into the man's hand as they disembarked. "We will not be needing anything else."

The doorman nodded, and Winifred watched in amazement as the tiny room descended once more, disappearing from sight. She was even more surprised when Charles led her down the brightly lit hallway to their suite and opened the door with his key.

The room was incredible. Winifred gazed shyly about as she took in the burgundy velvet furniture trimmed in gold, the good French paintings, the thick, plush carpet. A gold brocade sofa graced one side of the room, while an elegant marble fireplace warmed the interior. Several rosewood chairs stood invitingly about, while a silver champagne bucket cooled the sparkling wine, and sugared almonds waited on the table. A small table near the fireplace held dishes covered with silver lids, and the enticing aroma of broiled chicken wafted from the plates.

And in the center of the room was a bed, larger and more sumptuous than anything Winifred had ever imagined. Covered in burgundy satin quilts, filled with pillows of all shapes and sizes, and framed with carved brass, it beckoned like a sultan's dream.

Tearing her eyes from the bed, she gazed at the

floor, suddenly overcome with insecurity. Charles reached for her cloak and removed it from her shoulders. Noticing her change in mood, he handed her a glass of champagne and indicated the chair before the fire.

"Winnie, please take a seat and relax. Have some supper. We have all night. You are not having second thoughts, are you?"

"No," she said honestly, accepting the glass and sipping gratefully from its frothy depths. "It's just that I . . . I mean, I do not know how . . ." She gazed at the richly textured bed, feeling like a knobby-kneed schoolgirl.

"I know, darling." Charles stood beside her, then ran his hands down her arms, warming her with his touch. Instantly, Winifred felt some of the tension melt away. He smiled at her, the look in his eyes touching something deep within her.

"I want you to know that if at any time, you want to stop or feel uncertain, I will do exactly as you ask. In spite of what you proposed, I will not force you, ever. Do you understand?"

"Yes," she breathed gratefully. Charles seemed to understand everything. She drank deeply of the champagne, and when she held out the glass in a silent gesture, asking for more, he seemed not at all surprised. This time he filled her glass only half full and waited until she took a deep drink before speaking again.

"I want you to experience everything tonight," he whispered hoarsely. "Too much champagne would interfere with that." His gaze swept down her and took in the gold silk dress she wore, the sparkling earrings, and the scent of her perfume. "You look breathtaking."

Winifred smiled, her uneasiness disappearing at

his words. He thought her beautiful. All the time she had spent longing for this man, all of the wondering and wanting, would culminate in this night. Charles held out a chair for her, and she accepted it, feeling as if she were truly special. Having a man treat her in such a manner was heady, even more so because that man was Charles.

Removing the silver lids from the plates, Charles revealed beautifully prepared chicken, garnished with rosemary and sage, tiny potatoes, and crisp almond beans. Lifting his glass to hers, he smiled.

"To us," he said, his eyes bathing her in the warmth of his glance. "And tonight."

"Tonight," Winifred whispered, touching his glass to her own.

The ring of crystal reverberated to her heart. There was something magical about the whole evening. She tasted the wonderful bite of the beans, the smooth texture of the potatoes, the mouth-watering flavor of the fowl. The champagne, imported from France, was soft and bubbly, with just the right touch of sweetness. All of her senses were enhanced in anticipation of what was to come. Nothing had ever tasted so good; nor could she remember ever enjoying a meal more.

Charles's conversation was equally pleasurable. Although he knew her well, he wanted to hear everything about her, from the time she was a girl to this moment. Winifred laughingly told him about her exploits with her sister Jennifer, as a spiritualist. During their séances, she had been in charge of playing the harpsichord, in order to enhance the atmosphere, while her sister Penelope had jiggled the wires of the chandelier to convey a ghostly presence. One woman had been so taken by their performance that she had run out of the house, only to return the following evening with her entire sewing circle.

"I have to admire you girls," Charles said, shaking with laughter. "You did the best you could in awful circumstances. No wonder you are all so terribly independent."

"Is that so wrong?" she put down her fork and gazed at him seriously.

"Only when it keeps you from allowing someone else to help," he answered. "And forgetting that you still have needs."

"Such as?" she asked cautiously.

"This." He rose from the table and swept her into a kiss.

It was an incredible melting of hearts, a timeless communication that expressed all of the joy, desire, and anticipation that had built within them in the past few months. Winifred forgot everything in that moment, every insecurity, doubt, and inhibition. This was Charles, and this was right. It was so right that she thought she would swoon, and she clung breathlessly to his shoulders, her body trembling in his embrace. When he finally raised his face from hers, she gazed at him in wonder.

"Please, Charles," she whispered softly, more certain than she ever was of anything in her life. "Please, love me."

"I will, darling," Charles replied. "I will."

He kissed her once more, fiercely, showing her how much he wanted her, stoking her passion until it was as all-consuming as his own. His lips urged a response from her, and she melted against him, pressing her body along his. The subtle surrender sent his blood pounding through his veins.

It took all his self-restraint to go slowly, to cool the fierce ardor that arose within him, reminding himself that he wanted everything to be perfect for her.

"Charles!" she gasped. "It is so odd, I feel quite faint! I never knew—why is it each kiss feels like the first?"

"Because it's right," he said, smoothing his hands down the sumptuous folds of her dress. "It's good that you feel that way. Let's get you out of these clothes before we have to find the smelling salts."

Winifred smiled uncertainly, as he untied the bow at her neckline and began undoing the buttons. Lifting her arms in breathless anticipation, she allowed the gold dress to slip to the floor in a molten puddle.

"You are so sweet," Charles said in awe, pausing to place a tender kiss on her exposed neckline. "Let me help you with the laces."

It was wonderfully pleasurable, having a man do this for her. Accustomed as she was to the tight tugging of her housemaid, Charles's undressing was seduction itself. Every inch of skin that he bared he kissed, and through each peeling layer, he softly caressed her. She ached with longing.

"Oh, Charles, that feels so good. . . ."

"I know, sweetheart. I want you to feel good."

The silky material of her chemise slid to the floor, leaving her clad only in her earrings, silk stockings, and garters. To his appreciative gaze, she looked like Venus. Bathed in firelight, her body trembling, she was perfection itself. Below her waist, a dark gold triangle gleamed enticingly above her thighs. Charles's mouth went dry.

"Winnie," he said reverently, taking in the sight of her, "you are so beautiful." He kissed her, a soft, teasing, tantalizing kiss, very unlike the passionate one he had given her previously. This time he sought to arouse her to the point of begging for him, to make her forget everything except how badly she wanted him. His hand slid down her soft white skin and cupped her breast.

Winifred gasped but offered no protest as his lips followed. She leaned into him, encouraging him, feeling the warm flood of desire spread through her like a golden pool of heat. Her breast ached, her nipple throbbed enticingly as his tongue teased her, making her arch involuntarily against him. She cried out as his tongue flicked her hard puckered nipple, sending delicious rivers of pleasure pulsing through her, even as his hand swept softly to caress the golden curls below.

"Charles!" she cried in wonder, amazed at the sensations speeding through her. Her skin seemed amazingly sensitive. Each brush of his lips or touch of his fingers made her feel vibrantly alive. A throbbing ache grew deep inside her woman's core. Moaning, seeking more, she lifted her arms to his shoulders, giving herself up to him entirely, wanting him, needing everything his hard muscled body promised. . . .

"Charles, please—" Her eyes lifted to his and nearly took his breath away. Never had he seen such desire in a woman. Her eyes were smoky, filled with passion and need. Her lips were parted, soft and moist from his kiss. She was irresistible, a wanton and an innocent rolled into one.

"All right, darling," he whispered, barely able to speak. "Let me take you to bed."

His heart pounding, he slipped his arm beneath her knees and carried her to the bed. Placing her on top of the bedclothes, he tossed his jacket aside, then quickly rid himself of his clothing.

"Charles," Winifred breathed in awe, "why, you're . . . beautiful."

Her words stunned him. Never had a woman told him he was beautiful. Among his class, such phrases were reserved strictly for women. Men were considered rough breasts, crude and overwhelming, while women were delicate creatures to be handled carefully and put on a pedestal. Yet Winifred was hardly delicate. Even now, she did not modestly avert her eyes from him but seemed to appreciate him in the same way one would admire a sculpture or a painting.

"Do you think so?" he asked, his heart melting.

"Why, yes," she said without inhibition. "Your muscles are so hard. . . ." She let her hand run over his chest, and he groaned out loud.

Slipping into the bed beside her, he smiled warmly, entranced by her. "My God, Winnie, I don't know if I can wait—"

"Don't," she said earnestly. "Truly Charles, we've waited long enough. I want to know, to understand . . ."

The passion inside him throbbed violently at her words. Fires long repressed came roaring to the surface, with the reality of Winifred, ready and willing, in his bed. Taking her into his arms, he kissed her ardently, wrapping himself over her body. His hardness pressed against her hot, moist opening, and instinctively she arched against him, feeling the divine pressure against her most sensitive place.

"Yes, Charles," she panted. "Yes . . ."

He entered her, feeling the tight resistance, even as she moved restlessly beneath him, encouraging him to go on. Blindly he thrust into her. When he reached the silken obstruction to paradise, he forced himself to stop. "This might hurt for a minute," he said softly, his voice filled with regret. "I am sorry."

"It doesn't matter," she said, touched by his concern. "Please, Charles."

He groaned, then forced past the barrier and was deep inside her. He felt her stiffen, then relax as her body expanded to accommodate him. Instinctively he thrust forward, sinking deeply into her, feeling the almost unbearable heat of her body.

It was the purest pleasure he had ever known. It was as if she were made for him. Her body expanded, swelling around him, her warmth nearly driving him wild. She was so wet, so ready and slick, her hot sheath encasing him, raising the pounding within him to maddening intensity. He withdrew once, then thrust again deeply within her, feeling her rise up against him, her breath coming in quick little cries. Her face looked like that of a ravished angel. It took every ounce of his self-control, but he held back, pleasuring her, until he heard her break—

Her cry made him shudder, and he thrust deeply inside her, feeling the pulsing completion of her ecstasy. Never before had he experienced such profound and honest surrender in a woman, and never had his body enjoyed such an earth-shattering climax.

Her beautiful eyes fluttered open several minutes later, and he saw the same astonished pleasure there. "Charles! I did not believe it could ever be so wonderful!"

"I'm glad you feel that way," he said, kissing the tip of her nose. "It's supposed to be pleasurable. Especially when a man and woman . . . mean something to each other."

He watched her digest that thought, then she frowned. "Why don't they tell us this? Most women seem to consider lovemaking a marital duty."

"There are a lot of careless men out there," he said, "and a lot of fearful women. The consequences of making love unfairly usually fall to the fairer sex. Stop looking at me like that—I do not make the rules!" He smiled as he spoke, kissing her fingertips.

"Well, now that I know how astonishing it truly is, I will demand my share," she said, rising up to meet his kiss. "I hope you don't mind."

Charles smiled, then showed her how little he minded at all.

CHAPTER 7

Winifred awoke to the sun pouring into her room. Birds sang outside, and the winter seemed to be finally fading into a fresh spring. Tossing the covers aside, she stretched, yawning like a contented kitten.

Charles. Last night. Their lovemaking had truly been wonderful. She had been reluctant to leave the hotel, but Charles had insisted on escorting her safely home, leaving her with a kiss that, after the evening they had spent, was achingly sweet. Nothing could have prepared her for the sensual, erotic pleasure at the hotel, the feel of fingertips brushing across heated skin, the touch of a hot tongue on a throbbing pulse point, the emotional satisfaction of being really loved. . . .

Her eyes flew open as she mentally formed the word. She could not love Charles—she could not love anyone! Her mission in life was crystal clear and always had been. Love led to one thing: marriage, at least among women of her class. And once married, a woman became the property of her husband. Everything she owned, everything she was, became his.

When children arrived, becoming a lawyer would be impossible. As Mrs. Stanton once said, it is the unmarried women among us who must free us. Winifred knew exactly which camp she was in.

Her nerves calmed when she reminded herself that that was why she had agreed to make love with Charles to begin with. Now they could put all that behind them. Her curiosity satisfied, the physical part of the relationship out of the way, they could both fully concentrate on their work. She was certain Charles would see it exactly the same way.

Relieved, she bathed and dressed, her body aching in unaccustomed places after Charles's vigorous love-making. Fastening her hair up in a severe bun, she put on her most prim and proper gown—a stark gray dress that looked something like a male uniform. She decided it was important to send Charles the right message, just in case he was entertaining any other thoughts. As she marched down the stairs and stepped into the carriage, she saw Egbert's curious glance.

It was time to get back to the law.

CHARLES SPLASHED LIME WATER on his face, welcoming the cold sting. Nothing could trouble him this morning.

Winifred. For the hundredth time, he replayed that scene where she had propositioned him, then all the scenes that followed, right up until she cried out his name in the ultimate pleasure. She had been so hot, so tight, so erotic and yet so innocent at the same time. His blood boiled just at the thought of her. He could still see her now, her clothes falling from her, her body gleaming gold and white in the firelight, her face gently ravished and filled with bliss. . . .

His arousal throbbed achingly, and he realized

that after having her once, he only wanted her more. Surely she was experiencing the same thing this morning. He smiled, adjusting his tie, thinking of how exciting work had suddenly become. Why, they could enjoy little trysts in the library, he could tease her ruthlessly over lunch, they could play footsie under the table. Soon she would be begging him to love her, wide-eyed with desire, just as she had last night.

His conscience nagged at him as he recalled his previous resolution. Winifred was a lady. He could not continue to treat her like a mistress. But the thought did not trouble him unduly. He would simply ask her to marry him. That way, he could have the maddening hoyden all to himself and could enjoy her without consequence. His family would never approve, but Charles did not care. He wanted Winifred more than he'd ever wanted any woman. He would never be bored with her, would never have to endure conversations on the latest hair or dress styles. No, she would continue to enchant him, frustrate him, and confuse him, and after last night, he did not want it any other way. Winifred, he was certain, would feel exactly the same.

"MISS APPLETON, Mr. Howe would like to see you in his office," Miles Witherspoon said, his voice sounding ominous.

Winifred glanced up from the morning paper. There was a story in the *Times* about Mrs. Black, the woman who was accused of poisoning her husband and whose case she had researched. According to the paper, the tests had come back positive—arsenic had been found in the husband's tea. The case would now go to court, and it seemed almost certain the woman would be convicted. . . .

"Miss Appleton?" Miles questioned. "Did you hear me?"

"Yes, thank you, Mr. Witherspoon," she said, forcing a smile and putting the paper aside. She ignored the tension pooling in her stomach and started down the hall.

"Miss Appleton." Miles stopped her, his expression worried. Something about Charles's summons must have been daunting. "If there is any way I can provide assistance, you have only to mention it."

Winifred stared at him, then smiled more genuinely. "I appreciate the offer, but I am sure there is nothing to be concerned about. Thank you."

Walking past the clerk, she shook her head in wonder. Miles Witherspoon offering to help her. It was an odd world, indeed.

But why did Charles want to see her? Uneasy doubt swept through her as she pictured them entwined together the previous night. What if he wanted to continue the new state of affairs between them? What if he got angry? What if he felt she had used him . . . ?

She could not think of all that now. She would just have to try and explain her feelings to him, calmly and logically. After all, he was a gentleman and, as such, would have to respect her wishes. He might even be relieved.

When she got within a few yards of his office, she heard shouting. The door was open, and she could hear heated words from Jared Marton. Knocking timidly on the door, she waited for Charles's gruff, "Come in!" then entered with considerable trepidation.

"You called for me, Mr. Howe?"

His face was flushed with annoyance, but upon seeing her, he calmed somewhat. He started to respond to Jared, then his face turned quickly back to her, as if suddenly seeing her dour outfit and prim hairstyle. "Mr. Marton and I are just finishing up," Charles said, his brows coming together in disapproval at her appearance. He turned back to his colleague. "Jared, I do not want this case. Find the time."

"I am sorry." Jared stood before Charles's desk, holding a file of papers. "You know you are the only man here who can handle it. Not only do I not have the time, it would ruin me." At Charles's questioning look, Jared shrugged. "I cannot prosecute a woman. No girl in New York would be seen with me after that."

"So that is the real truth," Charles said sarcastically. "You are afraid to convict a woman of attempted murder because it would ruin your social life."

"Yes," Jared admitted. "Ask one of the married lawyers to take it. It cannot possibly harm them."

"Are you joking?" Charles asked incredulously. "Their wives would kill them. Oh, leave it here. I will do it."

His voice with thick with disgust and resignation. Jared slapped the file down on his desk, gave Winifred a jaunty look, then strode out of the office, whistling.

"What was that all about?" Winifred asked, puzzled.

Charles handed her the file. "The Black case. The woman accused of trying to poison her husband."

"I was just reading about that!" Winifred said in excitement. "That was the complaint I had researched. The woman was arrested before they could even prove there was poison—just on her husband's word."

"There is no question now." Charles's voice had an odd, disapproving note. "The tests came back positive for arsenic. Mrs. Black undoubtedly tried to murder her husband."

Winifred frowned, then began looking through the documents. "Does she have a lawyer?"

"Horace Shane," Charles replied. "She just hired him this morning."

"Shane," Winifred repeated. "Well, that's good. He is known to help women." Putting the file down, she faced him directly. "Charles, you cannot possibly mean to prosecute this woman. She was arrested without due cause, the evidence seems inconclusive, and her husband sounds like a wretch!"

Charles gazed at her in outrage. "Winnie, I have to prosecute her. No one else here wants the case. And how can you say the evidence is inconclusive? The man comes home, the woman gives him his tea, and within an hour, he becomes sick. They test the tea, and it is full of arsenic! How much more conclusive would you like?"

Despite his anger, Winifred locked eyes with him. "This woman will never get a fair trial. How can she? Where is a jury of her peers, when the entire jury is male? No one will see her side. Poor Mrs. Black!"

His face turned an interesting shade of purple.

"Winifred, there is no 'Poor Mrs. Black!' This woman tried to murder her own husband in cold blood! There is no excuse for that whatsoever! The law is the law!"

"She is 'alleged to have tried,'" Winifred corrected him. "You are not the jury."

She tossed her head tartly, and Charles swore under his breath. Taking a step closer, he grabbed the documents from her. "Stay out of this, Winnie. This woman is a murderess, not a cause célèbre for women's rights or a noble heroine. She is a ruthless, cunning woman who slipped arsenic into her husband's tea."

"And if it had been the other way around, would

anyone be batting an eyelash?" Winifred demanded hotly. "Why the male outrage, Charles? Because one woman stood up and tried to free herself the best way she knew how?" At his appalled expression, she continued self-righteously, "After all, marriage only benefits the man in our society! A woman loses all power. Maybe Mrs. Black was trying to regain hers!"

"By killing her husband?" Charles stepped closer, and Winifred backed up against his desk until her bustle stopped her. "Winnie, so help me God, you should be grateful for society's rules concerning the treatment of women. They are particularly convenient for you at a time like this!"

His eyes blazed hellfire, and Winifred swallowed hard. She'd seen him angry before, but never like this. Drawing herself up to her full five feet three inches—which still left her far short of him—she gave him her best icy stare.

"I can see that we disagree on this case, Mr. Howe," she said stiffly. "Perhaps it would be best if we did not discuss it in the future."

"I think that is a fine idea," he agreed, a muscle ticking in his jaw. He looked as if it were taking everything he had to maintain his composure and keep himself from throttling her.

"And I am sure you will understand what I have to do."

Winifred turned to leave his office—but she did not count on Charles moving faster, or closing the door firmly to block her way.

"What are you talking about?"

She felt the courage leaking out of her as if she had just sprung holes. "I have to try and help her," she said calmly, nearly flinching at the fire that burned anew in his eyes. "I am going to see Horace Shane and offer to assist the defense. I understand he is sympathetic to women's rights and will, no doubt, accept my help."

"Winnie," Charles spoke softly, his voice deadly, "you will do no such thing. I forbid it."

"I am afraid you cannot forbid anything," she said softly. "You are, after all, neither my husband nor my father. Unlike Mrs. Black, I am a free woman."

His eyes blazed, but he held himself in firm control. "Winnie, listen to me. You cannot do this. This trial will get a tremendous amount of publicity. You know it, and so do I. To assist in Mrs. Black's defense would destroy your credibility."

"Certainly the case will get publicity," Winifred said calmly. "But I am not afraid of that. If the papers want to call me a radical for women's rights, so be it. That will only help my cause. Charles, you are not going to talk me out of this. My mind is made up. I will not abandon this woman in need."

"I see," Charles said, seeing all too clearly. Fury swept over him as he realized he had been a fool ten times over. "Had you planned to do this all along?" The possibilities filled his mind, none of them flattering to her.

"Charles, you are being ridiculous," Winifred said flatly.

"Am I?" His indignation brimmed over, as his male ego took another bruise. "Were you just using me and my office as a way to learn the prosecution's case against her, so you could take that information to the other side? I must congratulate you, Miss Appleton, you have been extremely clever. Was it all just part of the game? Perhaps even our night together was part of your scheme—to keep me interested long enough to plot something like this?"

Winifred straightened abruptly. She felt as if he had slapped her. "I know you are angry, but there is no cause for these suspicions. None of this is personal."

"Isn't it?" Charles looked at her as if seeing her for the first time. Some of the anger lifted from his face, and his brows came together. "So that is what this is all about."

"What?" she asked, less sure of herself now.

"Last night. You do not want to work with me here, in this office, because you are afraid you will be tempted once more to make love to me." She started to sputter a denial, but he took her by the shoulders and continued fiercely. "You are afraid of even more than that. You are scared that I might start to mean something to you, that a man might become as important to you as your precious cause!"

"That is ridiculous," she protested, even though her conscience nagged at her. "I have no idea what you are talking about!"

"Good, I will be happy to show you." He slid his arms around her waist and yanked her into his arms.

None of this is personal. Her words had hurt him more deeply than he would ever admit. No one knew better than he just how personal their relationship truly was. With a muffled curse, he ignored her look of surprise and covered her mouth with his own.

He had a fragmented glimpse of her eyes getting impossibly wider, but he didn't care. Winifred whimpered, making a soft sound in the back of her throat as his lips possessed hers. It was an exciting kiss, filled with all the apprehension of two warriors doing battle, and two lovers undeniably attracted to each other. Charles deepened the kiss, refusing her half-hearted protests, deliberately arousing her and forcing her to admit that their relationship was indeed personal. Coaxing her lips apart, his tongue met hers, teasing at first, then plunging inside to take full possession of her sweetness. Winifred rose on her toes to meet him and melted into his arms, surrendering completely.

"Ah, so it wasn't all just an act," Charles said knowingly when he eased his mouth from hers. Her confused blush delighted him. "And it is not just all on my part. But I am warning you—I have no intention of reverting back to a friendship with you. I will not be tossed aside at the first provocation. I am more attracted to you now than ever, and I will win you, come hell or high water!"

Winifred's mouth dropped open, but he continued ruthlessly, shaking a finger in her face. "If you continue with this Mrs. Black folly, you will regret it. And if you think for one minute that I will go easy on you in the courtroom because of our relationship, you are badly mistaken. I intend to bring out all the big guns. This woman is a criminal, who committed a heinous crime. I will prosecute her to the fullest and put her behind bars where she belongs. Do you understand me?"

"Certainly, Charles." Winifred had regained her composure.

Charles had to hand it to her—never had he met a woman who was so clearly his equal, a thought that would appall his male counterparts. Something sparkled in her eyes, and he recognized with a sinking feeling, that it was a challenge—prosecution versus defense, male versus female—in a battle to the finish. Winifred, far from being intimidated or nonplussed by his kiss, was clearly invigorated by it. Yet in that moment, she looked more beautiful than he'd ever seen her.

"I would not expect anything else," she continued. "Give it your utmost, Charles, as I certainly intend to do. May the best attorney win."

With a flourish, she turned and stormed out of the room.

.

CHARLES STARED at the slammed door in chagrin. What in God's name had just happened? He had started that morning thinking the world was his oyster, and now he had lost the pearl.

Even after that incredible kiss, Winifred had dumped a bucket of ice water on him and shown him quite clearly that she did not need him at all. And now she would work on the Black case—against him! He groaned as he envisioned the circus the papers would make of this. Winifred's involvement in the case would only fuel that fire. Why did she not see that he was trying to help her find real happiness?

Because she was Winifred, a voice inside of him responded. And to be truthful, he would not be nearly so attracted to her if she were any other way. It was that fire inside of her, that passion for her cause, that had made him take notice of her to begin with. And it was her other passions, the ones that he felt when he kissed her, that made her impossible to forget.

There was but one thing he could do, he reasoned, a strange calm coming over him. He had to win the Black case. He had to show Winifred that he was right. Then she would see that courtroom life was not for her. She would surely lose, and the press would rip her to shreds. And when they did, he would be there to catch her fall. Hurt and disillusioned, she would turn to him for comfort, and he would provide it— and so much more. She would forget the law, dismiss her futile ambition, and come running into his arms, filled with love and gratitude. Then Winifred would finally be his.

"Crocker, get in here," Charles called, opening the door Winifred had slammed. "Call a meeting. We have a case to prepare—the case of a decade."

CHAPTER 8

WINIFRED MARCHED BACK to her desk and began to pack up her things. Her hands were shaking, but she determinedly piled her books into a box.

No matter what happened at Horace Shane's office, she could not work here anymore. Charles had no respect for her principles whatsoever. He could never understand why she objected to his prosecuting Monica Black. How could she have made love with such a man! The only thing he seemed to admire was her body, not her mind. The more she thought about it, the more she fumed. His smug assurance that he would seduce her again only inflamed her. He obviously intended to pick up right where he had left off.

Winifred paused. The case against the woman was, well, black, but Winifred could see a world of possibilities. The case would generate tons of negative journalism, but ultimately she could use it to an advantage. She would paint a picture of a distraught wife shackled to her brutish husband. What were her choices? she would ask the jury. Divorce was unthinkable, as were other legal resources. The woman had no other option but to submit to her husband, to give him control of her property and her own person. Poison, seen in that light, was the only way out. She had fought back the only way she knew how.

Winifred's eyes sparkled. It would be sensational, the talk of the country. And if the defense played the press right, and if they tried the case correctly, she could help expose the plight of women everywhere. In the process, she could help free Monica Black.

Picking up the box, she headed for the door.

THE DRIVE to Horace Shane's office was a short one. As Winifred alighted from the carriage and climbed the thirteen stairs to the prestigious law firm, she mentally reviewed everything she knew about this man.

Horace Shane was an eccentric, with long white hair and a beard that flowed down to his collar, lending him the appearance of a benevolent Saint Nicholas. His suits were always rumpled, and notes were absently stashed in his pockets, but beneath his careless appearance burned a brilliant legal mind. More promising, Horace Shane was also a vocal proponent for women's suffrage and advancement. He loved to upset social conventions and garner attention from the press with his radical views, supporting free love, divorce, the eight-hour workday, and equal rights for women. His wife was a beautiful, intelligent woman who doubtless influenced him, but even on his own, Shane was a Renaissance man.

Handing his secretary her card, Winifred waited politely in the foyer. She did not have to wait long.

"Miss Appleton?" A voice boomed down the hall. "Who the hell is that? I do not need any more of those women's righters coming through here to discuss poor

Mrs. Black. Just tell her to leave. I am not here. Damned suffragette!"

Winifred's stomach tightened. He was not going to see her. But surely within the next few days he would build his legal team. This might be her only chance. Instead of waiting for a dismissal, she strode directly into the room.

Shane appeared startled, but he stared at Winifred with interest, still fingering her card.

His secretary, pointing frantically, made it clear that she had nothing to do with this intrusion: "She came in here! I did not let her, I told her to wait—"

"That's all right, I will see her. Take a seat. I did not recognize your name immediately, but I do now. You work for Charles Howe, but it was something before that . . ." He gazed at her thoughtfully, then smiled. "Spiritualism, wasn't it?"

Winifred winced in embarrassment, then took the chair he indicated, trying to act as composed as possible. "That is all in the past," she demurred, wanting to change the subject.

"I am sorry to hear that," Horace said sincerely. "I was always partial to spiritualists. 'There are more things in heaven and earth, Horatio . . .' I am sure you know the quote. But I do not suppose you came here to discuss Shakespeare. I was wondering if perhaps I would hear from you, or someone from the state's attorney's office. The Black case does hold features of interest."

"That is why I have come," Winifred said, her hands trembling in excitement as she reached for her notes. "Mr. Shane, I am sure you are well aware that this case will be sensational. The newspapers will jump all over it, and the matter will be discussed in every drawing room. It could make you famous."

"I am already." The gruff attorney shrugged, gazing shrewdly at the beautiful woman before him. "And I, too, have thought of the implications of this case. Usually instances of suspected marital poisoning are considered private and are hushed up by everyone, including the police. It was only because Mr. Black did not die that the case is going to court."

"Then there is no doubt as to her guilt?" Winifred scribbled furiously.

Horace Shane broke into laughter. "Miss Appleton, I know you are an apprentice for Mr. Howe's office. Tell him I plan to fully disclose all my evidence, as required. But the case just came into my office."

Winifred put down her pen and looked directly at the older man. "Mr. Shane, I am not here on behalf of the prosecution. In fact, I would like to make you an offer. I will help you, do all the research, provide everything you need for a successful acquittal—in exchange for the opportunity to work on this case."

The attorney looked at her in confusion, then burst into laughter. Removing his glasses, he wiped his eyes with his handkerchief, shaking his head as if she had just told him the best joke ever.

"Miss Appleton, why on earth would I agree to something like that?"

Winifred was undaunted by his manner. "It benefits you entirely," she said confidently. "Think about it. Not only do I have real experience doing research for legal cases, but I have been clerking for the prosecution. I know the kind of research that the state's attorney's office does to win a case, and I know how they will approach this one. That experience alone will be invaluable to you. Also, there is the question of finances. Mrs. Black undoubtedly has little authority over the family money and will have a hard time paying you."

"I did not take this case for money," Shane said quickly.

"I did not think you had. Even more reason, however, to defray additional costs to yourself. If I can provide much of the research for free, it cuts your losses. Everyone benefits—most of all Mrs. Black."

Horace Shane's eyes narrowed as he thought her proposition through. "I must say it is unusual, Miss Appleton. And tempting. But how can I be certain that you are not simply an emissary from the state's attorney?"

Winifred grinned, even more certain of herself now. "Mr. Shane, it is no secret where my political affiliations lie. I apprenticed with Mr. Howe solely in order to learn from him and pass the bar examination. Mr. Howe has been extremely generous with his time and has taught me much. But this case is an opportunity not only to apply what I've learned but to support the female cause. There are many Mrs. Blacks out there, Mr. Shane. You know it, and so do I. Together we can not only win this case but draw attention to a cause that deeply deserves the light of day. If we can prevent one more Mrs. Black from resorting to poison, we will have accomplished something grand."

Horace Shane toyed with his watch for a moment. "I like your style, Miss Appleton. And I have heard your work is excellent. I do think you are right. Furthermore, my wife is an admirer of yours and thinks you demonstrate quite clearly that women are capable of anything. So you see, I do not dare refuse you— otherwise I may find myself in the position of poor Mr. Black."

Laughing, the excitement bubbling up inside her like water in a spring, Winifred accepted his handshake. She, together with Horace Shane, would fight for Mrs. Black, and for women everywhere. And they would win.

A twinge of conscience pulled at her as she thought of Charles, working on the opposite side. But she pushed the troubling image from her mind. Charles would not let thoughts of her stop him from proceeding, especially if he knew he was right. It was time she started thinking like a man, especially if she wanted to beat one.

"WE NEED TO DISCUSS our strategy for the Monica Black case."

The lawyers looked at each other and groaned. Jared Marton smiled knowingly as Charles slammed down a fist full of papers.

"But . . ." Edgar Whitcomb scratched his snowy head. "I thought this case was cut and dried! The woman attempted murder, poison was found in the tea . . . What else do we have to prove?"

"I want this case to be airtight," Charles stated. "Whitcomb, find out who tested the poison, then get a second opinion from an expert. Maybe Professor Doremuse, if he is available. Marton, interview everyone—her servants, friends, acquaintances. I want confirmation from neighbors that this Black woman was indeed at home that night. I want to know everything about her, where she goes, who she sees, what her true motivation was for trying to kill her husband. Was there a will? A lover? Abuse? McAlister, check the court records. See if there was a secret marriage, birth, anything at all. I want no surprises."

The lawyers looked at each other once more, all of them thinking of their heavy workload. "But why not ask Miss Appleton do to the legwork?" Drew McAlister said. "None of us have the time for this."

"Because Miss Appleton has gone to work for the other side," Charles said matter-of-factly.

A collective gasp came from the men. Charles glanced up from his file, but if he felt anything about what he'd just said, it was not apparent. Jared stared at him thoughtfully, a shrewd smile playing around his handsome face.

"You mean—" Miles Witherspoon seemed to have difficulty even forming the words.

"Yes. Mrs. Black hired Horace Shane to be her attorney, and Win—I mean, Miss Appleton is applying to him as a clerk. We all know Shane's bias toward women. I am certain Miss Appleton will win his favor."

A heavy silence fell around the room. Now they would have to do their own copying, filing, and researching. . . . And although not one of them would have admitted it openly, they had all come to respect Winifred's ability. More than one expression of regret stared back at Charles. They would have been far happier to have her on their side.

"Damn Shane!" Jared Marton swore. "That was really shabby of him to court Miss Appleton for this case. He probably means to gain publicity, as well as learn the workings of our office." Then his expression changed from outrage to sorrow. "I'm going to miss her. She was the only pretty face around here."

The men grumbled, all of them accusing Shane of unfair dealings until Charles interrupted. "Shane did not court Miss Appleton. She went there of her own accord. This case appeals to her as a women's rights issue, something she can use to publicize the plight of women. You all know what that means. The newspapers will be all over it, and our office put into the spotlight. A case that should have ended in an hour will now go on for weeks."

Everyone groaned, while Charles continued. "So now you see why we need full cooperation. We have to win this case. I want no slip-ups, no surprises. For every Shane trick, every clever action on the part of Miss Appleton, we will be prepared. Everything has to be perfect, or we will all suffer the consequences. Is my meaning clear?"

They nodded glumly. "Good," Charles said, and handed out the remaining assignments.

"I AM HERE to see Monica Black."

Winifred ignored the police officer as she stood inside the Ludlow Street jail. She knew what he was thinking. Ladies did not come to prison, not unless they were the immediate relative of an unfortunate inmate. And they certainly did not come as legal counsel. But since her papers were in impeccable order, he turned toward the interior of the prison, indicating that she should follow him.

Winifred walked through the narrow passageway, excitement coursing through her. The previous night, she had spent several hours with Horace Shane, going over the case and formulating how to best use the press. Mrs. Black had already given a few thoughtless statements to the *Times* that, although not incriminating, were damaging to public opinion. For the defense to use the papers effectively, she and Horace would have to approve every utterance Mrs. Black made and coach her on how to respond.

A pang of guilt hit her as she followed the man through the dank prison hallway. Charles would certainly not approve of her tactics, even though counseling defendants was a routine part of the job. Winifred quietly acknowledged that she intended to do much more than that, to escalate a common case of attempted

murder into a social cause. From her viewpoint, she
was entirely justified, no matter what Charles thought.

As she waited outside the cell, heat came to her
cheeks once more as she thought of that kiss she had
shared with Charles in his office. Why couldn't she
put it from her mind? She had thought making love
would kill the attraction between them. But instead it
was more intense than ever. Doubt crept into her as
she envisioned facing Charles in the courtroom. If she
could not control her emotional reaction to his kiss,
could she really defeat him using her wits?

"Mrs. Black, you have a visitor," the policeman
announced distastefully, as if he thought according a
would-be murderess any visitation rights at all was
unwarranted. He turned to Winifred. "You have thirty
minutes."

"Thank you, sir," she said politely, ignoring his
tone. She approached the cell, curious to see the
notorious Monica Black.

The woman behind the bars turned toward her,
and Winifred was immediately struck by the paleness
of her complexion. Large, luminous brown eyes stared
out of a face that might once have been called pretty,
yet now looked shopworn and fragile. She was dressed
in a frivolous pink gown that belied the seriousness of
her predicament, and she appeared younger than her
thirty-plus years.

Winifred frowned, recalling everything Shane had
told her about this woman. Monica had been a dance
hall girl, one of New York's shining sisters, who had
managed to snag a wealthy husband. While the cream
of society had never fully accepted her, the rising middle class, comprised of many Mrs. Blacks, was a lot
less particular. Friends had noted that after her marriage, Mrs. Black had lost her vivacity, and that she
seemed to fear her husband, but they felt it was not

their place to interfere. Marriage was simply a woman's lot to bear, for better or worse.

The huge brown eyes filled with tears, and Mrs. Black dabbed delicately at her face with a lace kerchief. "Hello. Who are you?"

"Winifred Appleton." Winifred extended a hand through the bars and took the fragile woman's, noting her cheap cotton gloves and worn ruffled sleeves. "I have come from Mr. Shane's office to help you."

"My lawyer sent a woman?" She stared at Winifred. "Why on earth would he do that? Is he coming himself?"

"Mr. Shane will counsel you in person, but right now he is preparing your case. I have come as his emissary, to gather information and to help you respond to the press."

"Oh, the *Times* has been here already," the woman sighed. "They keep asking the same questions, over and over. 'Did you try to kill him? Why did you do it? What was it like to watch your own husband drink poison?' It is enough to make a body mad."

Winifred experienced a thrill of apprehension. Mrs. Black did not seem to take her situation very seriously, and she did not come across as a sympathetic figure. That could be extremely damaging, for the press as well as the jury often made decisions based on the deportment of the accused. In an instant, Winifred's noble heroine disappeared, replaced by the picture of an unstable woman.

"Mrs. Black, I understand you must be irritated, but it is very important for you not to think of your case so cavalierly. The press may very well conclude that you not only tried to kill your husband, but that it does not trouble you at all. That could be very damaging to your case. Do you understand me?"

"I suppose," Monica appeared unconcerned. "Mr.

Shane said much the same thing when I first came here. Say, you wouldn't happen to have a flask of brandy on you, would you? I could use a stiff drink."

"No, unfortunately, I do not." Winifred was beginning to need a drink herself. "Mrs. Black, do you realize the seriousness of the charges against you?"

"What, that I tried to kill the old man?" Monica shrugged. "I do not remember if I did or not. I know I wanted to. I couldn't stand the old bastard another minute. 'Monica, get me a drink. Monica, get out of my sight. Monica, you are not as pretty as you used to be. You cannot do anything right.' I thought if I got rid of him, I could go to Europe for the summer and have some peace at last."

Mrs. Black spoke as if poisoning her husband were a way to rid herself of an annoying insect. Even if her motive was to escape an untenable marriage, one that society's mores had forced on her, she should seem more upset. Charles's words nagged at Winifred, but she pushed them aside. Her job was not to determine the woman's guilt but to help her get a fair trial.

"Mrs. Black," Winifred began, opening her notebook, "let us start at the beginning. How did you meet Mr. Black, and what was your marriage like?"

Monica settled into a chair, her brows knitted together, deep in thought. "I was a dancer, on the Broadway stage," she said softly, and her face brightened at the memory. "My, I had the looks then! I was going to try and be a singer, but the stage manager took a peek at my legs and said I was born to be a dancer. My dream was to become a real actress. I guess it wasn't in the cards."

Monica wiped at her eyes, and Winifred felt a pang of pity for the woman. "So you met Mr. Black at a show?" Winifred prodded.

"Yes. He was seated right in the front, passing

hundred-dollar bills around as if they were nothing. Can you imagine? Well, all the girls were impressed with him. He was good-looking, too, with his flashy silver vest and diamond pins. I didn't know at the time that it was all a show, that he was really stingy."

"Did he court you?"

Monica nodded. "I fell for him, just like the romance books say. I should have known on our honeymoon how things would turn out. He drank too much at our wedding, then passed out on the table. His butler had to carry him to bed, while I took off his shoes. The next day he had a powerful headache. Claimed it was all my fault, that he had made a mistake. He said I did not . . . could not . . . you know." The dark eyes stared plaintively at Winifred.

"Arouse him?" Winifred guessed.

The woman's head nodded vigorously. "Yes, that's it. What a nice way to put it! Anyway, it never got better after that. He was always yelling at me, everything I did was wrong. I wondered why he even married me, but I think he needed a wife for business purposes, you know? Then when I did not give him a son, he got even madder and would barely speak to me, though what he thinks I should have done about it, I can hardly guess."

Winifred felt a blush creeping up on her face. Dear God, it was a good thing she had come to see Monica Black right away! If the papers got hold of this. . . . Gently, Winifred continued with her questions.

"When you imply that Mr. Black treated you poorly, do you mean he struck you?"

For the first time, Monica Black looked embarrassed. Averting her gaze, she spoke softly. "Yes, he hit me once when he thought I was flirting with a gentleman at a party. I did not expect that! When I wrote to my pa, he wrote back that he could not interfere in a marital disagreement, that I had made my bed and could lie in it. There was no one else I could tell, not even my friend Delilah from the stage. So I hid it with powders."

She appeared as mortified as if she were confiding some secret shame for which she was personally blameworthy.

"Did you ever confront Mr. Black about his abominable behavior?" Winifred tried to keep the outrage from her voice.

Monica giggled. "I did one better than that. I waited until the old man fell asleep, and I conked him with a frying pan! He slept real well that night, I'll tell you. Never laid a finger on me again."

Winifred felt her mouth fall open. She admired the woman's pluck in fighting back, but her life had clearly been hopeless. She had no way out—no strong family background, no money of her own. Her plight was clear.

"So"—Winifred took a deep breath—"what do you mean when you say you are not certain that you tried to kill him? Wouldn't you know if you poisoned your own husband?"

"One would think," Monica replied. "Yet it was like a dream. Did I just imagine it, or did I really do it? I will tell you what I remember. He was drinking more than ever, calling me every name he could think of. I was sick of it. My neighbor told me she'd bought a large supply of arsenic, due to the rats. New York's full of them, you know. I saw her carting them out of the cellar the next day. I bought a supply myself. It occurred to me that if it worked on one kind of rat, it would work on another. I do not recall putting it in his tea—but I reckon I must have, mustn't I? They found it in the tests, all right. Funny, I can't recall for sure."

Winifred felt a thrill. Was the woman blocking out the memory, or was she being deliberately obtuse? "And the servant called for a physician?"

"Yes." Monica nodded. "After drinking the tea, Willy—I mean, Mr. Black—collapsed and began vomiting everything up. When he did not stop after an hour, Bridget went for the doctor. I tried to help him, but he was very ill. You wouldn't think a little poison would make him so sick."

As Monica stared out the bars of her cell, Winifred took a deep breath. The woman was like a child in some ways, acting on impulse with no clear thought as to the consequences.

Monica turned her gaze back to Winifred. "The doc said he recognized a poisoning case when he saw one, and the next thing I knew, I was brought here. When the policeman asked me if I did it, I told them the truth. I didn't remember. Can't you see?"

"Yes, unfortunately I can," Winifred replied softly, "Mrs. Black, we have to be very careful here. I know you did not mean for things to turn out the way they did, but an all-male jury and judge will not be likely to understand your viewpoint. They have never stood where you are, slept with a man they despised, been blamed for everything from sexual impotence to loss of beauty, and struck by a marital partner who is twice their size. Do you understand?"

"My Willy is not a big man," Monica said. "He is barely a hundred and a half—"

"It doesn't matter," Winifred said quickly. She rose and laid a comforting hand on the woman through the bars. "Mrs. Black, I am confident we can help you win this case. But you must listen carefully to my directions, as well as Mr. Shane's. Do not give interviews to any newspaper without one of us present. If anyone else tries to talk to you, tell them to speak to your attorney. Is that clear?"

"Yes," Monica said, appearing confused. "I think the papers are coming here today. That nice Mr. Dana from the *Sun* asked to speak to me. At three o'clock."

"Then that nice Mr. Dana will speak to both of us," Winifred said decidedly. "We have got a case to win, Mrs. Black, and I am here to help you."

The woman squeezed her hand in gratitude, and Winifred left the cell. She heard the policeman lock the door behind her, then escort her to the door. As soon as she reached the main hall, she heard a familiar voice behind her.

"Good afternoon, Miss Appleton. I would say I am surprised to see you here, but I am not."

She turned to face Charles Howe.

CHAPTER 9

M R . HOWE." A shudder of awareness went through her as she saw him. Charles. Her lover. Her opponent. . . . Was he still furious at her? Deciding not to take any chances, she assumed her best businesslike manner. "What are you doing here? If you are interviewing Mrs. Black, I respectfully request to be present."

"We have already talked to her," Charles said bluntly. "Enlightening conversation, I must admit." His expression changed, and he spoke to her sternly. "Winnie, you know what you are doing is wrong. This woman is guilty as hell. If you have interviewed her, you must have seen that much. Playing the 'poor female' angle is not going to do anything for you."

"You do not have any idea what angle I am playing!" Winifred said—rightly, because she didn't know. "And my name is Miss Appleton. Although I appreciate your advice, I certainly do not need it." She started to storm away, when he stopped her.

"All I am saying is, you have picked the wrong case to latch on to. Nothing good will come of this—

not for you, nor for her. I do not want to see you heartbroken, that's all."

He sounded sincere. Winifred felt her defenses crumbling. He was so much easier to handle when he was angry at her! Unfortunately, at that moment, he looked so handsome, his crisp white shirt a startling contrast to his dark tailored suit. Visions of their love-making scorched her as she suddenly noticed the sensual lines of his mouth, his hands. . . . She shook her head. She could not give in to her attraction to him, or all would be lost. Holding her head high, she gave him a cool smile.

"I appreciate your concern, Charles, but it is misplaced. I am a big girl, and I can take care of myself. Now if you will excuse me, I have a case to prepare."

"Winifred!" he called after her, but this time she did not stop. She turned and walked swiftly out of the building. The policeman looked up from his coffee and gave Charles a sympathetic grin.

"Women," he muttered. "Can't live with them, and can't live without them."

Charles could not have agreed more. How could one woman be so stubborn? What she was doing was wrong, yet she didn't care. All that seemed to concern her was "poor Mrs. Black."

Charles fumed, digging through the police reports. Apparently, Winifred was able to put everything else from her mind, including her relationship with him. Well, if she could do it, so could he. Taking the documents he was looking for, he slammed the file shut and stormed out the door.

The policeman shook his head, then went back to the newspaper. "Women," he muttered to no one.

•   •   •

"WHAT THE HELL is this?" Charles snatched the newspaper from his secretary the following afternoon. The headline screamed:

MRS. BLACK TRIAL TO BEGIN! PLIGHT OF
WOMEN EVERYWHERE EXPOSED! POOR MRS.
BLACK, NOBLE HEROINE FOR WOMEN'S RIGHTS!

Charles stared at the paper, appalled, as the secretary backed out of the room. This could not have happened so soon. Scanning the columns, he smothered a groan as he read an outrageous account of Monica Black's story.

Poor Mrs. Monica Black lived a life of torment with her abusive husband. Mr. William Black, an odious brute, treated her with singular contempt not at all befitting the marital state. Tearfully, Mrs. Black confessed in prison today that she tried everything to improve her marriage, but that her husband, a drunkard and a ruffian, refused to mend his ways.

"I tried to make him happy," she lamented, twisting a lace handkerchief between her fingers. "I was tied to this man, legally and morally, through eternity. I truly believe he would have killed me."

Mrs. Black at that point lifted her veil, showing a face of stark beauty. Her features were regular, her eyes soft and brown, filled with a moving sadness. As she articulated her plight, one could not be unmoved.

"I appealed to my father for help," Mrs. Black continued, "but he refused, saying that I must obey my husband above all. Even my minister could do nothing except offer his prayers."

Mrs. Black is going to trial for the attempted

poisoning of her husband, William Black. The case is to be heard by Judge Culvert on Tuesday, May 10. On March 8, Mr. Black, a successful New York businessman, was taken violently ill. Dr. Perkins, the family physician, examined him and determined that poison was the cause of his illness. Mrs. Black was taken into custody, although she declares she does not remember poisoning her husband.

A friend of Mrs. Black, who was present at the jail, indicated that Mrs. Black's plight is far from isolated. "Mrs. Black is everywoman," Miss A. declared. "There are many such marriages, hidden behind society's curtains, discussed in whispers in the best drawing rooms. It will be difficult for Mrs. Black to obtain a fair trial in this country, for an all-male jury and judge will certainly have little sympathy for a condition they will never experience. Poor Mrs. Black will, unfortunately, be denied a jury of her true peers and thus a fair trial."

Although male, this reporter can certainly sympathize with the fair Mrs. Black and can only hope the jury will as well. . . .

Charles tossed the paper into the nearest rubbish bin. " 'Poor Mrs. Black!' " he growled, pacing the room in frustration.

This was undoubtedly Winifred's doing. She was obviously the "friend" at the jail, the mysterious Miss A. with such decided political convictions. The battle had already begun, and Winifred had fired the first volley. She had taken a murderess and portrayed her publicly as a noble martyr.

Cursing under his breath, Charles flung open the door, facing the startled Crocker. "Get Marton, Witherspoon, and McAlister in here right away. I also want to see that reporter from the *Times*, the one who has been following me for weeks. *Now!*"

Crocker leaped to his feet and raced down the hall. Slamming the door shut, Charles returned to his desk and yanked out the Black file.

Winifred had beaten him to the punch. By noon today, most of New York would have read the paper or heard about the case, and their first reaction could well be "Poor Mrs. Black." To find a jury that had not heard about the case would be damned near impossible—exactly as Winifred intended.

Yet admiration swept over him as well. She had learned her craft well. Mrs. Black had committed a heinous crime, and her chances of acquittal were near zero. But by using the press to her advantage, Winifred could send a message to the jury.

It was damnably clever, but he intended to put a stop to it. This was the law, not a suffragette march, and a murder had been attempted. Mrs. Black deserved to be punished, no matter what her husband had done to her beforehand.

Still, that last thought nagged at him. Perhaps her trial would not be fair. Did Mrs. Black really have an equal chance? Did she have the same power as her husband in the relationship, or before the court? Quickly Charles dismissed such thoughts. Winifred was beginning to affect him!

As Marton and the other attorneys piled into his office, Charles indicated the paper.

"Gentlemen, the opposition has scored once already, and effectively. We are going to have to get this case off the ground as soon as possible. Let us begin our review."

The attorneys nodded, but Jared Marton gave Charles an odd little smile.

• • •

VERY LATE in the day, Winifred heard a knock on the door of the law library.

"Miss Appleton?" a male voice questioned. "I came to see if you needed any assistance."

Winifred was astonished to see Jared Marton standing outside the door. "Mr. Marton," she said in confusion. "Why on earth would you come here?"

Jared grinned, then offered her a chair. She hesitated, then took the seat, eyeing him intently all the while. Jared dropped into a chair across from her. His manner was charming, and he employed it to his best degree.

"I just wanted to offer my services, in case they were needed." His voice was rich with meaning, and Winifred wondered frantically if Charles had disclosed their tryst to him. But surely not—Charles was a gentleman, and as such, he would never reveal such a thing, especially to a coworker.

"Mr. Marton—" Winifred began, but he interrupted her.

"Jared." He smiled. "Call me Jared."

"Mr. Marton," she continued as if he hadn't spoken, "it is very improper for you to be here. I am now working for the defense in the Black case, as you must know. There is no reason for us to converse."

"I just wanted to let you know I was available if you needed anything—research materials, books from the library, legal assistance. Now that you are no longer at our office, I am at your beck and call."

His grin deepened, and Winifred understood his meaning. He saw her now as available, a woman he could flirt with and court, to add to his collection. But although he was handsome and charming, she was not at all attracted to him. He was too much of a ladies' man for her taste.

"Thank you for the kind offer, Mr. Marton, but I am in good hands here. Now if you will excuse me, I have work to do."

Instead of being put off, Jared chuckled good-naturedly. "All right, Miss Appleton. I had to try. I must tell you, though, you are truly missed around the office. Whitcomb and McAlister have been dour ever since you left, particularly since they now have to do their own work, and Charles has become a slave driver. And I find the office a whole lot less appealing."

"Charles—I mean, Mr. Howe—is all well with him?" Winifred asked, picking up her papers as if she were only casually interested.

She did not see his grin deepen. "Why, yes, he is just fine—except for the fact that he growls all the time like an old bear with a thorn in his paw. He does not seem very lonely, though. Yesterday a Miss Billings came to call on him. They had a little closed-door session. Quite interesting, wouldn't you say?"

For a moment, Winifred found it difficult to take a breath. Charles and Elizabeth Billings . . . closing her eyes, she wondered why it bothered her. Charles was certainly free to see any woman he wanted. She had made it clear that she did not intend to continue their relationship, so she could hardly blame him for looking for comfort elsewhere. Why then was the idea so wretched?

Jared watched the play of emotions on her face and then rose with a satisfied grin. "I just thought you might need a friend. If I can ever help you, please call on me. By the way, do you have an escort to the Governor's Ball? I know it is not for two weeks, but I would be very happy to take you."

"No—I mean, yes. I mean . . ." Winifred tried

to get her emotions under control. "I would love to go with you," she breathed.

"Good. I will come for you at seven. Good day, Miss Appleton. I very much look forward to that dance."

Whistling, he put on his derby and walked out the door.

AS SOON AS JARED closed the door, Winifred put down her papers. Good Lord, she had to get herself under control. The idea of Charles courting Miss Billings was far too upsetting.

Elizabeth was the perfect woman. She came from a good family, had all the right connections, and would make a perfect political wife. She was pretty, demure, and vapid—exactly the kind of girl most men adored. Everyone expected Charles and Elizabeth to marry eventually, and both families would be overjoyed at their union. Winifred should be happy for him. Yet all she could feel was an odd kind of sickness.

But what did she want from him? Charles had to marry someone. He would want his own family, stability, children—these were all things that would greatly appeal to someone like him. And he would make a wonderful father, for he was intelligent, honest, and firm, but understanding. . . . All the qualities that any woman would want in a man.

Winifred squeezed her eyes closed, fighting the suspicious tightness in her throat. She startled when the door flung open and Horace Shane burst in.

"Working late again, I see, Miss Appleton. I saw the light outside. Who was that?" he gestured to the stairs.

"Mr. Marton. He is from the prosecutor's office. He offered to help," Winifred said thoughtfully.

"I see. Damned generous, seeing as he is on the other side." Horace's voice was rich with inflection.

Winifred smiled. "Don't worry, I declined. I made it quite clear that I had all the help I needed."

"If only that were true," Horace said slowly. When she looked questioningly at him, he continued softly. "Miss Appleton, while I admire your dedication, I think you ought to know what you have gotten yourself into. Cases like this one never run smoothly. People do not like to think of women as murderers. That can either work for us or against us."

"And you are afraid in this case it will work against us," she hazarded.

"Yes." Horace tugged on his long white beard in an age-old habit. "You see, I do not think Mrs. Black can win. The prosecution has a pretty tight case. I am going to do a little investigating, see if I can find anything to help her, but frankly I do not hold much hope. Best we can do is probably to raise some issues, garner some attention for her, and maybe arouse some sympathy with the jury. But even that is a long shot."

"Why?" Winifred asked, perplexed.

"Public opinion can be ugly," Horace said. "The mentality can quickly revert to that of the Salem witch trials. Conventional thinking finds something repugnant about a female, who is supposed to give life and nurture, doing anything that goes against her nature or the fabric of society."

"But that is so unfair!" she protested. "That puts women on a pedestal, but it also makes them less than human! Such nonsense assumes that Monica Black does not feel the same pain, confusion, or desperation that a man would feel in her place!"

"Exactly." Horace nodded in agreement. "I am not saying the judgment is right or wrong. I'm just telling you what to expect. The publicity will be awful. For helping this woman, you will be talked about in every drawing room, and you will be ostracized from society. I want you to be prepared for that."

Winifred looked at him solemnly. "It will mean much the same for you, too, will it not?"

Horace laughed benignly. "My dear, I do not give a tinker's damn what they say about me. I am long past all that—I have certainly been called everything from radical to fanatical. I have gotten quite used to being snubbed. I am actually looking forward to the ruckus this case will cause. But I am also not a beautiful young woman, just embarking on life. The price I pay will be far different."

"I understand." Winifred smiled softly. Charles's warnings had been much in the same vein. "Thank you for your concern. I have given the matter a good deal of thought, and I have known ever since I was a child that this would be the role I would fulfill. So to answer your question, a little gossip is not about to stop me, either."

"Good." Horace patted her shoulder. "I knew you were made of stern stuff, but you deserve a warning. Now get out of here. It's getting late."

"Yes, sir." Winifred beamed at him, proud to have earned his respect.

CHAPTER 10

"MRS. COSTELLO?" Charles stood on the doorstep of the fashionable brownstone. A woman had just cracked the door, and he peered inside the half-inch opening.

"Yes, that's me." The strident voice nearly shattered his eardrums. "You aren't one of those door-to-door salesmen, are you? Ever since Harry bought me this new house, they've been pestering me every day!"

"My sympathies," Charles said, suppressing his impatience. "No, I am not a salesman. I am from the state's attorney's office. I came to ask some questions about Mrs. Black, your neighbor."

The door immediately opened, and a woman dressed in rich brown taffeta smiled prettily. "Mrs. Black! Why yes, I do know her, though I don't think I'll be of much help. We weren't exactly friends, you know."

Something in her tone told Charles that the woman hated Mrs. Black and that she would be a veritable font of information. "May I come in?" he asked.

"Please." She led him into the parlor, then

shouted for the maid to bring tea. "The help these days," she grumbled, then lowered herself into a tiny curved sofa. "Those are opera singers on the armrests," she confided, indicating the carved heads on the arms of the loveseat and chairs. "I forget her name, but it is considered very classy."

"I see," Charles said, fighting down amusement—the furniture was ghastly. "Mrs. Costello, I will try not to take up much of your time, but I need to ask a few questions. You did hear about what happened across the street?"

"Oh, yes!" The woman leaned closer to him, her brown eyes wide with excitement. "It's the talk of my ladies' club! Imagine, poisoning your own husband!" She gave a delicate little shudder. "Not that he didn't deserve it, the brute!"

"What do you mean by that?" Charles took out a notebook and began scribbling.

"It's well known that he spent more time at the tavern than he ever did at home," she confided. "Not that that excuses anything. My Harry, he takes a drink now and then, but not every night."

"So Mr. Black drank heavily?" Charles made a notation.

"You didn't hear it from me," the woman simpered. "But yes, that is correct. He even—no, I can't tell."

"What?" Charles smiled encouragingly. "I won't use your name. I just want to get a feel for what their marriage was like."

"Well, then." Mrs. Costello shrugged as if coerced into speaking. "One time at a Christmas party, he was so . . . intoxicated that he . . . you know . . ."

"No," Charles said. "Know what?"

"Relieved himself in the fireplace!" The woman's eyes sparkled as if relating the best possible gossip. "I wasn't there, but I heard about it later. Terrible, isn't it?"

"Yes." Charles was beginning to feel a lot less self-righteous. Although the man's behavior didn't justify an attempt at murder, he couldn't imagine being tethered for life to the kind of person Mrs. Costello described.

Suddenly, he could see Winifred Appleton standing over his shoulder like an angel, with "I told you so" written all over her face. Quickly, he put the ridiculous vision from his mind.

"Mrs. Costello, what else can you tell me about them? Were there ever any other problems? Visitors?"

Turning away demurely, she nodded to the maid, who set the tray down before her. "There was a visitor," she answered softly after the maid left, pouring two cups. "As I mentioned, Mr. Black was away a lot. A man came to see Mrs. Black upon occasion. I don't know his name, but he dressed very handsomely. He was fond of striped trousers, if I remember correctly."

Charles's pencil stopped. "How often did he visit?"

The woman blushed, then sipped her tea delicately. "I'm not implying anything," she said carefully. "And you didn't hear it from me, but at least once a week. They would sit on her front porch, talking for hours. One time he came at night. Harry and I were scared half to death that Mr. Black would come home, but he must have been out of town. In any case, the parlor lights were on very late."

"And did he stay over?" Charles asked, his voice rising.

"Oh, how naughty!" Mrs. Costello slapped his wrist flirtatiously. "No, I don't think he did. At least his carriage was gone when Maggie, my maid, dumped the slops in the morning. I was sure to ask her. Now it seems it's a good thing I did."

She gave him a coy look, and Charles felt his collar getting tight. Evidently the women on Third Avenue did not have enough to do all day. "Mrs. Costello, is there anything else you can tell me that might help my case?"

"Well . . ." She gazed thoughtfully into her tea-cup. "Mrs. Black did ask me once how I killed the rats in my basement. Devilish things." She shuddered, her little finger extended from her cup. "I told her I bought arsenic from the local druggist. It did the trick."

Charles stared at her in amazement. "You told her that! When?"

"About a month before the arrest." Mrs. Costello gazed at Charles as if suddenly realizing what she just said. "Oh my, I couldn't be considered an—accessible, can I?"

She looked terrified. Charles hastened to reassure her, "No, you would not be an *accessory*. You had no idea what Mrs. Black would do with that information. Who is the druggist?"

The woman mentioned the shop, then gazed at Charles as if he were a truffle. He forced a smile. "Is there anyone else I should talk to?"

"You might want to see Bridget, her maid. The woman is devoted to Mrs. Black. I'm certain she was there the night of the poisoning."

"Alleged poisoning," Charles said, hearing Winifred's remonstrance in his head. "We have not proven anything yet, and Mrs. Black is innocent until proven guilty."

"Oh, yes, that's in the Constitution, right?" Mrs. Costello preened, pleased with herself.

Charles rose and handed her a card. "If you think

of anything else, Please contact my office. You have been a great help already."

"I have! Well, that's grand, but remember—"

"I know," Charles recited. "You didn't hear it from me."

The woman looked startled, then broke into laughter. He could still hear her when he reached the street.

SO MRS. BLACK may have had a lover. Charles gazed across the road at the Blacks' house. Mrs. Costello certainly had a good vantage point. But who could the lover have been?

Charles walked back to his carriage, shaking his head. Adultery was not always a motivation to murder, he reminded himself. But it now seemed that Mrs. Black may have had more than one reason to wish her husband dead.

Charles was about to get into his carriage when a hansom cab pulled up. As Horace Shane disembarked, he recognized the white-haired figure instantly.

"Morning, Charles." Horace extended his hand. "Fine weather we're having."

Charles chuckled, taking the huge paw in his own. It was impossible not to like Horace. Even now, with the additional provocation of Winifred working with him, he still had to smile.

"Yes, it is fine weather. But it is suddenly turning cloudy, with what the newspapers report."

"I see." Shane pulled a pipe out of his vest and lit the fragrant tobacco. "Care to save me an hour?"

"Certainly. Mrs. Costello told Mrs. Black how to kill rats. Evidently, she took the advice to heart." Briefly, Charles related the arsenic story. "It also seems that Mrs. Black may not have been the lonely house-wife she pretends to be."

"Another bird in the nest?" Horace guessed.

Charles nodded. "No name, just that he wears striped trousers. William Black is not much liked, either. Apparently, the man is known for drinking and urinating into fireplaces on Christmas."

"Charming," Horace said again, drawing on his pipe. "Anything else?"

"No, but I think I was lucky to get out alive. Mrs. Costello obviously saw me as a way to relieve her own boredom."

Horace snorted. "You will be finding arsenic in your own tea if you start that. Married women are nothing but trouble."

Something in his tone, almost a warning, gave Charles pause. Still, Horace appeared to be his usual jovial self. "How is Miss Appleton?" Charles asked quietly.

"Very well. Hell of a worker. We are glad to have her." He gave Charles a penetrating look. "Why don't you come by and see for yourself?"

Charles shrugged. "Wouldn't that be a little awkward, seeing as we are on opposite sides of the case?"

"That does not seem to stop one of your coworkers," Horace said, his voice thick with amusement. "Nice-looking chap. Dashing, I would even call him."

Charles could not stop his look of shock. "Jared Marton! He came to see Winnie—I mean, Miss Appleton?"

"I thought it a little odd myself." Horace shrugged. "The man seems to genuinely care about her. Offered her help . . ."

Charles swore under his breath, and Horace shook his head in sympathy. "Can't trust anyone these days, can you? Even what this Mrs. Costello says is circumspect." He turned and started toward the woman's stairs.

"You don't have to interview her," Charles said. "I told you everything she knows."

"I think I will anyway," Horace said thoughtfully. At Charles's puzzled look, he grinned. "I have not been propositioned in a long time. It will do my heart good."

"COME IN, Miss Stone. How happy I am that you could come!"

Winifred beamed, as the carriages lined up outside her aunt's mansion the following evening, and one by one, the women strode up the porch. Egbert grumbled, shaking his head as one stormy visage after another passed through the wrought-iron gate. Young women in the first bloom of their youth came, followed by others who, in his muffled opinion, ought to be home knitting booties for grandchildren. But his eyes widened when he recognized Mrs. Stanton and Miss Anthony. The two fabled dragons disembarked from their coaches and stepped smartly past him to the open door.

"Ladies!" Winifred cried in delight. "I am honored that you could come! We certainly need your help, as you will soon see!"

Susan B. Anthony managed a smile which lightened her serious countenance for a moment. Her hair was parted in the middle and swept back, and her dress was somber black with a white collar—her famous deportment. Elizabeth Cady Stanton followed, her eyes twinkling merrily, her snowy hair framing a face of pure mischief and intelligence. Leaning forward, she pressed a kiss on Winifred's face and squeezed her hand.

"Would not miss it for the world. Had a devil of a time getting everything settled at home, but when I heard Miss Appleton needed my help, there was no question in my mind."

Winifred glowed, acknowledging the praise as rare indeed. Mrs. Stanton, while elderly, was president of the Woman Suffrage Association. It had often been said that while Mrs. Stanton forged the thunderbolts, Susan Anthony fired them. A male opponent declared them the most "pertinacious incendiaries in the country." They were great friends.

The house was soon filled with women from all walks of life: members of Socios, the intellectual women's club, advocates for women's rights, Quakers and Baptists, wives and spinsters. Penelope and Aunt Eve hastened to bring more teacups, their maidservant gasped at each new arrival, and Jennifer, draped in robes, her pregnancy well advanced, enjoyed the ladies' attention. So many came that they spilled from the parlor into the séance room and even into the kitchen.

When everyone was settled with refreshments, Winifred stood before the fire, fanning her flushed face, and began to speak. All of the women quieted, their attention firmly fixed on the lovely legal siren they had heard so much about.

"I am very grateful that you could all come today," Winifred began. "I summoned you because I need your help. A woman is in prison for a crime she committed out of desperation, a crime considered so heinous that it may result in her spending a good part of her life in jail. Yet there is mitigating evidence to show that while the woman did wrong, she had reason."

A murmur went through the crowd, and Winifred explained the details of Monica Black's case. When she finished, the women began to argue in earnest. Some deplored the fact that one of their sex had attempted to murder her husband, while others were more sympathetic. As the noise level rose, Mrs. Stanton rapped the floor sharply with her umbrella.

"Ladies, please. We all have an opinion here, and each of you will have a chance to speak. But we must proceed in an orderly fashion, or little will be accomplished."

The noise died as the women turned respectfully toward the elderly lady, whose grandmotherly appearance hid a shrewd and calculating mind.

"Mrs. Stanton, please lead us," Winifred said softly.

Mrs. Stanton rose and faced the crowd, determination on her merry face. "All right, my dear. Some of you here may be familiar with my views. Woman has been done an immense disservice by her fellow man. Taught that education is indelicate, she is kept ignorant. Taught that a low voice is an excellent thing, she is trained to subjugate her vocal cords. Not permitted to run and climb, her muscles deteriorate and her strength weakens. But worst of all, forbidden to enter the courts, her sex is unjustly tried and condemned for crimes that men are incapable of judging."

The women applauded, and even Aunt Eve clapped her hands as loudly as possible. The maid paused and cheered, and even pretty Penelope, the recipient of many male admirers, thrust her fist into the air in support of Mrs. Stanton's words.

Mrs. Anthony joined her friend and began to speak in her clear, schoolmarm tones. "Mrs. Stanton is right. Certainly Mrs. Black should not have tried to poison her husband, but it is apparent that she had attempted to obtain help without success. If we let the matter drop, she will surely hang, and once more man will have shown woman that she has no voice, no chance, and must submit to him in the most humiliating of circumstances without complaint."

"One of my most fervid desires is to achieve for women the freedom to end a marriage if her partner is a confirmed drunkard," Mrs. Stanton said firmly. "Mr. Black, I understand, fits that description fully."

"May I speak?" Mrs. Smith waved a handkerchief at the crowd of women. Winifred nodded, and the woman began softly.

"I, too, was in a loveless marriage, such as Mrs. Black's." A silence fell upon the crowd, as Mrs. Smith fought back tears. "I know full well the despair that becomes one's life. I tried everything, to no avail. One bitter night, I dosed myself with arsenic, in the hope of passing into a better place than this. Instead of dying, as I had hoped, I became violently ill. My physician gave me an emetic, along with a stern lecture, and I recovered fully. Yet, had I been successful, no one would have thought my husband responsible for my death."

Winifred saw a dozen heads nod, and a pang of pity went through her. Charles, she knew, would never treat her so shabbily, nor any other woman. Still, while many women enjoyed good marriages, a silent minority clearly did not. Her mind worked feverishly as she saw first hand the evidence that no jury would ever witness.

"But still, the Black woman may have tried to kill the man!" another woman protested. "We cannot be saying that we agree with murder?"

A horrified murmur went through the crowd, and Winifred tried in vain to calm the disagreements. Once more Mrs. Stanton rapped the floor, and once more order was regained.

"I think I understand what Miss Appleton wants here," Mrs. Stanton declared. "She sees Mrs. Black, not just as a murderess, but as a voice for all women who are trapped by marriage and have no escape. Having studied the genus Homo on the heights of exaltation and in the valleys of humiliation, I know there is only one way to get his attention. We must elevate this case, much as Miss Anthony has done with other cases, to shine the warm light of day on such plaintive misery. We must encourage all women, the obedient little spaniel wives, to stand up for themselves and take notice. Women like Miss Appleton will give us a voice in court. Let's loosen our stays, fill up our lungs, and use them!"

The applause exploded once more, and this time the women—even the very round Jennifer—stood and cheered. Mrs. Stanton nodded, winked at Winifred, and exchanged a smile with Miss Anthony. That noble woman was already taking notes, putting together a strategy, and anticipating the next steps. She smiled back at Mrs. Stanton, the reins of progress already in her hands.

JARED MARTON AND CHARLES strode up Broadway the following day, having just finished lunch. They had been discussing the Black case and were pleased to learn that the appointed judge, Culvert, was known to be fair and not at all partial to females.

"It seems our case is complete," Charles said, indicating his notes. He could not moderate the tension in his voice as he addressed Jared, although he knew he had no right to say anything to him. Jared could see anyone he chose, just as Winifred could entertain any man she wanted. Yet the thought of Jared visiting Winifred made his jaw tighten. "We have the physician, the maid who saw her serve the tea and who summoned help. We also have the neighbor who showed Mrs. Black how to kill rats with the poison."

"It appears to be conclusive," Jared agreed. "William Black will also testify. Although he is not a sympathetic sort, he is bound to tell his story, which is damning, no matter how you look at it."

"Let's interview him first," Charles said prudently. "I do not want to take any chances. This Black trial has to be a sure-fire win for us." The smile faded from his face, and he spoke almost to himself. "You know, I almost feel sorry for Miss Appleton. Her first case is certain to be a loser."

Jared stopped abruptly, his face filled with astonishment. "I don't know if you want to feel that sorry. Take a look!"

Charles looked in the direction his compatriot pointed, and his mouth fell open like a shucked clam. Marching down Broadway was a contingent of females in bonnets and shawls, waving banners and furling ribbons. Even before reading the blaring banners, Charles had a sinking feeling that told him what this was all about. As the parade of women drew closer, their banners held high, their petticoats swaying in the breeze, he could easily read their message:

FREE POOR MRS. BLACK! RIGHTS FOR ALL WOMEN! VOTES FOR VICTORY!

Jared gave a low whistle, staring at the women with both admiration and outrage.

"She could not have! . . ." Charles said incredulously to Jared, stark confusion written all over his face. "Surely Winnie didn't do this!"

Jared shrugged, and Charles glanced back quickly at the growing crowd. Both sides of the street were now lined with supporters, hecklers, children who clapped cheerfully, witnessing what they thought was a parade, and policemen who kept the mob at a respectful distance. Groaning, Charles recognized Susan B. Anthony and Elizabeth Cady Stanton at the front of the line. There were other familiar faces, women whose Zincographs had graced several newspapers, women who had fought to become doctors and merchants, shopkeepers and writers. Charles watched them pass, growing more outraged with each minute. It seemed that the most prominent female suffragettes in the country had all gathered into Mrs. Black's camp. Even Amelia Bloomer marched by, waving, in her scandalous trousers.

"My God," Charles swore under his breath, barely able to speak.

"Look, isn't that Reverend Manly?" Jared asked. "He hates suffragettes."

Across the street, the self-righteous reverend was addressing reporters, pointing a virulent finger at the women, calling them jezebels, radicals, and—even worse—Democrats. Miss Anthony ignored him, Mrs. Stanton smiled, and one of the younger women blew him a kiss. The minister shouted to be heard, but the cries of the crowd and the shouts of the marching women drowned him out. Scandalized, the reporters scribbled furiously.

"This will be all over the papers tomorrow," Jared said. "So much for our airtight case against poor Mrs. Black."

"My God!" Charles repeated.

"He's probably planning to write a brief for her, too," Jared said ironically. He turned toward his friend. "Charles, this has got to stop. Even the papers that do not support women's rights will report on this demonstration, which will only add to the publicity. And the reverend will undoubtedly speak about this in church, unwittingly playing right into their hands. Miss Anthony and Mrs. Stanton are real trouble. The two of them have been very effective in the past in petitioning on behalf of women whose cases they endorse. The newspapers quote them constantly, and they have a large following. Those two voices could give us a mountain of problems."

"Yes, but they also have enemies," Charles pointed out. "Some men will turn against their cause simply because of Miss Anthony. And the facts are still the facts."

"I would not depend on that," Jared said dryly. "The men may feel that way, but they still have to go home to their wives—wives who will make their life miserable if they do not support Mrs. Black. It looks like Miss Winnie has struck a real blow for her client."

Charles started to protest, then he thought of his own parents and closed his mouth. His father would bluster, but eventually his mother with cool reason and persistence, would make her opinion felt. Her weapons would consist mainly of reproachful glances and poignant silences, but they would be utterly effective.

"Surely Winifred could not have organized this," Charles objected again, disbelievingly shaking his head. "The suffragettes often take on cases on their own. Surely she would not be so devious . . ."

Yet even as he spoke, Charles recognized the figure pulling up the rear, a very familiar woman, one who knew how to wrench his heart with a smile but who today made him absolutely furious.

Winifred looked even more beautiful than usual. Dressed in her navy-blue suit, with its short jacket and white blouse, she looked very efficient and totally in control. She waved and smiled at the crowd like a princess greeting her loyal subjects, ignoring the epithets that some of the men shouted at her. When a tomato plopped directly before her, she only lifted her skirts and delicately stepped over it, giving all the men a wonderful glimpse of her white petticoats and slender ankles. Applause broke out among them, and more than one shouted encouragement for her to lift her skirt higher.

Jared whistled again, this time almost a wolf whistle mingled with incredulity. The crowd rumbled, threatening to turn into a mob at any moment, even as Winifred raised a FREE MRS. BLACK! sign above her head. Charles thrust his papers into Jared's hands and turned toward the street.

"Where are you going?" Jared asked in surprise.

"I am putting a stop to this," Charles said furiously. "By God I will."

CHAPTER 11

WINIFRED EXULTED as she marched through the streets, waving to the throng and carrying her sign. It had been Mrs. Stanton's suggestion to hold a march, and judging by the results, it had been an excellent idea. Reporters filled the streets, rushing up to the ladies with their notepads and pencils, while artists sketched depictions of the event. In the morning every newspaper in New York would carry the story.

A thrill of excitement shot through her as she anticipated the effects. How effective this would be! And she and Horace desperately needed to turn the tide. They really hadn't anything solid to go on. Mrs. Black simply did not remember whether she had poisoned her husband. The prosecution would have little trouble proving an attempted murder. Winifred planned to research a self-defense theory, but she knew it would be weak, so they needed as much public support as possible.

As the watching crowd pushed toward them, she felt someone staring at her. She turned just in time to see Charles and Jared looking at her. Apprehension rushed through her when she saw Charles's expression. He was furious. Even Jared looked disapproving and embarrassed.

Raising her sign even higher, she spun around and resolutely continued her march. Charles Howe had no right to interfere. She would help her client no matter what, and if he did not approve of her tactics, so be it.

"Winifred!" Charles shouted. Ignoring him, she paraded down the street, her fingers tightening on the sign. Surely he would just go away, not wanting to find himself in the headlines. . . . A moment later, her hopes were dashed as he grabbed her arm, effectively preventing her from going anywhere. Her sign toppled to the street.

"Unhand me, sir!" she protested indignantly, but her confidence ebbed as she faced him directly.

Never had she seen him so outraged. His black eyes blazed hellfire at her, his jaw was locked, and his nostrils flared. In answer to her protest, his fingers tightened on her, dragging her closer to him. She felt a moment of unreasonable panic as he pulled her up against the hard, muscled length of his body.

"Miss Appleton, I want you to come quietly with me to my carriage, and I will take you home. Now."

He appeared to be struggling to keep his emotions under control, as if it required every ounce of effort. Even his voice sounded forced through his clenched teeth. Swallowing her fear, she drew herself up to her full five feet three inches and spoke much more coolly than she felt.

"No."

"What did you say?" Charles gazed at her in disbelief, astounded that she would defy him so openly.

"I am sorry, Charles, but I have to do what I think is right for my client. You may not approve, but that does not matter. Poor Mrs. Black is in a very bad spot indeed, and I am grateful for Mrs. Stanton's and Miss Anthony's help. Now if you will excuse me, I think they are beginning the speeches."

She tried to step away from him, but he refused to release her. Instead, he turned her in his arms. "Winifred," he said softly, his voice like silk, "what you are doing is wrong, and you know it. This woman is a murderess, and you are parading on her behalf as if she were some noble heroine. If you think I will let you proceed with this because of the night we shared, you are sorely mistaken."

Her brows flew upward with incredulity at his bold reminder of their lovemaking. "It appears you are the one to presume," she retorted haughtily. "If you think because of our past association that you can order me around, you are sadly mistaken."

His jaw tightened, even as he quietly admired her audacity. No woman had ever turned him so completely upside down the way she did. He was torn between admiration, outrage, and a flaming passion that threatened to rob him of control. Part of him wanted to kiss her senseless, while the other part wanted to thrash her firmly. Instead, he locked his gaze on hers, and a wicked smile came to his face.

"I think exactly that, Miss Appleton, for you see, when you allow a man certain privileges, you cannot prevent him from taking other privileges as well. We have two choices here. Either you come with me willingly, or I will be forced to take action. I promise you will not like the second option."

The warning in his voice was unmistakable. Winifred eyed him warily, taking his measure, and then the corners of her mouth turned upward.

"Well, then. I'll see you in court, counselor," she said loftily. Yanking her arm out of his grip, she picked up her sign and stalked once more toward the street.

Charles swore under his breath. She meant it—she would openly defy him, and the devil take the consequences. In that case, he had to take a stand. Winifred had sorely underestimated him, and it was high time she understood that.

He caught up with her in three strides. Winifred gasped as he whirled her around to face him. Before she could let loose with a hail of recriminations, he stooped down, rammed his shoulder into her waist, and then straightened. Winifred found herself draped ignominiously over his back—like a sack of potatoes, she would later recall—her fists pounding into his muscled flesh, her legs kicking furiously.

"Put me down! You have no right—"

"I have every right," Charles said calmly, ignoring her protests. When a well-placed kick caught his groin, he groaned but only tightened his grip around her knees. She pummeled him furiously with her fists, even as the men standing on the sidelines began to cheer. "As your former mentor, I have an obligation to prevent you from utter foolishness."

"Charles!" Winifred struggled. Suddenly a bevy of reporters came on the scene, attempting to scoop each other. Moaning in misery and humiliation, she tried to hide her face, but she was immediately recognized.

"Miss Appleton, do you have any comment?"

"Miss Appleton, do you consider today's march a success?"

"Miss A., will you retract your former statements about your client, now that Mr. Howe has taken charge?"

That last question infuriated her. Bracing herself upward on Charles's back, she could only glare at the reporters in outrage. "Poor Mrs. Black is a woman wronged!" she cried. "We shall see her set free, just as all women in bondage will be freed!"

Charles rewarded her statement with a smack on her rump, and she yelped. The reporters chuckled, enthralled by this turn of events, their pencils scribbling furiously.

"Mr. Howe." Mrs. Stanton suddenly appeared like an avenging angel, standing directly in his path. The saintly old lady had her own hellfire in her eyes, and she braced her hands on her hips. "I demand that you put Miss Appleton down! This is an outrage!"

"It certainly is," Charles agreed, tightening his hold on Winifred's legs. "You see, I am a believer in the law, not in theatrics. Mrs. Black will get a fair trial, I will see to it!"

"Is it your intention to thwart the defense in the same way once the trial starts?" Mrs. Stanton demanded, refusing to let him off easily.

A rumble of laughter came from deep within his chest. "I certainly hope so!" he exclaimed.

The reporters guffawed. Just as Charles reached the carriage, Winifred landed another well-placed kick and had the satisfaction of hearing him grunt, even as he dumped her unceremoniously inside. Furious, she righted herself and faced Charles directly, her eyes spitting fire.

"Mr. Howe, there is no excuse for your actions! You will answer for this, even if I have to take you to court for . . ."

"Obstruction of justice?" he suggested helpfully.

His amusement earned him another glare. Charles locked the door, shouted Winifred's address to the driver, then peered once more inside. "You will thank me for this tomorrow, Miss Appleton, when you see the headlines. No doubt you have made the front page."

Winifred did not dignify that with a reply.

THE FOLLOWING MORNING, as Winifred opened her eyes, she heard her sister giggling.

"Winnie, wake up! Did you really participate in a suffragette march? Were Mrs. Stanton and Miss Anthony there? Goodness, this Mr. Marton sounds terribly attractive. Did Charles really fling you over his shoulder to get you out of there?"

Winifred groaned, drawing the covers over her face. More than her pride was bruised this morning. She rubbed her posterior, remembering the bold smack Charles had given her. "Is it really in the *Times?*" she asked softly, hoping it was all a dream.

"Front page," Penelope said proudly. "Look, there is even an illustration of Charles carrying you. How romantic! He looks like a knight in shining armor," Penelope sighed dreamily.

"Hmmp," Winifred snorted. "Let me see the paper." Forcing herself to brave the worst, she peered at the front page.

"Oh, no! Look at this headline! 'Legal Siren Gets Prosecutorial Comeuppance!' " Horrified, Winifred sat up and scanned the story. "There is nice coverage of the march . . . plenty of material about Mrs. Black . . . well, that's good. But then it goes on to justify Charles's interference! 'Many men cheered the handsome attorney's actions when he swept the troublesome Miss Appleton over his arm and out of the fray.' They even speculate about the nature of our relationship! Oooh, that man!"

Winifred fumed, whipping through the pages so quickly that Penelope felt windblown. "Is it that bad?" her sister asked innocently. "I mean, after all, Winnie, you have been sweet on Charles for a long time—"

"I am not sweet on Mr. Howe," Winifred announced firmly, finding the continuation of the story. "Look at this sidebar. 'Outraged Prosecutor Seeks Revenge!' They make it sound more like a lovers' quarrel than a political disagreement!"

"Well, isn't it?" Penelope shrugged. "I think it is all terribly romantic, and it shows the depth of Mr. Howe's feelings for you. He obviously is not comfortable with you being portrayed as a suffragette, and he feels what you are doing with the Black case is wrong."

"I am not doing anything illegal," Winifred insisted. "Charles is just angry because I outwitted him with the march. He has won a battle, certainly, but the war is far from over." She glanced at the clock, and her face brightened. "I think there is still time to influence the *Evening Post*. With any luck, we can give them an exclusive story and change the tide of public opinion."

"Winnie! Where are you going?" Penelope exclaimed as her sister jumped out of bed, dropping the paper in her haste.

"To the *Post*, silly," she responded, as if the answer were quite evident.

"MR. HARRISON, could we speak for a few minutes?"

The reporter looked up from his work, annoyed at the interruption. Then he recognized the woman standing before him. "Miss Appleton!" he said, getting awkwardly to his feet. "I did not expect—"

"I came on my own accord." She gave him her best smile. "I thought you might appreciate a scoop."

"Yes! I mean, that would be great! But why"—his ill-kept brows drew suspiciously together like two caterpillars—"have you come to me? I thought Shane's office used the *Sun*."

"Have you seen this morning's paper?" Winifred asked softly, displaying the *Times* with an air of the injured party.

"Quite a picture, wasn't it?" The little man grinned, eyeing the sketch of Winifred, her rump in the air, being carried from the street. "Say, that's you, isn't it?" He cocked his head, as if trying to see her upside down.

"Yes, I am afraid it is," she sighed, closing the paper up when he seemed more interested in her posterior than her story. "It has all been terribly misconstrued. I am here to set the record straight."

"I see." Harrison grinned, then reached for his notepad, sensing a good tale. "We didn't get our version out yet. We are an evening newspaper. If your story has merit, we'll try to get it in tonight." He opened the *Times* to the front page again and glanced at the picture. "Mr. Howe certainly seems infatuated with you. Did he actually carry you off like that?"

"Charles—I mean, Mr. Howe—has had . . . rather a fatherly feeling toward me for quite some time," Winifred sighed, as if explaining something painful. "That is why he offered me the apprenticeship in the state's attorney's office—as a way of helping my career."

"Damned nice of him," the reporter scribbled. He eyed her shrewdly. "You consider his interest fatherly?" His gaze traced the soft curves outlined by her stark dress, and his expression became hungry.

Winifred wished she had something to cover her chest with. "Yes, that is absolutely the nature of our relationship," she said. "That is why he forcibly escorted me from the march. It was his way of protecting me."

"Interesting. The prosecutor protects the defense. I don't think I have ever heard of a case like that before."

"But this incident should not distract us from the real reason for the march," Winifred insisted, changing the subject. "Miss Anthony and Mrs. Stanton are firmly behind poor Mrs. Black. Mr. Howe's demonstration with me clearly shows what is wrong with men in our society. They treat women as children, just because they are stronger physically than we are! They refuse to give credence to the fact that we have a brain."

She rose, flushed with indignation, her eyes flashing. She was no longer pretending; this was truly how she felt.

"That makes good press," the reporter said gleefully, fascinated by the change in her appearance, "but the men will be outraged."

"None of them want to face the truth," Winifred continued indignantly. "But women are people, too— even the notorious Mrs. Black. And her husband may well have abused his power over her. I understand that he is a brute. Who knows what he did to drive her to her alleged action? Yesterday's events make one wonder, don't you think?"

"That's a hell of a transition," Harrison remarked, "if I do say so myself."

"I think it would make a good evening news story, don't you?"

The reporter grinned. "Yes, Miss A., I believe it would. Let's get started."

• • •

THAT EVENING at Horace Shane's office, Winifred yawned, rubbing her eyes and forcing her attention back to the work at hand. Horace had long ago left, leaving her free use of the library and an admirable opportunity for peace and quiet. Egbert waited for her below, grumbling as usual, but she had given him a few coins to purchase a "wee dram," so she knew his discomfort was not unreasonable.

There was so much to do, yet the clock was already ticking a late hour. The suffragette march had been hugely successful, and afterward had come speeches, with the suffragettes pleading passionately on behalf of Mrs. Black. But organizing it all had eaten up precious time needed for preparing Mrs. Black's defense. Fortunately, Mrs. Stanton and Miss Anthony would take the lead in organizing public events from here on, and Winifred would not have to be directly involved in their activities. Thanks to their talents, Mrs. Black would be a household name by the week's end. Surely most New Yorkers would be sympathetic.

Charles would not be. The publicity campaign would make him furious, but it mattered little. Mrs. Black had the deck stacked against her. In fact, no man, without a woman's influence, would see her side. Any typical judge and jury would send her to jail without thinking twice. The defense's only hope lay in publicizing and escalating Mrs. Black's cause.

Glancing at her pile of books, Winifred yawned again, fighting sleep. The work itself was fascinating. This was her first real case, a case that would make history.

A carriage pulled up outside. It must be the secretary, Winifred thought, flipping open another law book and reviewing yet another case. Hearing steps on the staircase, she frowned—Shane's man was slight of figure and probably would not command such a noise. When the door flung open, she gaped in startled amazement.

"Charles!" Winifred dropped her pencil. "Whatever are you doing here?"

He strode over to her and thrust the *Evening Post* across the desk at her, his eyes glittering in black fury. "Miss, how do you explain yourself?"

Winifred glanced warily at the glaring headline. She did not have to read the article to know why he was outraged. Shoving the paper aside, she faced him directly like a schoolmarm. "Charles, I am aware of the story. I had to do what I could for poor Mrs. Black. What is your point?"

" 'Poor Mrs. Black'!" Charles sneered. "If I hear that phrase one more time, I am going to punch someone. You've deliberately manipulated the press! This must end! You almost imply here that I had a personal motive for preventing you from making a fool of yourself yesterday!"

"Well, didn't you?" Winifred answered hotly. "You said yourself you felt entitled to special privileges, just because we—we—"

"Were intimate?" Charles suggested, his eyes narrowing dangerously.

"Well, yes," Winifred replied, her cheeks heating. "I did not say anything that wasn't true."

"You made my office look like a bunch of misguided Romeos," Charles spat, his black eyes glittering. "You are trying to influence public opinion, even the prospective jury. You know you cannot win legitimately, so you are resorting to these tactics! It is wrong, and you know it."

"I really do not understand why you are so upset,"

Winifred said defensively. "Mrs. Black suffers from the same injustices that afflict many, many women."

"Mrs. Black is no noble heroine, as you well know. I do not care how many suffragettes embrace her—nothing changes the fact that she has committed a crime. She attempted to murder her husband. Murder! And you have made her out to be Joan of Arc!"

"Charles." Winifred rose and placed a cool hand on his shoulder. The man was obviously distraught. "You have your view and I have mine. You have never heard the woman's side of this. Her husband is a brute—"

She stopped suddenly when she realized he wasn't listening but instead was staring at her hand. His gaze turned back to hers, and she inhaled sharply. Passion burned there in his eyes, along with his fury. There was something dangerously exciting about his fiery rage, something that made her own blood flow hotter and her fingers long to touch him more fully.

Had she pushed him too far? No, they were simply on opposite sides of this case. She must never forget that.

Then Charles recovered himself. "I did speak to Mrs. Black." His voice was deceptively soft. "I know all about her marriage. Granted, her husband is no saint, but he did nothing to justify her action. He did not try to kill her. Lots of people have unhappy marriages. Instead of trying to murder each other, they usually separate!"

His voice had risen an octave, and Winifred swallowed hard. He stepped smoothly around the desk, to her. All her memories of his seduction flooded her. She couldn't protest, couldn't do anything except experience a longing for him that was more intense than any she had ever known.

He was so close, she could smell his cologne, breathe the sensual scent of man and lime water, and see the blazing fire in his eyes. "I know how this must seem to you," she said. "But truly, you cannot understand the woman's viewpoint. You cannot know what it is like to be completely within a man's power and then to have that power abused. There are many Mrs. Blacks out there, living in silence and shame, desperately unhappy. It is disgraceful that they have no voice, no escape—"

"Fine." Charles put his hands on Winifred's shoulders as if to shake some sense into her, but the warmth of his palms only made her long to feel them caressing her, touching her, arousing her to the point of forgetfulness. As angry as he was, even Charles seemed affected by their contact. "I agree," he said hoarsely. "Perhaps the divorce laws should be made easier. Maybe there should be some other mechanism to help women in unhappy marriages. I would not object at all if you fought for that. But damn it, Winifred, this woman is guilty as hell! You know it, and so do I!"

He gazed into her eyes, and the intensity of his words made her breathless. Swallowing hard, she realized with a sudden sense of female vulnerability that she was alone with a deadly furious man. She tried once more for sanity.

"Charles, be reasonable," she said coolly. "There is no sense in getting . . . passionate about it."

Charles swore silently, completely exasperated, and the fire in his eyes blazed out of control. "I have been too reasonable," he said hoarsely. "And too permissive where you are concerned. I have let you have far too much say in our relationship. I have given you free rein thinking that you would soon come to your senses. Instead, this is the result. You consider my interest 'fatherly.' I think it is time you learned something about the true relations between men and women. I will show you just how passionate I am about this."

With that, he took her roughly into his arms and kissed her.

THE KISS WAS incredible—defense meets prosecution, man meets woman, softness yields to strength. Winifred was completely undone. The passion inside her rose to an overwhelming force, and she eagerly returned his embrace, amazed at the heat she felt in his arms. Sensing her response, Charles deepened the kiss, teasing her tongue with his own, then plunging in to take full possession of her sweetness. At the same time, he undid the buttons of her dress, and his hand slid beneath the coarse cotton to cup her breast. Breathless with excitement, she rose up against him, eager for his caresses, wanting to feel the full length of him against her, wanting his kiss, wanting . . .

The sounds that came from her throat surprised even her. Opening her eyes, she was dimly aware that she was sitting on the desk, half naked, her desire spiraling out of control. Then his fingers moved cleverly to the place where she was dying for him to touch her. Breathlessly, she arched her back, loving everything he was doing to her. All else was forgotten: the case, Mrs. Black, male versus female. All she cared about was fulfillment, which seemed to hover just beyond her reach.

"Charles, please," she begged, "I need you to love me. Please."

"I will, darling, I will." His voice was filled with a husky promise. "Put your hands on my shoulders. That's it. Trust me, Winnie."

His reassurance made the emotion inside of her grow golden and melting. She did trust this man, really and truly trusted him. He loosened the drawstring on her drawers and pulled them to the floor, giving him even greater access to her most secret place. All her inhibitions gone, she closed her eyes and felt the sweet, seductive pressure of his thigh against hers.

"Lift your hips. That's it. Let me, sweet Winifred. It will be all right, I promise."

Eagerly, she positioned herself on the edge of the desk and lifted herself toward him. She felt his hard male shaft poised against her soft fullness. Slowly, torturously, he entered her, and to her delight, her desire began building once more.

"Hold on to the desk, darling," he whispered, his voice strained. "It's going to be a rough ride."

Excited by his words, she did just as he suggested. Clasping the sides of the desk, she felt him fulfill his sensual promise, sliding into her again, this time with a hot, penetrating thrust. Winifred gasped, feeling her body expand to accommodate his fullness. He slammed into her again, this time impossibly harder and even more wildly exciting. The books crashed to the floor, followed by the candle and the research work. Everything was forgotten in those few minutes except what was happening between them—all their senses were riveted on the splendor of their loving. Each thrust brought Winifred to a higher plane of sheer, erotic pleasure. Rocking furiously against him, she felt the pressure explode into a frenetic volcano of sheer, unadulterated bliss.

That moment of pure, perfect eroticism obliterated all reality. She heard Charles's hoarse cry, then opened her eyes to see his head thrown back, totally immersed in the moment, even as her own body sang with hot sweaty delight. For a second, joy flooded through her, that she could do this to him, that she had the gut-wrenching ability to tear him from himself in the most intimate way possible. But even that thought was short-lived as she gave herself up to the riot of sensations that consumed her.

Time hung suspended, even as the moon rose outside the window. When Charles finally collapsed and held her tightly in his arms, Winifred knew that she had experienced the utmost in a woman's pleasure. Making love could never be so wild, so uninhibited, and so . . . erotic. No other man would ever fulfill her the way Charles did, she was certain, nor would any other man ever understand her the same way. It was a frightening thought, with implications she didn't dare to examine.

Charles lifted his head and gazed at her tenderly. Pressing a kiss to her throat, he smiled down at her.

"I take it you didn't think it was so bad," he said softly, through the light shining in his dark eyes.

"I thought it was wonderful," Winifred sighed, blushing brilliantly. "Truly wonderful."

"Good. You are so sweet, so sensual. My darling Winifred."

All along, Charles had been concerned with her own pleasure as much as his. Few men were this way, she knew from the whispered conversations of other women. She thought of how he had tried to help her, the hours he had spent teaching her, the support he had given her even at his own expense. A welling of emotion rose within her, and tears stung her eyes. *My darling.* No other man ever called her that.

Even as the tender feelings warmed her, panic started somewhere within her. What on earth was she doing? Quickly she sat up and began to button her dress. She was becoming far too involved, even after all her precautions. She had a case to win, everyone was depending on her—Horace and Mrs. Black—and here she had given herself to the prosecutor!

"I had better go," Winifred whispered suddenly, frightened by the feelings that roiled within her. "Egbert's waiting. He must have finished his dram by now."

"Are you certain you have to leave?" Charles questioned softly. "Winifred, I really think we should talk. I want to tell you how I feel about you, about this. After tonight, surely you are thinking the same way I am. There is no need for you to continue with this case, no need for us to be on opposite sides. We could be together. You could come back to the office, if you so desired. Once the publicity died down, it would be a perfect time to . . ."

Winifred gazed at him incredulously. "What makes you think I would consider such a thing? Did you think, just because we made love, that I would forget all this like some simpleminded maid?" Her eyes narrowed in outrage. "You have never taken my ambition seriously, have you? Were you waiting all along for me to back down? To confess that I was not capable of being a lawyer, that I was just another help-less woman—"

"I never said that!" Charles answered hotly. "You're making too much of this."

"Am I?" Winifred gazed at him with new eyes.

"Isn't this why you came here tonight? To seduce me into abandoning the Black case?"

"Of course not!" he insisted with righteous anger. "How could you even conceive of such a thing?"

"It seems entirely too coincidental to me," she answered logically. "First you show up, barging in here, making all kinds of accusations, and the next thing I know . . ." She gave him a haughty look. "Well, I am certain you recall."

"I refuse to dignify that absurd accusation with a reply," he said, furious now. "I seem to remember that you were an active participant. You certainly did not need much encouragement from me! If I had to quantify the passion, I might even think it was the other way around!"

His last words came as a shout. There was something dangerous about the way he looked at her, and something in his expression that appeared to be hurt or disappointed.

Winifred faced him stubbornly. "Charles, I refuse to get drawn into this. We are both adults. We are also on opposite sides of a court case. There is no commitment between us, nor do I think either of us desires one. What happened between us tonight was simply physical release of the accumulated tension between us. I read all about it. We are programmed through evolution to reproduce, so of course our mating instincts—"

"Is that what you think this is all about?" he thundered. "Mating instincts? Woman, you tempt me—"

He took a step toward her, then seemed to think the better of it. Instead, he picked up his coat and slammed his hat onto his head with such force that the crown nearly met his eyebrows.

"Where are you going?" she cried.

"Out." He swore silently, adjusting his hat brim.
As he approached the door, he spoke without turning
to face her. "I will win you, Winifred, come hell or
high water. You can pretend all you want that this
means nothing, but I will show you otherwise. One
last thing. I know you want to help your client, but
using manipulative journalism to do so is wrong. This
woman is guilty of attempting cold-blooded murder.
The case goes to trial on Tuesday. I don't care if the
jury must be illiterate, I will see this case tried fairly.
Mrs. Black is guilty as charged, and she will be
punished for her crimes."

Her heart tightened. He didn't understand—he
never would. Until he could see this case from a female
perspective, he would always think of Mrs. Black as
just another murderer.

Winifred spoke, her voice firm. "As I said before,
may the best attorney win."

CHARLES STORMED OUT, the memory of their
lovemaking still burning in his memory. How could
she, after what happened between them, revert so
quickly to her ambition? Her last words stung him.
He had thought that taking her to sensual fulfillment
would make her more sweetly reasonable.

What had gone wrong? He had her right where he
wanted her, in every possible way, but still Winifred
had pulled the rug out from under him—again.
Didn't she feel anything for him at all?

He was certain she did. The look in her eyes, the
softening, their emotional connection—it could not
possibly be faked. Yet she almost looked, well afraid,
when he tried to discuss feelings. But that was ridiculous. Still, he reminded himself, he was dealing with a
charlatan spiritualist, a woman of uncanny ability to

get what she wanted. What did she mean about no commitment between them? Was she thinking of making love with someone else? Jared Marton, perhaps?

The flash of jealousy that went through him made him furious. She couldn't have meant that—she was just being obstinate. Yet Horace had warned him that Jared had visited her, ostensibly to offer his help. Charles knew all too well the character of his co-worker. As much as he liked Jared, the man was a notorious womanizer.

Yet he had misjudged everything else, and all of his plans so far appeared to have backfired. Instead of growing less enamored of becoming a lawyer, Winifred was now much more so, especially with the Black case. Her need for independence, far from diminishing, seemed to have grown. Frustrated beyond measure, Charles realized that more than another man, his adversary was a courtroom!

Even as he swore, he secretly admired her. As a lawyer, her tactics were effective, even if they were wrong. Already the Black case was becoming the talk of New York. Even before the trial began, Winifred was getting her message out. And he was certain that the reporters enjoyed looking into her hazel eyes much more than they did reviewing the facts.

Yet the facts would stand. Charles calmed down as he thought of this. They had to. And when she lost the case, as she surely would, she would come running back into his arms, begging for forgiveness. He would lovingly sit her down and explain the facts of life to her: that she couldn't continue marching with the scandalous suffragettes and defending hapless murderesses. Then he would forgive her and take her into his arms, and she would promise to be obedient. His confidence returning, Charles climbed into his carriage.

When he looked up, he saw her light still blazing at the window.

WINIFRED HEARD his carriage pull away, then nearly collapsed onto her desk. A thousand emotions whirled inside of her, all of them begging to be explored.

How on earth had she let this happen? The last thing she had intended to do was make love to Charles, particularly after his behavior at the march yesterday. Yet he had hardly touched her, kissed her, before she melted into his arms.

More than that, she had turned into a wanton. She looked at the desk where Charles had made such exquisite love to her. Appalled at her own behavior, she covered her mouth with her hand, remembering all too vividly the way he'd positioned her there, then driven into her over and over, making her want him so badly that she shook even now, thinking about it.

"My Lord!" Winifred gasped, fanning herself as the heat suffused her. No wonder Charles has accused her of actively encouraging him! He could easily have said much more than that, Winifred realized to her shame. Once again, the gentleman in him didn't allow such behavior. She knew that most men wouldn't have restrained themselves.

And now she would have to face him in court.

The thought scandalized her. How could she face him at all, let alone before a judge, defending Mrs. Black? True, her work would be behind the scenes— she would not actually be speaking in the courtroom. That was Horace's job. Still, she would be there, would see Charles each and every day, would have contact with him. . . .

Winifred groaned out loud. This was a fine mess.

But she forced herself to remember Charles's proposal that she drop the case now, just because he made love to her—and grew infuriated all over again. How could she have fallen for his seduction? Charles Howe obviously had no respect for her ambition, or her ideals. Well, she meant exactly what she had told him, and if anything, she was even more bent now on winning. All she had to do was keep her mind on the case. What had happened with Charles was purely physical and was nothing to concern herself with.

It was, as she had told him, simply a mating instinct.

CHAPTER 13

O RDER! ORDER!"

Judge Culvert entered the court and immediately rapped his gavel. The courtroom was filled with spectators and reporters, whose disheveled hair and harried appearance betrayed their battle to get inside. The doors had been forced open from the rest of the crowd outside. Deputy sheriffs stood by the entrance to the courtroom, holding back the mob, while the reporters scribbled furiously. Before the proceedings had even begun, the Black case had already made headlines.

Within the bar, counsel had already arrived, along with the stenographers, talesmen, witnesses, sheriffs, and others. The judge, a man of about sixty years, with thin, silvered hair and a stern, immobile face, appeared annoyed at the disruption and ordered the sheriffs to gain control.

Winifred sat in the first row, watching intently as Horace Shane conferred with a junior counsel. Much as she would have liked to sit with them, they had all agreed that if she did, her presence would draw too much attention. From the corner of her eye, she could see Charles, looking devastatingly handsome in his dark blue court suit and sparkling white shirt. He looked businesslike, confident, and—sexy. Immediately, visions of their torrid lovemaking sprang into her mind. She quickly looked away. Good Lord, the last thing she needed was to be harboring seductive thoughts about the prosecution! She had to keep her mind on the case, or all would be lost.

Beside Charles was seated William Black. Unfortunately, he did not appear to be a brute, nor even a man inclined to violence. Instead, he looked more like a dandy. Winifred remembered Monica's tale of how they had met, and she could easily envision him in the dance hall, buying rounds for everyone. Yet she knew the man could be harsh if crossed. She could only hope that sometime during the trial, he would show his true nature.

Her gaze flickered unwillingly back to Charles. The state's attorney conferred with his associates, jotted down notes, and appeared entirely self-assured. Swallowing hard at the prospect of facing him, she reminded herself for the hundredth time that she had to do this. Many women's lives depended on it.

"The State of New York v. Black."

Winifred repressed a shiver as the case was called. It was beginning. Horace approached the bench and made a motion for postponement.

Winifred closed her eyes nervously. It was standard procedure for the defense to ask for more time in order to build its case. For Mrs. Black, it was even more important, simply because Horace felt their case was not yet strong enough to win.

"Your Honor," Horace began, "the reason for the postponement is that the defense has requested the testimony of Professor Jenkins, an eminent toxicologist. The professor is out of town, and we have not been able to locate him in time for this trial."

A murmur went through the crowd, and Charles rose before the bench. "Your Honor, the defense has had ample time to prepare. There are plenty of experts in the State of New York who are available to testify regarding poison, including several that the defense intends to call. It is also unknown whether Professor Jenkins can be located within a reasonable time. We cannot afford to drag this case on interminably. The publicity has already been extraordinary."

His argument was succinct and effective. Winifred never appreciated just how good he was until now. A strange mixture of emotions—pride, annoyance, and awe—surged through her, mingled with apprehension. Clearly, Charles was in control here, much as she would have liked it to be otherwise. Instead of being put off by his tactics, she only admired him and desired him that much more. She found the entire situation unbearably seductive.

The judge appeared to consider the matter for a moment, then turned to Horace. "I normally try to be lenient in these matters, and I appreciate the rights of an accused person to a good defense. However, it seems that Mrs. Black has excellent counsel and more than enough witnesses. If Professor Jenkins's presence is critical, I am certain that he can be found. I favor making any necessary expense required to contact him. In addition, Mr. Howe makes a good point—the professor's testimony will only augment what the other witnesses will have to say. I am certain that Mrs. Black will receive a fair trial, with or without him. Motion denied."

Horace glanced back at Winifred with a shrug, and she felt her heart stop. Round one lost. Although Horace had warned her that the motion would probably be denied, it wasn't a good beginning. Glancing secretly at Charles, she saw that his expression contained no triumph but looked expectant, as if certain of the outcome.

The clerk began calling the jury, and Winifred watched the men file into the room. Charles approached the first man, asked a few questions, then nodded to the clerk. "Accepted!"

Horace walked over to the same man and fiddled with his notes. Winifred smiled. Horace's manner was completely different from Charles's. While Charles was businesslike and sharp, Horace appeared warm and comfortable, someone to whom a witness would divulge just about anything. Yet he hid a keen mind and a wealth of legal knowledge beneath his demeanor.

Horace chatted casually with him about the weather. Winifred guessed the man to be a middle-aged Irishman, a rustic farmer or builder by trade. He seemed nervous, but true to form, after a few minutes Horace had him talking easily. Finally Horace pulled out a newspaper and indicated the front page.

"You read the paper much, Mr. O'Reilly?"

"Not if I can help it," the man responded, earning a titter of laughter from the court. "Damned rags these days, beggin' yer pardon, but that's all they are."

"I quite agree," Horace answered, smiling indulgently. "Then you have not read anything at all about Mrs. Black?"

"Well, some," the Irishman admitted. "I mean, it would be impossible not to know who she is, what with all the talking and papers and such."

"Have you formed an opinion, then, about the accused?"

"Glad I'll not be wed to her," the man answered honestly, earning another peal of laughter. "I'd have to watch my damned whiskey, to make sure she didn't drop something in it."

"Dismissed!" Horace declared.

The Irishman looked genuinely puzzled, as if not at all certain what had gone wrong. The judge leaned toward him.

"You can step down, Mr. O'Reilly."

The man reluctantly departed, casting a rueful glance at Horace, who was already consulting his notes about the next juror. Winifred began to relax a little. Horace was certainly thorough. He already knew which jurors he preferred to dismiss: misogynists, men who disliked suffragettes, men who were of the old school and thought a woman who asserted herself in any way was a threat, men who were overly sanctimonious and who would enjoy the spectacle of seeing a woman imprisoned.

"Mr. Kendricks, do you know the defendant, Mrs. Black?"

The man looked askance. "No, and I don't want to," he said emphatically, arousing another peal of laughter from the galley.

"Dismissed!" Horrace waved for the next juror to approach.

He kept the next juror and dismissed two more. Winifred glanced toward Charles and could see his impatience, but remarkably, he restrained himself from objecting. Surprised, Horace rushed on, as if aware that for some reason, Charles was granting him considerable leeway. Suddenly it occurred to Winifred why: he was keeping his promise—that Mrs. Black would get a fair trial.

A warmth ignited inside her. How honorable Charles was! Yes, it was very unlikely that he had deliberately seduced her in order to get her to quit the case. It was just not in his character. As much as he wanted to win, and as strongly as he felt about Mrs. Black's guilt, he was giving the woman every possible advantage. Could he have finally begun to realize, as

Winifred and the suffragettes preached, that women were not fairly tried by the legal system?

It was a heady thought. Still, as the approved jurymen were finally assembled, Winifred felt a rush of dismay. None of them were female. They were middle-class men, bankers and businessmen, tradesmen and merchants, most of them married and comfortable, beneficiaries of the system. Not one would ever really understand Mrs. Black's plight. Instead, they would most likely relate her attempted poisoning as a personal threat, and see Mrs. Black as an upstart woman who must be made an example of. Her heart sinking, Winifred tried to find one sympathetic eye to whom Horace could appeal, but it did not look good. Although they had gotten the best of the heap, the best were not at all likely to help.

She cast a meaningful glance at Charles, who surprisingly seemed to understand. His eyes met hers, telling her wordlessly that he couldn't help it. There was something else in his glance as well, a bold reminder of their sexual encounter that made the blood rush to her skin. As if reading her mind, he sent her a seductive wink. She turned away quickly.

"Order! Order!" the judge called out as a collective gasp went through the crowd. Mrs. Black had entered the room. Heavily veiled, she was being led by the jailer to the defense table. The eyes of every man there were on the prisoner. Breathing a sigh of relief, Winifred saw that the clothes she'd ordered for Mrs. Black, a somber dress with a simple brooch for ornamentation, had arrived on time. Instead of appearing like a showgirl, she now looked like a serious woman.

Delicately, the prisoner lifted a lace handkerchief beneath her veil, dabbing at her eyes. A small smile crept across Winifred's face. She and Horace had spent hours coaching the woman on her deportment, her manners—all of the things that should not count but always did. Even Charles appeared startled by her appearance, for he glanced twice at her as if to make certain she was indeed the notorious Monica Black.

The judge banged the gavel, and the court came to order. As the charges were read out loud, Mrs. Black shuddered then lifted the lace handkerchief once more. The judge spoke:

"Will Dr. Perkins take the stand!"

The elderly physician rose and put his hand on the Bible. After promising to tell the truth, he took the stand, facing the people directly. He was handsome and convincing, and Winifred knew that his testimony would be damning. She and Horace had wanted him to testify first to get it out of the way, in the hope that by the end of the proceedings, the jury would have forgotten its impact.

Charles strode toward the man and indicated the courtroom. "Dr. Perkins, can you tell us what happened on the night of March 8?"

The physician absently pulled on his short beard, but he answered succinctly while the crowd strained to hear.

"Yes. I was summoned to the Black house at around ten P.M. by Bridget Flynn, the Blacks' servant. Miss Flynn roused me from my sleep, explaining that her master was violently ill, and I should come at once."

"Did you?"

"Yes. I knew the Blacks, having treated Mrs. Black in the past for an occasional illness or injury. I also saw them socially upon occasion. In any case, I dressed quickly, then left in my carriage, arriving at about half past the hour. I found Mr. Black lying in bed, gravely ill, almost unconscious. I proceeded to examine him, taking note that his pulse was very weak and his complexion abnormally pale. He had been vomiting steadily since earlier in the evening, when, Bridget declared, her mistress had brought him tea."

"And what was your conclusion?"

"Objection!" Horace called out.

"Sustained," the judge said firmly.

Charles reworded the question. "So what did you think caused Mr. Black's condition?"

The doctor turned and looked directly at Mrs. Black. "I immediately suspected poison. Someone had tried to kill Mr. Black in his own home, in his own bed."

A shocked murmur arose in the room. The reporters scribbled furiously, then rushed from the room, undoubtedly to supply the day's headlines. In the jury box, stone-faced men stared at the veiled figure before them in horror and indignation. Even the judge, after banging his gavel, sent a distasteful glance toward Mrs. Black.

"Dr. Perkins," Charles said smoothly, allowing the man's words to settle in the minds of the jury, "have you treated poisoning cases before?"

"Many times." The doctor leaned forward, warming to his speech. "They are much more common than people realize. Many poisonings are unintentional, such as when improperly stored food becomes toxic, or when an overdose of medication is unwittingly administered. The symptoms are similar. Vomiting. Breathlessness. Paleness of the complexion. Sometimes shock and death follow, accompanied by a certain rigidity of the features."

"Then how do you know this was a deliberate poisoning and not just the consumption of, let us say, a spoiled dinner?"

"The victim had taken only tea before the incident occurred," the physician said, assuming a self-important manner. "That fact, coupled with the symptoms, led me to believe that something had been put in the man's tea, something lethal."

"What did you do next?" Charles paused by the jury box, making sure they heard every word.

"I administered an emetic, designed to remove every trace of poison from the victim's stomach," Dr. Perkins said. "Mr. Black began to recover slowly, and I no longer feared for his life. Upon realizing that a toxic substance may have been forced on the man, I questioned the servant and asked her to give me the teapot and cup that had been Mr. Black's undoing. I was determined that his wife not get away with attempted murder."

"Objection!" Horace stood up.

"Sustained." Judge Culvert glanced at the doctor. "Please just answer the question."

"I apologize." The doctor didn't appear sorry at all but continued in the same manner. "I then told the servant to fetch a policeman. Bridget did so while I attended Mr. Black."

Charles let the man's testimony sink in before continuing. "Where was Mrs. Black during this time?"

"She flitted in and out of the room. I bade her sit still, for I did not want her removing any evidence or altering what appeared to be a crime scene. She wrung her hands in her handkerchief but did not attempt to assist her husband at all. It was that which made me suspect her."

Horace objected again, and the judge spoke more sternly to the witness. "Doctor, please confine your answers to the question. It is the jury's job to determine who is guilty."

Winifred glanced at Horace, who gave her a nod. Then she looked at the jury. While listening to the judge, they were staring at Mrs. Black. Not one among them seemed friendly or in any way open to the possibility that the woman could be innocent.

"Dr. Perkins, would you consider your examination thorough? Could there have been any other reason for the man's condition other than poison?"

Winifred glanced over at Charles, confused. It was Horace's job to put the witness on the defensive and to introduce the possibility that his testimony was mistaken. Yet as soon as the man answered, Winifred realized what Charles was doing.

"I did a thorough examination of Mr. Black. His heart, liver, and intestines all seemed healthy. Some illnesses and natural toxins can induce similar symptoms to poisoning. It was for that reason that I summoned the police. If poison is suspected, then an examination of the food or drink taken, immediately after the incident, will prove conclusive."

"I see. No further questions, Your Honor."

Charles strode from the witness box, and Winifred's heart sank to the floor. Horace had planned to question the doctor along the same lines, but after Charles's skillful maneuvering defusing the point, there wasn't much left for him to say. Still, Horace rose as if unconcerned, and he approached the witness in a friendly manner.

"Dr. Perkins, how long have you been practicing medicine in this state?"

"Over thirty years," the doctor said, puffing up importantly.

"I see. Have you seen many cases of intentional poisoning in your time?"

"A few," the doctor replied. "More in recent years. They seem to be epidemic."

The crowd tittered with laughter, and the judge banged the gavel.

When the noise died, Horace continued in his seemingly absentminded way. "Doctor, you indicated that you had treated the Blacks for many years. Is this so?"

"Yes. Mr. Black has been my patient since he was a youth, and Mrs. Black after they wed."

"And for what condition did you treat Mrs. Black?"

Winifred leaned forward in anticipation. She knew where Horace was going with this, and only prayed that it worked.

"Mrs. Black had the usual—influenza, colds, that sort of thing. Overall she was healthy, so I only saw her when she had viral complaints."

"Anything else?" Horace asked pointedly. "You mentioned injuries. Did you ever treat Mrs. Black for an injury?"

To Winifred's surprise, Charles did not object but simply waited for the man's response.

"Yes, I did once treat Mrs. Black for an injury. She had several bruises and contusions on her face."

"To what did you attribute those injuries?"

"She said she had walked into a door," the doctor answered.

Another murmur swept through the crowd. Mr. Black sat up warily, like a rabbit sensing a hunter. Mrs. Black sobbed beneath her veil, loud enough for the jury to hear.

Horace paused for a moment, then spoke as if to himself. "Bruises about the face. Contusions. Dr. Perkins, I am no physician, but I think I would have difficulty obtaining that sort of injury by walking into a door. Can you enlighten me?"

The physician looked indignant, glancing at Charles as if for help. Charles simply returned his stare.

The doctor shrugged. "I wouldn't know. I have never walked into a door." The crowd chuckled nervously.

"Would you say that her injuries were consistent with what one would happen if one actually did something so ridiculous?"

"Objection!" Mr. Black rose from the table, his outburst astonishing everyone. "She hit me with a frying pan!"

The judge banged the gavel amid the uproar, ordering silence. "Order in this courtroom! We will endure no more outbursts like that," he warned, measuring each word. "You will have an opportunity to speak, Mr. Black. Please wait until you are called."

Mr. Black sank back down into his seat, apparently disgruntled by his dismissal. The judge turned to Horace. "Proceed, Mr. Shane."

"Thank you, Your Honor." Horace appeared more than pleased by what had transpired. "Doctor, is it your opinion that Mrs. Black's injuries could have been caused by a door?"

The doctor struggled hard for a moment. "I did not question her. That is what she said."

"I understand, but in your professional opinion, does it make sense?"

The doctor looked at the veiled prisoner, the judge, and then finally Horace. Taking a deep breath, he admitted, "No, it does not. I do not know how Mrs. Black received her bruises, but they probably could not have resulted from what she claimed."

"No further questions." Horace walked away as the crowd broke into excited commentary.

One volley fired, Winifred thought. It wasn't much, but it was a start. She could not resist taking a peek at Charles. Instead of appearing annoyed or dismayed, he was devouring her with his eyes, mentally undressing her. He focused first on her collar, and she could envision him peeling the linen away from her throat, placing scorching kisses on her flesh. Then he lowered his gaze to her bodice, fastening on the row of buttons marching between her breasts. As surely as if he were actually doing it, she could feel him slipping each button out of its sphere, exposing her bare breasts. His smile grew wicked as he lowered his eyes still further, and she could only guess what he was thinking now. . . .

Her hands flew up to her face, and the heat stung her cool fingers. Charles saw her reaction, and then his smoldering gaze met hers with a sensual promise that brooked no argument. Winifred heard him as clearly as if he'd spoken in her ear.

I will win you, come hell or high water.

Gasping, she looked quickly away, as a rush of erotic energy filled her. Her body flushed with heat, and her blood pounded in her veins. Good God, this man was dangerous! He could seduce her with little more than a glance! Forcing her attention back to her notes, she could not stop her pencil from trembling.

It was going to be a long case.

CHAPTER 14

CHARLES HID a chuckle as he saw Winifred tighten her lips and lift her head, trying desperately to appear unaffected by his sensual eye play.

Not that he could blame her. She was on the opposite side of the Black trial from him. But far from being dismayed by the situation, he found it unbearably stimulating. Every ounce of male predator inside him rose to the challenge, and he became even more determined to win her.

Especially after her blatant dismissal of him the other night, it gave him some satisfaction now to see her squirm. Yet every time he envisioned her in Horace's office, bent over her desk, pleading with him to love her, his own arousal pounded. It was all he could do not to cross the courtroom and pull her into his arms.

It was amazing and more than a little disconcerting that she had this power over him. He didn't at all like the lack of control he felt whenever she was around. He found it increasingly difficult to focus on the case, a case he had to win, because of her beautiful and sensual presence.

So he was not at all sorry he had laid down the law with her after they made love that night. Winifred Appleton was entirely too headstrong for her own good. That their argument had taken a sensual turn only showed him that her feelings were much more complicated than she admitted. What he needed to do now was to court her, to prove to her that what she felt was much more than "mating instincts," to get her outside the courtroom, where she could see him as a man and not as the prosecutor. He also had to win this case.

The defense was doing a damned good job, he had to admit. Charles had always admired Horace's technique, but the elderly lawyer had brought all his skills into focus for this trial. Charles didn't know whether Winifred's influence had something to do with Horace's interests but he would not doubt it—Horace was not so old as to remain unaffected by his bright and lovely apprentice.

Still, he would have felt better if his own office had been able to find Mrs. Black's lover. As he stared at the notepad before him, he remembered Mrs. Costello's testimony. There was another man—he felt it in his gut. A woman like Mrs. Black would not resort to murder unless she had a compelling alternative—someone or something to move on to. And the jury would be much more likely to convict if they knew such a strong motive. Juries liked to know why someone perpetrated a crime.

"Officer Lafferty to the stand!"

The burly policeman appeared in the rear of the courtroom, then strode up to take the stand. After the preliminaries, the officer glanced around the room with interest, his gaze settling on the veiled figure seated at the defense table.

"Officer Lafferty, would you mind telling us what

happened on the night of March 8?" Charles asked him.

"I was on night duty. I was just finishing up when the clerk told me that a possible poisoning case had been reported by the Blacks' maid, and that Dr. Perkins was in attendance. Normally, I would have waited until the next morning to see if the victim wished to sign a complaint, but I decided to stop by the house instead."

"Why did you do that?" Charles asked.

The policeman, perfectly comfortable, shrugged. "The maid indicated the man was pretty sick. I'd been involved in a few poisoning cases before—the victim lingers for a day or so, then passes on. I thought it might be a good idea to stop by right away, since I had the following day off."

"And what did you discover?"

"When I arrived at the house, Mrs. Black was in the dining room, sobbing quietly and wringing her handkerchief, much like she's doing now. When I asked for her husband, she seemed too upset to answer me, but the maid indicated that he was in his bedroom. When I approached Mr. Black, Dr. Perkins was still tending him, but he indicated that he could speak. Mr. Black appeared to have been poisoned."

"Objection!" Horace said quickly. "The officer is not a physician and is not in a position to make that determination."

"Let me ask the question another way." Charles glanced at his notes. "Officer, you say you have witnessed other poisoning cases. Is that correct?"

"Yes."

"How many?"

"I'm not sure—probably at least a dozen."

"So you are familiar with what a poisoning victim

looks like immediately after ingesting poison," Charles continued.

"Unfortunately, yes. In all the cases I've seen, the victim gets a sudden attack of severe vomiting, which lasts for several hours. There are other symptoms as well, including a pale complexion and, in advanced cases, a peculiar stiffness of the limbs. There are additional symptoms once the person dies."

A gasp came from the gallery at the policeman's casual description. Charles persisted asking, "Can you cite other cases where the victim had a similar appearance?"

"The Wilson case last year, the Peterson murders, and the Royce case, just a month ago. They all appeared remarkably the same."

Charles made a note and then glanced at the judge. "I think that Officer Lafferty's experience establishes him as something of an expert, but we will note that his testimony is not medical evidence."

"Agreed," the judge said, satisfied, and nodded to the clerk. Charles glanced at Horace, but the defense lawyer didn't challenge him.

"After you decided that a crime did take place, Officer Lafferty, what happened next?"

"I interviewed Mr. Black. He was still vomiting, but eventually could speak to me. He told me he had come home and drunk a cup of tea given to him by his wife. It was after that that he became violently ill. He believed that his wife had deliberately tried to kill him."

A deadly silence fell over the courtroom. Even the gallery was quiet—the shuffling and coughing ceased for a long moment as the spectators digested the idea of a wife attempting murder. Mrs. Black lowered her veiled head as if in shame, while her husband simply stared at her.

"Then what did you do?" Charles asked gently.

"I asked him if he wanted to press charges, and he said that he did. I brought him the forms, and he signed them in my presence. I then ordered the maid to bring the tea, the cups, the sugar, spoons, and the tea tin, and any other implements used to brew the tea. It turns out the doctor, suspecting the same thing, had already asked her to bag everything up. It was funny, but the tea tin itself was missing."

Charles glanced up, instantly alert. "What do you mean, missing?"

"It was not in the house. Bridget, the maid, could not explain its disappearance, and neither could Mrs. Black. I had the place searched, but the tin was gone. It didn't matter much in any case, since we had the teapot and cups, which were sent out for testing."

"I see." Charles glanced at Horace, who shrugged, as if unable to answer the question himself. "So after Mr. Black agreed to press charges, and you wrapped up the tea implements, what took place next?"

"I escorted Mrs. Black to the Ludlow Street jail, where she was placed under arrest."

Mrs. Black sniffled, reaching pathetically for her lace handkerchief. Charles realized that Horace must have tutored her well.

She appeared to know exactly when to sob, when to lower her head, and when to look directly toward the witness with her head cocked in disbelief. Using the veils was a clever move by the defense, since they hid a demeanor that Charles knew could be very immature and less than serious. Horace was playing every card he had.

"What was Mrs. Black's state of mind at the time of her arrest?"

"Horrified," the officer admitted. "She begged her

husband not to let us take her in, but he wasn't sympathetic, particularly since he still had his head in a bucket. The doctor gave her a sedative, and she cried all the way to the jail."

"Did she seem particularly remorseful, or more concerned with herself?"

"Objection!" Horace shouted. "There is no way the officer could know why Mrs. Black was crying."

"Sustained." The judge gave Charles a warning look.

"I apologize," Charles said, although he wasn't sorry in the least. He had to dispel the doleful picture that the policeman had painted. Mrs. Black, as he knew from talking to her, hadn't been at all sorry that her husband had almost died. If anything, she had seemed disappointed that he had survived.

"When she arrived at the jail, did she say anything about the crime?"

For the first time, the policeman grinned. "Yes. She said she could not remember if she did it or not."

AS WINIFRED LISTENED to the testimony, her heart sank. Although she and Horace had interviewed the policeman and knew exactly what he would say, it was damning. Lafferty was the perfect prosecutor's witness. He was sure of himself and spoke with authority, but he didn't exaggerate or fill in with information he didn't know. His testimony about the missing tea tin clearly showed that. By admitting he didn't have all the answers, he came across as even more credible.

Lafferty had also successfully cast Mrs. Black in a bad light. And with Charles's parry and thrust, making sure the jury was aware that there could be more than one reason for her tears, the Black case was beginning to look very black indeed.

The missing tea tin, however, was a mystery. Someone, it appeared, was trying to protect—or convict—Mrs. Black. If the tin contained only tea, it would show that any poison present in the teacup had been added after the beverage had been prepared, incriminating Mrs. Black. But if the poison was already in the tea, perhaps she had not been the one to add it and was guilty only of giving her husband the tainted cup . . .

Her eyes flew open at the thought. Scribbling a few lines on a sheet of notepaper, she handed the note to the bailiff, then watched Horace read it. He glanced up at her with a nod of agreement. Excitement began to build inside her as she envisioned the possibilities. If they could find the tin, they could go a long way to throwing doubt in the minds of the jury about Mrs. Black's guilt.

The judge called for an adjournment until Friday, and Winifred rose with the rest of the gallery. She would question everyone involved and see if she could find a clue to the missing tin. There had to be something the police had overlooked, someone they hadn't talked to.

AS SHE STARTED for the door, she heard a shout behind her: "Miss Appleton!" Turning, she saw Charles approach, a determined look on his handsome face.

"Yes, Mr. Howe?" she said in her best starched tone.

"Winnie"—Charles glanced around, and seeing no reporters, he continued—"I would like to speak to you. I think we need to talk."

Winifred ignored the thrill that raced through her

at his words. "Not now, Charles. I have to do some investigating about the case."

"What kind of investigating?" His eyes narrowed, and he took her arm, propelling her to the rear of the courtroom where they could talk more privately. "You are not doing anything dangerous, are you?"

The concern in his voice was real. "I do not think it wise to reveal what I am working on at this time," she responded loftily. "If I find anything of use, I will let your office know."

Charles's fingers tightened on her arm. "Stop it. I only want to protect you. I have more resources at my disposal than you do, and I could possibly assist you."

She forced a smile. "Thank you, Charles, I will keep that in mind, although I think it strange that the prosecution wants to help the defense."

"Winifred," he said evenly, fighting to control his impatience, "just because we are on opposite sides of this thing does not mean we have to be enemies."

"Well, I think it means exactly that," she said, trying not to react to the excitement of being in his presence. Never had he looked so handsome, so charming, or so desirable. "We do not have to be enemies exactly, but neither can we be friends, at least for now. You have to agree with the wisdom of that, Mr. Howe, particularly given our history."

She had the pleasure of seeing a dangerous flash in his eyes, but it was gone in a moment, followed by a gleam of amusement. "I see," he said sympathetically. "You are afraid to be alone with me. I understand that, given—"

"I beg your pardon!" she gasped.

"I am flattered that you find me so irresistible."

"I do not find you irresistible," Winifred hissed, forcing her voice down as several reporters glanced their way, "in the least."

"Good! Then you won't mind accompanying me to the Governor's Ball tomorrow. I cannot possibly seduce you there, so there is no reason for you to refuse."

Her lips parted in astonishment, the emotions tying her stomach into knots. It would be wonderful to go to the ball with him. Their evening would be filled with witty repartee, interesting conversation, and seduction. And taking her to such an event would signal his serious interest in her, something that would become publicly apparent to everyone.

But then she remembered she had agreed to go with Jared. Her heart sank as she recalled her impulsiveness, fostered by Jared's admission that Charles had seen Elizabeth Billings. It could not be undone now. She lifted her face to his.

"I cannot, Charles. I'm sorry, I would have liked to go with you, but I"—she exhaled regretfully—"I have made another commitment."

"I see," Charles said. Releasing her arm, he gave her a cool smile. "I am sorry to have troubled you, then. Good afternoon, Miss Appleton."

Winifred's stomach tightened as he walked off, and the coldness in his voice reached all the way into her heart.

As court closed for the day, Charles flipped through his notes, trying to forget his irritation. Winifred could be so absolutely maddening. He had little doubt that her escort to the ball was Jared, whose smug looks and odd comments over the last few days suddenly made sense. But he could not blame Jared—the man simply got to her first.

And yet Winifred must have known that her choice would infuriate him, seeing as Jared worked in his office. In fact, that was more than likely her motivation. It would be just like her to try to throw him off balance, to win emotional points regardless of the outcome.

Well, two could play that game. Elizabeth Billings had made it more than clear that she was interested in going to the dance with him. Perhaps it was time he gave Winifred a taste of her own medicine, Charles thought shrewdly. It would be interesting to see her reaction to another woman hanging on his arm. He didn't like the manipulation, but extreme times called for extreme measures, and dealing with an Appleton sometimes meant exactly that.

His gaze fell back to his notes from the trial. The tea tin. Today was the first time the officer had thought to mention it. The missing vessel was extremely important. Normally, a policeman would disclose something like this long before the trial, but apparently, it had been overlooked until now.

Where was it? Who had hidden it? Was someone trying to protect Mrs. Black, or to incriminate her? He packed up his notes and started for the door. Someone had to know something about it. All it would take to find out was a little persistence.

CHAPTER 15

SHE WOULD find it. She had to.

Winifred stood on the porch of the Blacks' house, knocking on the front door. The place was shrouded in darkness, with nary a gaslight to illuminate the inky black windows. The curtains appeared to be drawn, probably to discourage curiosity seekers. Where was Mr. Black? Was there not even a servant around?

Her knuckles ached from knocking. Yet the tea tin could either make or break their case. She had to find it before Charles or the police did, or else Mrs. Black would surely be seeing a jail cell for the rest of her life.

Somehow it must have been overlooked. That was the only explanation that made sense. As a woman, Winifred was certain she had a better chance of locating any domestic article than a burly policeman. It was probably sitting right behind the flour, or beside the sugar. If she could only get into the house. . . .

She quietly opened her lantern and allowed just enough light to escape to illuminate the few inches beneath the doorknob. She could see the keyhole just below the knob. It did not appear terribly complicated. Now if she could just get it to open. . . .

It would be breaking and entering. But, her cause was desperate, and no one was around. She certainly didn't intend to steal anything, just to borrow— evidence.

Whipping a hairpin from her bun, she jiggled it back and forth in the keyhole. Nothing happened. Frowning, she recalled that in every novel she had ever read, this worked. Why, even New York gangs were experts at picking locks in little more than a few minutes. She continued to move the wire back and forth in the keyhole, yet was rewarded with only a backache.

A twig snapped somewhere behind her, and she froze. A dozen ugly scenarios rushed through in her mind. If she was caught, she would have a terrible time explaining this to the press or to the judge. She could just see the headline now. Worse yet, if Mr. Black came home, he wouldn't be delighted to see her, his wife's law clerk, breaking into his house.

The shrouded moon rose high in the velvet sky, smothered by an occasional cloud. A dog barked somewhere, and down the street, she could hear people talking. Everything else remained quiet.

It must have been a squirrel or some other animal, she thought. Stooping back down, she jiggled the hairpin again, trying to push it even deeper into the lock.

"Damn!" she whispered in frustration as the pin fell to the floor. She was about to look for it when a voice from the darkness stopped her cold.

"May I be of some assistance, Miss Appleton?"

"Charles!" she hissed in horror as he stepped into the feeble lantern light. "What are you doing here?"

"I could well ask you the same question," he said dryly.

Frantically, Winifred wondered how long he had been standing there and what he had seen. Straightening, she tried to appear nonchalant.

"I was just knocking to see if anyone is home. No one answered, however, so I suppose I will be leaving."

"I see," Charles drawled. Stooping down, he picked up the silver hairpin. "Forget this?"

Winifred tried to take it from his hand, but he held it firmly. "Thank you, it must have fallen from my hair."

"And right into the lock," Charles surmised. "You do know that breaking and entering is a crime in this city, don't you?"

"I was not—"

"And as a prosecutor, it would be my duty to report you."

Her bravado fell at that. Charles was on the side of the law, and breaking into a man's house was something he would not abide. She had no alternative now but to throw herself on his mercy. "I—Charles, you know how important it is to find that tea tin. The entire case hinges on it. I just thought—"

"That you would break into the Blacks' house and find it yourself," he hazarded. He took a step closer as Winifred backed up to the door, then lifted her chin to look into her face. "Did I not tell you to stay out of trouble?"

A door creaked across the street. Charles pressed up against Winifred in the shadows, trying to make them as inconspicuous as possible. She started to protest, but he held a finger to his lips, warning her to be silent. It took every ounce of her self-control to obey him—especially standing so close to him. The scent of him, the feel of his body against hers, the warmth of him, all brought back memories she'd been struggling to forget.

Suddenly, a head popped out of the door of the house across the street. The female face looked directly toward the Blacks' doorway, peering into the blackness like a cat. It seemed impossible that the woman couldn't see them. Holding her breath, Winifred waited for her to shout for help. But to her astonishment, the woman disappeared, slamming the door behind her.

"That was close," Winifred breathed.

"Yes. Mrs. Costello is a bit of a busybody," Charles said softly. "Seeing you here on the Blacks' porch would have made her day."

Winifred eased awkwardly away from him. "So will you report me, then?" she asked.

Charles gazed at her for a good long moment. "I ought to do much more than that. But since we are here, we might as well make the best of it."

To her stunned amazement, he squatted down, inserted the hairpin into the keyhole, and then expertly wiggled the instrument. Within a moment, the tumblers fell, and with a sharp click, the lock sprang open. Winifred held her breath as he picked up the dark lantern, then stepped quietly into the house.

"Wait here," he whispered when she started to follow him.

"But—"

"Unless you prefer to spend the night in jail?" Charles looked at her, one brow lifted quizzically. When she continued to glower at him, he was forced to smile. "Besides, I need you to keep guard."

Fuming with impatience, Winifred did as he ordered. As she waited, hearing him moving about the rooms, each minute seemed to take forever. Glancing at the house across the street, she breathed a sigh of relief when the lights went out. Mrs. Costello was apparently going to bed. Winifred was just beginning to relax when a carriage lumbered up the street.

"Charles!" she hissed into the door as the vehicle slowed. Within a few moments, she heard a slurred voice speaking casually to the driver.

"I told you to pull right up to the porch, didn't I?" Mr. Black said drunkenly. "Damn, I have to walk now. A man should not have to walk after being out all night, Kelly, you know that."

The carriage was as close to the steps as it could possibly get. Mr. Black disembarked, then wove across the lawn. Frantic, Winifred rushed into the house, careful to close the door softly behind her.

"Charles!" she whispered loudly, tiptoeing into the parlor. A moment later, she stubbed her toe on a piece of furniture hidden in the darkness, then hopped about on one foot, rubbing the injured member.

Footsteps sounded on the porch, and she could hear Mr. Black fumbling with his keys. Feeling her way into the kitchen, Winifred found Charles by following the sound of moving pots and pans.

"He's here! Mr. Black!" she said in a panic.

Charles remained strangely calm, as if being confronted by a drunken lout were an everyday occurrence. Snatching up the lantern, he grabbed Winifred's hand and ushered her toward the back door.

"Quickly!" he whispered, pushing her down the steps and into the backyard. He followed a minute later, pausing to quietly relatch the door.

"Damn maid!" the slurred voice continued. "Never leaves a light on! Lucky I don't break a leg."

Winifred's eyes widened as she heard Mr. Black slamming around the house. A gaslight went on somewhere, throwing a triangle of illumination into the yard. With considerable dismay, she looked down and saw they were standing in a slop pile. Immediately,

Charles pulled her out of the light toward a gap yawning in the fence.

"Quick! Through here——"

He pushed her through the rubble, then followed just as a dog began barking violently. Winifred saw a light come on in the next house and heard a male voice shouting above the dog. Her heart in her throat, she felt Charles yank her through the adjacent yard to the street beyond. There were more voices, and the sound of water running through a gutter, then someone was yelling for them to stop. Finally, they arrived at Charles's carriage.

He shoved her inside, shouted to the driver, and then joined her. The carriage pulled away from the curb at a good trot just as the neighbor appeared in his nightclothes and cap, shaking his fist into the air. Winifred and Charles looked at each other, then simultaneously burst into laughter as the carriage left the street behind.

"My God, I was so frightened!" Winifred said between choked spasms. "I thought that dog would be on our heels in another minute!"

"He probably would have," Charles said dryly, peering through the rear window of the carriage. "He could still be following us now. I must say, Miss Appleton, your choice of scent tonight is entirely appropriate."

She glanced at her soiled boots, wrinkling her nose at the smell. "How was I to know we were in a slop pile? The back door was your idea, remember."

"I suppose I should have let us get caught," Charles said sarcastically. "We might have both spent the night in jail."

"Well, we didn't, did we? Did you find it?" she asked anxiously. "The tea tin?"

"No," he replied, suddenly serious. "I looked everywhere, too. It seems to have vanished into thin air."

"It has got to be somewhere," Winifred said. "Perhaps the trash bins, Mrs. Black's room . . ."

"Oh, no," Charles said sternly. He turned to her in the carriage and faced her directly. "You are not pulling another stunt like that one anytime soon. We will get the police to obtain a search warrant, and they will look for it legally. But it may not help your case to find it."

"I know," Winifred sighed. "I just thought—"

"That if you found it before me, you could decide for yourself if it was helpful. Damnit, Winifred, that is obstruction of justice. Not only was what you undertook tonight illegal, but you could have gotten yourself in a lot of trouble. Suppose Mr. Black had caught you fumbling around in his house? Suppose that neighbor had called the police? Anyone could have seen you, a servant, a friend—"

"Charles, I think you exaggerate," she said smoothly. "Everything turned out fine. I greatly admire your adeptness with the hairpin. However did you learn such a thing? You must teach me sometime."

He swore under his breath. "There are times, Winifred, when I deeply regret that you are not a man. It would make things so much simpler. Then, of course, there are times when I am very glad you are not."

Before she could reply to that astonishing statement, he kissed her firmly.

Winifred lifted her arms around his neck and surrendered to his kiss.

She was so soft, he thought, so giving. Yet a half hour ago this same bold woman had been attempting to break into a man's house. Once more Charles was reminded of her dedication to her mission, her stubbornness and single-mindedness, without regard for the consequences. It was difficult to stay angry at her, especially with her so close and so damned tempting. . . .

When he finally eased his mouth from hers, she seemed as surprised as he was by the turn of events. Straightening her dress, she attempted to fix her appearance. When she could finally speak, her words were disapproving.

"Really, Charles, you shouldn't, you know. It is not proper for us to be . . . consorting in this manner."

"Consorting?" He teased a curl that had fallen from her knot. "Is that what you call it?"

"You know what I mean," she said indignantly.

"Yes, I do think I understand you. We have had this conversation before. You would prefer to keep our association on a more formal level because of the case. Unfortunately, Miss Appleton, I do not have a choice in the matter, and I do not believe you do, either."

"Charles!" Winifred huffed. "You are grossly overestimating your charms."

"Do you think so?" He shot her a wicked smile. "You almost tempt me to prove you wrong. I do not suppose you will find it offensive if I ask you for a dance at the ball tomorrow evening?"

She gave him a flustered look. "I suppose a dance would not do much harm. But really Charles, you know as well as I do that we should limit our socializing. The press would never understand."

"Yes, I know. And that is more important than anything else, is it not? Winifred, you can try to pretend there is nothing between us except mating instincts, but it won't work. Sooner or later you will have to face this, along with a lot of other things." He held open the door for her, then assisted her along the walkway to Aunt Eve's mansion. When they reached the door, she turned to him, her expression contrite.

"Charles, about tonight, I"—she seemed to struggle with something, then gave up—"I do appreciate your help. Mrs. Black may have been set up. That's why it was so important to try and find that tea tin."

"Mrs. Black was not set up," Charles began grimly. "I know you don't want to accept that your client is guilty, Winifred, but nothing changes the facts. The woman wanted her husband out of the way, and she tried to murder him to do it."

"You don't know—"

"Unfortunately, I do. You see, Winifred, there is something that you do not know. Mrs. Black has a lover."

"What?" Winifred's eyes grew wide. "I don't believe it."

"You will soon, if I can find the man, for I will certainly call him to the stand. I would suggest you talk to your client as soon as possible, however, and see if you can divine the truth. If Monica Black is hiding a lover from you, it's better to find out from her than in court."

"And if she denies it?"

Charles shrugged. "I will find out the truth on my own."

CHAPTER 16

"MISS APPLETON, here for Mrs. Black!"

The jailer called out to the guard, apparently more than tired of receiving visitors for the notorious Mrs. Black. Giving him a smile, Winifred waited while the guard went to fetch the prisoner.

She took a seat on the bench, thinking of the previous evening. *Mrs. Black has a lover.* Charles had seemed absolutely certain. How had he found out? How much did he know? He was doing her a tremendous favor, tipping her off in this way. But why? Was he so utterly confident that he would win this case, or did he actually want to help her?

It was all so confusing, especially with the physical attraction she felt for him. Her experiment, she realized now, had been a dismal failure, for Charles was quite right—she now felt more drawn to him than ever. When he kissed her in the carriage, it had taken all of her willpower not to kiss him back just as thoroughly. He was the last man she should be involved with, especially now, yet she couldn't seem to stay away from him. Worse, she was beginning to experience increasingly tender feelings for him, in spite of her declarations to the contrary, and it frightened her.

No man could ever understand why it was so important for her to achieve her goals, no man could comprehend her fascination with the law, no man—except Charles. Try as she might, she could not banish that thought. True, even Charles assumed that she'd tire of it eventually and give up the law. How could she make him see that she had no choice in this matter, either?

"Hello, Miss Appleton. How do you think things are going?" Monica Black approached, her veils lifted to reveal her pale but pretty face.

"We had been more hopeful, before now." Winifred said, reaching out to straighten the brooch on the woman's dress. "We need to talk."

Something in Winifred's tone sobered the woman's expression. She shrugged guiltily, as if resigned to her fate. "All right then, but I thought you already asked me everything. What now?"

Winifred waited for the guard to leave. As soon as he was out of earshot, she turned to the prisoner. "Mrs. Black, I'm going to have to ask you this question straight out. I have reason to believe you are involved with another man, besides your husband. Is this true?"

"Do you mean Robbie?" Mrs. Black asked, as her eyes lit up and a pink flush came to her cheeks. Then she dropped her eyes quickly to her lap. "What has he got to do with all this?"

Winifred hid a groan. She had been hoping against hope that it was just a groundless rumor, that Monica would deny it indignantly. But the expression in her eyes told Winifred it was the truth.

The guard glanced at the two women curiously. Winifred lowered her voice.

"How long have you been secretly seeing Mr.—"

"Albright," Monica finished for her. "Oh, I dunno. A few months, maybe? But it's not like you think! He had nothing to do with what happened! Besides, the old man did it first!"

"Do you mean your husband had an affair?" Winifred asked incredulously.

"Yes." Monica nodded vigorously, then reached for her handkerchief. Finding none, she accepted Winifred's, then dabbed at her eyes. "I knew he was seeing a couple of them floozies from the dance hall. That ain't supposed to count, is it? He said since I couldn't . . . he didn't . . ,"

"I think I understand your meaning," Winifred said softly. "Go on."

"He was entitled." At this, the former dance hall girl burst into real tears. "I never thought to have anyone else, I really didn't."

"When did you meet Mr. Albright?"

"At Stewart's," Mrs. Black said, stifling her sobs. "He took me to lunch. It had been so long since someone treated me kind. Like I was pretty or something. Do you know what I mean?"

A strange welling of emotion arose within Winifred. Six months ago she would not have had any idea what the woman meant. But now—

"Go on," Winifred urged.

"Well, it went right to my head. I didn't see nothing wrong with it at first. But after a time things got more . . . involved."

"Did you write to him, send him presents, accept anything?"

The woman stared stupidly at Winifred, then nodded. "I gave him a book and a money clip with my initials on it. I thought that looked real classy. Don't you think?"

Winifred hid another groan. She looked heaven-ward, trying to keep the impatience from her voice. "How about Mr. Albright? What did he give you?"

"Poetry." Monica's eyes went dreamy. "His own and a book. Why, he writes the most beautiful things. 'Your eyes are like daffodils, your lips like cherries.' You know, that sort of thing."

A sense of despair came over Winifred, and she glanced once more at the guard. The papers would have a wonderful time with that one! It wouldn't take the reporters long to find someone to talk, and when they heard about the poetry . . .

"Mrs. Black, I want you to answer me honestly. All of this is liable to come out in court. Have you ever . . . been physical with Mr. Albright? In the way you are only supposed to be with your husband?"

Mrs. Black nodded, then faced Winifred with a strange sort of expression. "It's almost like a drug. I don't know how else to say it, except I felt like those street blokes who have to have a whiskey. It was . . ."

"Intoxicating," Winifred supplied thoughtfully.

The woman, obviously pleased to be understood, nodded vigorously again. "Yes, that's it!" She seemed astonished that this elegant, sophisticated lawyer would have any idea what she meant.

"Mrs. Black, did Mr. Albright ever give you any indication that he was . . . serious about you?"

The smile died on the prisoner's face. She glanced at the guard, at the floor, then out the window again. Winifred gently touched her sleeve.

"To help you, I must know. Please be truthful with me. It's your only chance."

The woman nodded, blew her nose furiously into Winifred's handkerchief, then lifted her reddened face.

"He said if anything ever happened to my old man, he'd find a way to marry me."

WINIFRED WALKED SLOWLY HOME after her visit at the Ludlow Street jail. Ignoring the toughs who shouted at her from the alleys, the Irish laborers who huddled over a weak fire, and the endless procession of horses and carts, she thought carefully about what Mrs. Black had told her.

Charles had been right—the woman did have a lover. A Mr. Albright, to be exact. Although Mr. Albright had disappeared since Monica's arrest, Winifred had little doubt that the story would leak to the press. The only thing more scandalous than murder was sex, particularly if the perpetrator was a woman.

The defense had to find the man, hopefully before the prosecution did. They would talk to him, attempt to understand his role in the Black case, and to coach him on how to answer in court. Yet it still looked bad. A lover, even a cooperative one, would only give Mrs. Black more of a motive to murder.

Worse, Mrs. Black still didn't seem to take any of it seriously. What a poor witness she would be if Charles called her to the stand! She came across as shallow and silly, immature and naïve. Winifred could just see her telling the jury about her Robbie. She groaned out loud.

Instead of getting easier, this case became more complicated by the minute. When she had questioned Monica about the tea tin, she didn't know what happened to it, either. Another mystery.

Even Mrs. Black's female supporters, the suffragettes and Miss. Anthony, could well be less sympathetic if they thought Monica had tried to kill her husband so she could be with another man. Yet for all her childishness, Monica was oddly sincere. The woman was desperately unhappy and had reached out for a chance to enjoy life, even for a short while. Was that so wrong?

As Winifred entered her aunt's house, she heard Penelope's cheerful voice, and much bustling in preparation for the ball that evening. She sighed, removed her gloves, and placed them carefully on the side table. It would not do at all to show up at the ball morose or distracted. Charles would immediately guess she had found out something, and he would hound her relentlessly until she told him what it was. Monica Black's secret had to remain a secret, at least until they located Mr. Albright.

"Winnie! There you are. One would think you were not looking forward to tonight at all. I have drawn your bath. Come and help me choose a wrap."

Penelope bubbled merrily, and Winifred followed her upstairs.

THE GOVERNOR'S BALL was held at the St. Nicholas Hotel, which was not in the most fashionable location but was beautiful. Winifred and Penelope disembarked from their coach, and Winifred barely noticed the Italianate marble structure, the glittering gaslight chandeliers, the black walnut wainscoting, the satin damask draperies—or her handsome escort, Jared Marton. Her visit to the jail that morning still haunted her, and it took every ounce of effort to pretend she was happy to be here.

Jared took their coats and handed them to the attendant, while Winifred tried to mask her glum mood.

"May I fetch you ladies a glass of punch?" he asked, unfailingly polite. He looked very handsome this evening, dressed in a stylish dove-gray coat with a paisley vest and diamond tie pin. Even his gloves were pearl gray and impeccable.

"Champagne punch," Penelope said coolly. "I believe they have it in the ballroom."

"And you, Miss Appleton?" he asked Winifred.

"The same," she said softly, giving him a reserved smile.

When Jared went to get the refreshments, Penelope frowned. "Mr. Marton is very handsome, but I thought you would want to go to the dance with Charles."

"Mr. Howe and I are not seeing eye to eye these days," Winifred said. "As you know, we are on opposite sides of the Black case. It would have been unseemly for him to escort me."

"Pooh!" Penelope brushed aside any such reservations. "Mr. Marton is from the prosecutor's office, also. If you can go with him, I cannot see why you could not go with Charles. Besides, I don't trust him. He seems like too much of a rake for you."

Winifred glanced at her sister in surprise. Even in such a short time, Jared had obviously made an impression on her. She had thought perhaps the two of them might find an interest in each other, since in some ways they were very much alike. Yet her aunt had told her that one of Penelope's suitors had recently died in an accident, so she was in no frame of mind to be receptive to any man, even refusing an escort to the dance. Still, her irritation with Jared seemed telling.

"Penny, Mr. Marton is just being kind. Let's talk about this later. It is much too complicated for me to explain here," Winifred said. The last thing she wanted to admit to her sister was that she was jealous.

"All right," Penelope said, unconvinced. She glanced around at the beautiful setting. "Winnie, will you look at all that food! And the decorations, and the gowns! You must tell me who all the political people are, for I daresay I only know the fashionable ones!"

Winifred smiled. Her sister, clad in cream-colored lace with a trail of carnations pinned to the back of her dress, looked even more astonishingly beautiful than ever, outshining almost every woman there. Even Jared could not remain unaffected, although Penelope gave him only the simplest courtesies.

"I will try to point them out." Winifred scanned the room. "That's John Kelly, who took over after Mr. Tweed's ouster. They call him 'Honest John.' Then there's August Belmont and Horatio Seymour, Richard Croker and Plunkitt—all of the new Tammany leaders are here."

"I only know the rich ones," Penelope giggled. "There is that terrible Mr. Gould. It is a wonder he can be seen in public after the last year's panic. And there is Cornelius Vanderbilt—this is going to be a wonderful party!"

Jared returned with the champagne, handing a golden flute to Winifred and another to her sister. Penelope drank hers quickly, giggling at the bubbles as they tickled her nose. Before long, she was surrounded by eligible young men, all of whom wanted to be introduced to the most beautiful of the notorious sisters.

Winifred was conspicuous as well, and soon she was barraged by questions about the Black case, from the curious, the well-meaners, the suffragettes, and the reporters. She weighed her answers carefully, knowing how easily her words could be distorted, and responded as graciously as possible. Yet the effort was wearing. Rather than enjoying herself, she had to be constantly on guard and could not relax for a moment.

Thankfully, Jared Marton saw her dilemma and

sought to rescue her. "Miss Appleton is needed on a matter of state business," he told the crowd, then whisked her away to the dance floor. Winifred's mouth parted in surprise, but then she giggled at his ploy.

"Mr. Marton, that was not very nice. That reporter from the *Times* will surely name you in his article in the morning."

"I have always enjoyed seeing my name in print." He smiled. "Besides, this is supposed to be a party, not a political convention. If it were left to them, you would never get to dance." His gaze wandered down her throat to her gown. Admiration burned there, and he spoke hoarsely. "I must admire your gown, Miss Appleton, which is far different from your office attire. You really are a very handsome woman."

"Thank you," Winifred said. His admiration was like a balm to her raw nerves, and she smiled gratefully as they twirled around the dance floor. "I was afraid this gown would appear terribly old-fashioned, for I have not paid much attention to styles. They change so quickly."

"It suits you," Jared commented. "The gown's simplicity only enhances the jewel inside, like a diamond in a gold setting."

"You flatter me, Mr. Marton," Winifred said, her eyes meeting his.

"Not at all, Miss Appleton," Jared protested flirtatiously. "I only speak the truth." He cocked his head to listen to the music, then smiled as he recognized the quick beat. "I daresay they are playing Strauss. Do you waltz, Miss Appleton?"

"Occasionally," Winifred responded, "and not very well."

"Nonsense! You are amazingly light on your feet. This dance is called the Boston, and it is extremely popular. I will show you. Now just let me hold you a

little closer . . . that's it. You have wonderful, slender hips."

As Jared whirled her around the dance floor, she
found herself laughing and more than a bit breathless.
The music was brisk, and although she could not follow the steps, Jared was proficient and soon was dip-
ping her and swinging her around.

When she finally dared to look up, the smile on
her face died.

Charles had entered the ballroom with Elizabeth
Billings on his arm. At the same moment, his eyes
met hers, and Winifred felt as if she were an insect,
pinned by a madly determined scientist.

"Miss Appleton?" Jared asked softly. "Are you all
right? You look a little pale."

"Fine, I'm fine. I'm just a little breathless, that's
all," Winifred said quickly. "I suppose I am not used
to such a fast pace."

"Perhaps we should get some air?" he offered.
"There is a balcony just beyond."

"Yes, I think that is a wonderful idea," she replied, trying hard not to look at the handsome couple.

Charles and Elizabeth. She felt the same sinking
feeling she'd felt when Jared had told her that Elizabeth had come to see him.

Yet there was absolutely no reason for her to feel
that way. Charles was a grown man and was certainly
free to see anyone he liked. And he had asked Winifred
to the ball—she was the one who had declined. Still, it
tore at her heart to see Elizabeth look up into his face
and laugh, then smooth a piece of lint from his jacket
as if he belonged to her.

"Here. Try to smile. You have to at least appear to
be happy." Jared handed her a glass of champagne, a
sympathetic look on his face.

"Is it that obvious?" Winifred said, taking a sip.

"No. But now that we are talking about it, what the devil is going on between you two?"

Winifred gazed at him over the rim of her glass, uncertain of how much to trust him. "Well, there is this case—"

"Bah!" Jared waved a hand dismissively. "If you were mine, that would not stop me."

"It is not Charles, it's me." Suddenly Winifred wanted to talk to someone about it all. "It is more than just the case. It's what I want to do with my life—to become a real lawyer and help other women. That does not reconcile with being a wife and mother."

"I see." Jared tipped his own glass thoughtfully. "And have you discussed all this with our esteemed prosecutor?"

"Charles?" She smiled. "Mr. Marton, you of all people have to know that Charles never took my ambition seriously. I am grateful for his help—do not misunderstand. Yet he clearly expected me to fall flat on my face and give up."

"Yes, he can be sort of opinionated, now that you mention it," Jared smirked. "And old-fashioned, stubborn, high-handed—"

"He is not! Why, he—" Winifred stopped when she realized Jared was laughing.

"Forgive me, Miss Appleton, I could not resist the opportunity to tease you a little. So you are in love with Charles Howe, and now he is on the other side of a case. And not just any case but the Black case, which thanks to your efforts will go down in history as a women's rights case. And Mr. Howe, who I think is in equally dire straits, is here tonight with the beautiful and ambitious Miss Billings. So what do you do?"

Winifred looked at him miserably. Somehow she thought she'd feel better after talking about it, but hearing her dilemma so succinctly summed up was even more depressing. "What would you suggest?"

"Dinner," Jared said, holding his arm out to her. Even as she gazed at him warily, a slow smile crept across his face. "Miss Appleton, do not tell me you are ready to concede defeat? I suppose I could just take you home, and Charles would know you could not bear to see him with another woman—"

"No!" Winifred cried indignantly. "No, I won't do that."

"Good." Jared chuckled, rubbing his hands together. "This is going to be an entertaining evening after all. Thank God. Now, shall we go in?"

Winifred took his offered arm firmly. Charles was here with an escort. He saw nothing wrong with it. Why should she?

CHARLES WAS about to burst from frustration. All through dinner, Winifred, looking incredibly beautiful and sophisticated, had been seated across from him with Jared Marton, laughing and flirting outrageously. His own dinner companion, Elizabeth Billings, had tried repeatedly to engage him in conversation, but he simply was not interested in this year's fashions or the Merryways' soirée. Instead, he could not take his eyes off the lovely Winifred, who seemed to be doing everything in her power to drive him crazy.

So he could only watch helplessly while his cohort, Jared Marton, thoroughly enjoyed himself. Besides Winifred's beauty, her company would be equally stimulating. Charles attempted to hear what they were talking about, hoping to join in the conversation, but the clanging of silver platters and the noise of hundreds of guests made it hopeless.

Worse, his feelings of frustration didn't appear to be at all reciprocated, for Winifred seemed perfectly content with Jared's company. When her napkin fell to the floor and Jared gallantly picked it up, a hot flash of jealousy rent Charles. It seemed to him that Jared took an inordinately long time in doing it. Was he treating himself to a view of Winifred's pretty ankles? Charles was about to dive beneath the table himself when Jared finally reappeared, shaking out the napkin with much fanfare, then placing it on Winifred's lap. He lingered over the task, his fingers brushing over her thighs. Charles took a deep drink of wine, wanting nothing more than to strangle the handsome young lawyer.

"Charles? Are you all right?" As if from a huge distance, he heard Elizabeth.

"I have a bit of a headache," he replied to the pretty woman.

"Oh, I am sorry. Perhaps some tonic would help. You should probably try that instead of drinking so much wine. I think it only aggravates a headache."

"I am certain you're right," Charles said, ordering the servant to refill his wineglass. Drinking deeply of the rich burgundy once more, he scowled as Winifred said something, then Jared threw back his head in mirth. When Winifred accepted the glazed carrots from the waiter, Jared insisted upon arranging them on her platter. He used any excuse to touch her, admiring her ear bobs so he could finger her soft white lobes, then commenting on her hair so he could smooth a stray curl from her face. And when the servant came by with an assortment of cakes for dessert, Jared teasingly insisted that she sample more than one, personally feeding her a bite from his own plate.

They looked like a courting couple, Charles thought bitterly. Why did propriety never seem to concern his associate? But he knew why. Whispers of a romantic liaison with the notorious Winifred Appleton would only enhance Jared's reputation. By flirting with her, Jared had nothing to lose.

A sudden vision of his future flashed into Charles's

mind. Numbly, he reached for another drink. Without Winifred, he would probably wed Elizabeth Billings. He would buy a good house on Fifth Avenue and raise a brood of children who would go on to Harvard or Princeton. And he would forever sit across the table, watching the woman he truly wanted enjoying herself with another man.

In that one moment, everything crystallized for him. He had to have Winifred. His need was more than sexual desire, although he felt that intensely. It was even more than a need for intellectual stimulation, although that was important too. The fact was, she was his other half, the one whose opinion mattered more to him than any other's, the face he looked for in a crowd. He was desperately in love with Winifred Appleton.

The guests rose after supper, and Jared slid his arm around Winifred's waist, his hand resting possessively on the delicate curve of her hip. A blind red rage swept over Charles. All he could think of was Winifred standing before him, naked in the firelight in their hotel suite. All he could see now was Jared Marton, sliding his hand across her naked flesh, enjoying that same pleasure. All he could envision was Jared, bringing Winifred to fulfillment, seeing the way she closed her eyes in ecstasy, hearing those sharp little cries as she reached her climax.

Years of restraint, legal education, and observance of propriety went right out the door. Charles could see nothing but a blaze of outrage as Jared led Winifred toward the ballroom.

"Will you excuse me?" he said thickly to Elizabeth, who opened her mouth in surprise. Nothing mattered except that he stop the blatant seduction of the woman who should be his. Stepping across the floor, he accosted Winifred and Jared.

"Charles, old boy!" Jared boomed. "I am delighted to have a chance to speak to you. I must say, I have been enjoying Miss Appleton's company so much, I forgot everyone else!"

"I'll bet," Charles said, then punched him as hard as he could.

The contact was solid, and his years of boxing lessons paid off. With immense satisfaction, Charles saw his tormentor stumble backward, cupping his chin, then crumble to the floor. Almost immediately a crowd gathered murmuring in shock.

Winifred gasped. "Charles, are you insane? You hit him!" Shocked, she reached for Jared in an attempt to help him to his feet.

But the young attorney wisely stayed where he was, refusing her help. Something sparkled in his eyes, then was gone in a second as reporters flocked to the scene. Pencils scribbled furiously, and they shouted questions, each of them trying to get a scoop on the scandalous story.

"Mr. Marton, are you hurt?"

"What precipitated this?"

"Why did Mr. Howe strike you?"

"Is it true, Miss Appleton, that you are Mr. Howe's mistress?"

"Has the Black case become a lovers' quarrel?"

Belatedly, Charles understood that he had precipitated this feeding frenzy. The warm drunkenness he had felt earlier vanished. Astonished at his own lack of control and the depth of his anger, he now felt deep remorse and shame. Helping Jared to his feet, he began to publicly apologize, but Jared quickly interrupted.

"Gentlemen, I simply slipped and fell. There is no story here. I suggest you all go back to the party."

The reporters jostled each other to get closer. Charles flashed Jared a look of profound gratitude.

Jared refused to respond in any other way, repeating the same tale over and over. But the reporters, scenting a scandal, were relentless.

Penelope quickly escorted the besieged Winifred away, giving Jared a meaningful glance, while the lawyers attempted to control the damage. Still, the episode was too hot to cover up. Within minutes, the story had circulated through the ballroom, and spectators added their own version of what had transpired. It had been, everyone agreed, a night to remember.

SCANDAL AT GOVERNOR'S BALL! FIGHT
BETWEEN PROSECUTORS OVER LEGAL SIREN!
COURTHOUSE RUMORED A LOVE NEST!

Charles groaned, tossing the morning paper aside in disgust. In spite of the three cups of coffee he'd already had, his head pounded fearfully, and he had to shade his eyes from the dim sunlight pouring in through his window.

It could not have happened. He had been hoping and praying all night that it had just been a nasty dream, one that, upon awakening, he could put from his thoughts. But the newspaper, blaring the headline in black and white, would not let him entertain that hopeful fantasy.

He had completely lost control. He couldn't remember ever doing such a thing before. Even as a child, he had resisted schoolroom bullies, using his brains instead of his brawn to settle disputes. Yet in the course of last evening, in a fit of jealous anger, he had struck a fellow lawyer and shocked the woman he cared deeply about.

What had come over him? He scarcely recognized

himself. Jared had been enjoying himself at his expense, but that was no excuse for his own behavior. Technically, he had no rights to Winifred. He was not engaged to her, he was not courting her, and he had no prior claim to her. She could see Jared or anyone else she chose.

Suddenly the man he had been thinking about stepped into his office and closed the door. Charles stood up instantly, more embarrassed then ever when he saw the bruise on the attorney's chin. Lifting his hands helplessly, he felt like sinking through the floor.

"Jared, I am so sorry," Charles said softly. "I hope one day you can forgive me. I was just thinking about it when you walked in. I honestly do not know what came over me."

"Oh, I have an idea." To his amazement, Jared seemed more amused than upset. He dropped into a seat and lightly fingered his chin, wincing when he touched the bruise. "You have a hell of a left there. I guess those boxing lessons paid off. You should have warned me."

Charles took his own seat. "Say what you want— you are perfectly entitled. I will even let you take a swing at me if that would make things better. I can not believe I did such a thing."

Jared laughed, helping himself to some of Charles's coffee. "I did not come here to rub it in. I just wanted to clear the air. Charles, I understand what happened, and truth be known, it was partly my fault. I should apologize to you."

"What?" Charles gazed at him in disbelief.

"It is perfectly apparent that you have feelings for Miss Appleton, deep feelings. I knew that, yet I entertained myself, knowing it was likely to bother you. I admit, however, that I am attracted to her as well. She has the most beautiful—"

"Jared." Charles cleared his throat. The possessive feelings rose in him once more, surprising him again in their intensity.

Jared laughed. "Charles, what is going on between the two of you? It is obvious you cannot leave each other alone, yet you are not engaged, not even courting—unless I am deceived."

Charles choked on his coffee, aware that he owed Jared some kind of explanation for his behavior, but he was unwilling to divulge the full extent of his relationship with Winifred. "Miss Appleton is not like other women," he finished lamely.

"I'll say." Jared grinned. "Do you know that she believes you do not take her seriously? That you think she will just quit and forget about being a lawyer? I have to admit, I reminded her of what a closed-minded scoundrel you can be—"

"Thanks," Charles said dryly.

"Interestingly, though, she rushed to your defense. Miss Appleton has a blind spot where you are concerned. Along with a great deal of loyalty. I would hate to see that wasted."

"Jared, what are you getting at?"

He shrugged, his jaunty demeanor gone. "I suppose I have decided to befriend the lady and am thus concerned about her welfare. Have you seen the morning paper?"

"Yes." Charles buried his face in his hands.

"Miss Appleton's name is in serious jeopardy."

"I know." Charles lifted his head and stared at the front page once more. "It will take everything in my power to restore it. This is entirely my fault, and I am prepared to do just that. I feel terrible about it."

"There is one other option," Jared shrugged. "You could marry her."

"What?"

"Sure, why not?" Jared asked casually. "After all, this entire scene will then be described as romantic. You will be seen as a modern-day Byron, and Winifred the damsel in distress. You could stay up well into the night, discussing legal dilemmas. . . . It could work."

"Thanks for the advice, but I think I will figure out my own solution," Charles said smoothly. The last thing he wanted to admit to Jared was Winifred's reluctance to wed him.

"Well, if you decide you don't want her, I will be more than happy to stop in and console her—"

"Jared," Charles cut him off quickly, "if you do not mind, I am not entirely rational where Miss Appleton and you are concerned. Trust me, I will put things right where she is concerned—and without your help."

He ignored the other man's laughter.

IT HAD BEEN a wretched morning, and Winifred groaned. Penelope had thought last night's events incredibly romantic. She had wanted to know every detail that had led up to Charles striking Jared, and she had gigglingly suggested he was madly jealous. Winifred dismissed such talk as nonsense.

Thankfully, Aunt Eve's presence had quieted the exuberant Penelope, for neither of them wanted to alarm the elderly lady. Talk would reach her soon enough. Still, Winifred could not help the feeling of guilt and shame that swept over her.

Somehow she was responsible for all this, she felt. Jared and Charles had been friends and associates for a long time—until now. She had come between them. Deep down, she knew she had flirted with Jared on purpose, in order to hurt Charles for being with Elizabeth. Every time Charles had leaned his dark head close to Elizabeth's to listen to her chatter, or called the waiter to refill her glass, Winifred had felt a pang of possessive jealousy.

In vain, she tried to explain to Penelope that this situation was not funny at all. She had fought to gain an equal footing with the other lawyers, but she would now only be seen as a silly woman, caught in the midst of a lovers' scandal.

Worse, as she couldn't tell Penelope, her own actions had made Charles do something foolish, something that would no doubt make him sorry he ever knew her. His own good name had been besmirched last night. It would be best for everyone if she never saw him again, as much as the prospect hurt. She had to go see him one last time, to tell him that, and somehow make things right again between him and Jared. Snatching up her cloak, she headed for the state's offices.

"I am here to see Mr. Howe."

Mr. Crocker took Winifred's card, holding the farthest corner of it as if the thing were poisoned.

"I will tell him you are here."

The little man left, and Winifred, left in the familiar surroundings, glanced down at his desk. The newspaper lay there, the headline blaring last night's events. She winced. No wonder the secretary had treated her like a pariah.

"He will see you." Crocker indicated the door disapprovingly.

Winifred swept down the hall with as much dignity as she could muster. She could not blame Crocker for thinking ill of her. He was loyal to Charles and had every reason to see her as a jezebel, a woman who had disrupted their office and come between the two attorneys.

When she entered Charles's office, he was busy scribbling something, his dark head turned down, concentrating on his work. Winifred took a moment and openly admired the square cut of his coat, his muscled shoulders, the elegant line of his profile, and the sensual curve of his mouth. She had started to think of him as hers, and last night had shown her clearly that he was not. She forced herself to swallow hard, refusing to give in to the emotions that threatened to overwhelm her. She had to keep control. This would be hard enough without her making a fool of herself.

As if sensing her presence, Charles glanced up, a smile coming to his face. "Winnie, I am glad you came. I was going to come to see you today. Please, take a seat."

"No, thank you," she said formally. She had to make this quick, or she'd lose her nerve. "This won't take long. Charles, I just want to tell you how very sorry I am for what happened—"

"I was about to say the same thing to you," he admitted, then looked puzzled. "What on earth do you have to be sorry for? You, of all people, were innocent in this."

"Not so innocent," she said softly. "I knew you might be upset when you saw me with Mr. Marton, and I took advantage of that. I suppose I was upset with you because—"

Her voice broke as she realized what she had been about to admit. Charles must have sensed it, too, for he got to his feet and quickly shut the door, then locked it. Then he came to her side.

"Yes?"

He was standing so close, she could lean into his

embrace. Winifred wanted more than anything to throw herself into his arms, beg his forgiveness, and tell him what he meant to her. But she could not do that. Instead, she fought the tender feelings inside her.

"Never mind. It is foolish, I know. But I think it is best if I do not see you anymore. Socially, I mean."

"I see." Charles did not seem the least surprised or disturbed by her pronouncement.

"No, I mean it this time. I know I said that to you before, but after what happened . . ." Tears stung her eyes. "I know your name and position are important to you. I never meant to hurt you or cause you any trouble. You have to believe that."

Charles looked at her for a good long moment, then lifted her face gently to his. "Why, Miss Winifred, do I detect a softening in your emotions toward me? I thought you would be more concerned about your own reputation."

"Not at all," she said uneasily. "I am, after all, an Appleton. I am quite used to being drawn and quartered in the press. When I practiced spiritualism with my sisters, it was common to see my name splashed all over the papers in a deprecating way."

"I am aware of that," Charles continued. "I am beginning to believe that that is the reason you know how to use the press so effectively."

"Precisely," Winifred admitted. "But that does not excuse what happened here. You did not deserve this, and I—I am partly responsible."

"That's very noble of you, Winnie, but I am capable of taking responsibility for my own actions. Unless you are implying that I was so bewitched by you, I cannot be held accountable for what I did—"

"No, not at all!" Winifred looked appalled. "I do not think anything of the kind. I also want you to know that, about you and Elizabeth . . . well, I understand."

"Understand what?" Charles looked surprised. He lifted one boot onto a chair and leaned on his bent knee.

"That you want to be with her," Winifred said quickly. "She is, after all, perfect for you. She comes from a good family, has social connections and her own income, and is very much a lady. I can see why you are attracted to her as well. She does have a sort of fashionable prettiness."

"That is very kind of you."

Winifred smiled wanly. "Yes, I just wanted to make you aware that I do not hold you to anything because of . . . what has transpired between us in the past. It is better all the way around, when I think about it."

With an oath, Charles stepped closer to her and pulled her into his arms. "Winifred," he exclaimed in exasperation, "what if I do not want Elizabeth? What if I were to tell you my taste runs to a far different kind of woman, one who has a mind as sharp as a tack, one whose social activities run to breaking and entering, one who causes me to punch out other men simply because I am beside myself with jealousy?"

Winifred's mouth dropped open. "But you cannot—"

"I cannot what? Want you? Marry you? See you every night when I come home, and wake up beside you each morning? Watch our children grow up together? Grow old with you? I cannot do any of that? Tell me why not, Winifred."

She gazed at him in astonishment, while a little flutter began in her heart. Could it really happen? Could she really be with him every day, have that dark, handsome head leaning on her shoulder each day, hold his warm, wonderful body each night? The picture he painted was beautiful, and it struck a chord deep within her. But how could she reconcile it with her dream?

"Winifred, this is not how I had planned it, but after what happened, there is no reason to wait," he said softly, drawing her more deeply into his embrace. "We cannot deny what is between us. Why not make the best of it?"

He kissed her, a soft brushing of his lips against hers. She sighed, feeling an overwhelming rush of emotions. All of the bottled-up passion, longing, and desire broke over her like an ocean wave, sweeping her completely under with its force. Her arms lifted by their own accord around his neck, and her feet stood up on tiptoes to better receive his kiss. She couldn't help it—all she knew was that she wanted him, and that he was hers.

Sensing her surrender, Charles groaned and deepened the kiss, plunging his tongue recklessly inside the sweetness of her mouth to taste her fully. She was like a good wine, complex and heady, more intoxicating with each sip. His own needs thundering out of control, he turned her in his arms, cupped her head, and thoroughly enjoyed his plunder.

When his mouth finally eased from hers, she looked stunned, her lips swollen from his ardent kiss, her eyes dark with desire. He knew she was experiencing the same riot of emotions he was and was just as confused. Tracing a tender finger along her profile, he smiled.

"Will you come to me tonight? My servant has the evening off. No one will be there. I can hold you like this, make love to you. . . . Darling I want you so badly."

"Charles, you know I shouldn't—"

"Yes, I know. I can think of a thousand reasons why you should slap my face and tell me no. And only one to say yes." He gently lifted her face to his.

Winifred opened her eyes and looked deeply into his. "Yes, Charles," she breathed. "Yes."

CHAPTER 18

YES, OH PLEASE, Charles, you must stop that!"

Winifred writhed beneath him, her body drawn and taut, every inch of her tense and quivering and incredibly sensitive. He had slipped his hand between her legs and teased her, even as he drove into her. She cried out in fulfillment, her body visibly reacting to her climax. The sight of her, so uninhibited and erotic, caused him to lose his last ounce of control. Rising upward, he thrust into her deeply, feeling her body clench around his as the spasms shuddered through her.

"Winifred, you are so beautiful, so sensual, so unbelievable . . ." he whispered hoarsely, driving fiercely into her, taking her to new levels of pleasure. Her cries became more vocal and soon she was straining against him, thrashing beneath him, twisting and turning, wanting to get everything she could out of the experience. . . .

When he heard her break, he could not hold back any longer. She was so tight, so responsive, and so exquisitely sensitive that it took every ounce of his willpower to hold back and give her pleasure. She truly was Joan of Arc, Helen of Troy, and Morgan le Fay all captured in one beautiful body.

When her breathing finally returned to normal, she opened her eyes and looked at him with shocked innocence. "This cannot be legal! It is entirely too enjoyable."

"Actually, it would be legal if we were married. I think the laws were written to protect tender young damsels like you from foul seducers like myself." He laughed with her then turned serious. "Winifred, have you given any thought to what I said earlier?"

She shivered, as if the conversation itself left her cold. "Charles, I appreciate your offer, you know that. And I am honored. But you know why it would never work between us. I have to do what I was born to do—"

"Yes, I know, your damned destiny." He tossed the cover over her and moved away to sit upright. "Is it really more important than us?"

Her eyes grew moist, and she plucked at the covers. "Do we have to talk about this now?"

"Yes, I think we do," he said, his voice firm. "Winnie, be reasonable. You know how slim the likelihood is of you ever really becoming a lawyer. You could counsel women, help them, give them legal advice. You could also help me with my work. You might even pass the bar. But you could never really have a practice the way you would like, have real clients, appear before the Supreme Court."

"I do not believe that—"

"I know you do not want to, Winnie, but hear me out. There was a case a few months ago in Wisconsin where a woman who had passed the bar wanted to appear before the court on an appeal. She was flatly denied. I followed the case, hoping for a precedent, something to encourage you, but there it is. Other females who have been successful in passing the bar fail to obtain paying clients. It is not that I don't think you can do it. I just cannot see you setting yourself up for more pain."

"I know it is not acceptable for a woman to practice Charles. But it will be soon. I recently heard of a Miss Robinson who's forming a club for aspiring female lawyers. I've submitted my application. And the Black trial will surely advance my cause, even if I just get people talking about it. Surely you can understand that?" She looked at him pleadingly.

"For the last time, Winifred, Mrs. Black is not some noble heroine whom you should be defending! She tried to kill her husband in cold blood! Do you really plan to remain a spinster and forgo a husband and children of your own, just to try and save her?"

"That is so unfair!" Winifred cried. "And why do I have to choose? Oh, Charles, it is so different for men. No one came to you and told you to pick one or the other. Why is it that women are expected to make all the sacrifices?"

"Because you are the ones to bear children," he answered simply. He placed a hand on her stomach, then gently reached down and kissed it. "You might even be pregnant now."

"That is not likely since I have been counting the days," Winifred said with a sigh of relief. "Still, I know no method is foolproof. That is why I cannot wed. I am sorry, Charles, please understand."

When he saw that she was not going to budge, his expression changed. He rose and pulled on his trousers, yanking them on one leg at a time.

"Get dressed. I think I had better take you home."

"You are angry with me," she sighed, reaching for her clothes. "I shouldn't have come here tonight. I'm sorry I cannot just say what you want me to say. Life would be infinitely easier."

"No, I do not want you to pretend," he said harshly, snatching on his shirt. Then he helped her to dress, wrenching each button as if it were personally responsible for his disappointment. Finally one of them popped and rolled across the floor.

"My button—"

"Forget the damned button. I will buy you a new gown," he growled. Whirling her around, he held her shoulders firmly. "Winifred, just look at me once and tell me you do not care for me. Maybe then I can just forget about you and leave you to your own devices."

She looked up at him and felt pain rush over her again. More than anything at that moment, she wanted to tell him she loved him, would marry him, would give up everything for him. But to do so would betray herself in a way she did not think she would ever get over.

Yet she could not lie to him, either. "I cannot . . ." She faltered. "Charles, being married to you would be wonderful, except—"

"I see. You care for me but not enough. I am good enough for this, but not good enough to be your husband." He gestured to the rumpled bed.

"You cannot possibly think that—"

"What else am I to think? Or is this another one of your experiments? Let's go, Winnie, before I say something I truly regret."

She did not think it possible to hurt any more than she did. But she soon discovered just how wrong she could be.

"ORDER! ORDER!"

The judge rapped his gavel, glaring at the public

gallery. "I will close this courtroom if these outbursts continue!"

The crowd fell to a grumbling silence, like children deprived of their entertainment. A heavily veiled Mrs. Black took her seat at the defense table, her presence inciting the crowd to jeer "Murderess!" As the judge continued to glare threateningly, quiet finally settled on the room. The jury looked annoyed, the judge was incensed, and the prosecution simply waited patiently. At the judge's nod, Charles began questioning the prosecution's next witness.

"Professor Caldwell, I understand you are a professor of chemistry. Which college are you affiliated with?"

"Buffalo Medical College in New York," the professor answered somewhat pompously.

"How long have you been so employed?"

"Over fifteen years."

"And in your normal course of work, are you accustomed to testing materials and foodstuffs for evidence of poison?" Charles asked.

"Yes." Professor Caldwell nodded, his goatee just brushing his collar. "I am a chemist by trade, and I have often been called to assist in cases like this."

"I see," Charles said. "And can you tell the jury what happened in relation to the Black case?"

"I was contacted by the New York police and was asked to test a sample of tea, in an effort to determine if arsenic had been added to the liquid."

"Please tell the court how you made your determination and what the results were."

"The items sent to me for examination included the teacup the plaintiff drank from, and the teapot, which still contained tea grounds."

"Can you tell the jury the procedure for testing?"

"Yes." The professor picked up his notes and read

from them. "Generally, there are two kinds of poison that can sicken or kill someone—vegetable and metallic. Vegetable poison tends to break down and is harder to identify than metallic. First, I tested the teacup itself. To extract any possible vegetable poison, I started with alcohol and a trifle of acid. There was none in this case. Next, I used a solution of hydro-chloric acid, then sulferetted hydrogen, which gave a brownish precipitate. This was saved, washed in ammonia, then filtered. The sulfur and nitric acid was then driven off, and the solution so obtained was subjected to a pure hydrogen test. This resulted in a positive arsenic stain."

The crowd erupted once more, and the judge pounded his gavel. Winifred glanced at Horace. Although they knew the results of the professor's tests, there was something coldly horrible about hearing them recited in court, something that made the attempted murder even more real.

"What did you do next?" Charles asked softly after the judge warned the mob again.

"I performed the same tests on the teapot and the grounds."

"And those results?" Charles waited expectantly.

"All positive," Caldwell said firmly. "All of the articles contained arsenic."

A sinking feeling came over Winifred once more. Caldwell was bright, articulate, and obviously well versed in his field. As brilliant as Horace Shane was, this testimony was unshakable. Horace must have thought so as well, for when Charles finished, he declined to cross-examine the witness, obviously wanting to get the man off the stand as quickly as possible. Without the tea tin, there was nothing they could say about the evidence.

Winifred sighed. Even though they had known what the testimony would be, it seemed damning.

Next the prosecution would have the maid testify that it was Mrs. Black who brought the tea to her husband, and that the woman stood there and watched him drink it. After that, the gallery of working-class men, the jury of middle-class merchants, and the judge were unlikely to view Mrs. Black with anything but horror and disgust. Women, Winifred thought, were either the Madonna or Eve, and there was no in-between. And when the papers caught hold of the Albright story, which they eventually would, Mrs. Black would be not only a murderess but a whore as well.

All of her plans seemed to be for naught. Not even a hundred suffragette marches could turn this tide around. A shadow of doubt crept into Winifred's mind. Maybe Mrs. Black was not a noble heroine after all. Quickly she pushed the treacherous thought out of her consciousness. Even if she wasn't, it didn't negate the social issue of women trapped in bad marriages. Mrs. Black was shackled to a cheating brute who beat her, drank, and blamed her for his inability to perform as a husband. Winifred could not even imagine the woman's life. All she sought to do was help her.

As they awaited the next witness, Mrs. Black turned around and stared fixedly at the crowd. Curious, Winifred followed her gaze and saw a man pushing his way into the gallery. He was very handsome, dressed in a shiny black coat over a mother-of-pearl-gray vest. His walking stick was polished ebony with a gold handle, and his top hat gleamed. He wore a jaunty red cashmere scarf around his neck, which he quickly untwisted, then took a seat beside a fat old farmer who seemed none too happy to share the bench.

Looking back to the prisoner, Winifred saw that her gaze hadn't moved. Mrs. Black could not seem to tear her eyes from the handsome stranger.

It had to be him. No other man could have had

such an effect on Monica Black. No man except her lover, Mr. Albright.

Winifred studied the man once more. He was handsome all right, but he looked like a cad. That he had come to the courtroom was audacity itself, but Winifred doubted that he paid much attention to either morals or scruples, particularly since he had seduced a married woman. This man had promised Mrs. Black marriage if anything happened to her husband, while probably never intending to do anything of the sort. . . .

The stirring in her brain exploded. Catching Horace's attention, she indicated that she wanted the court to take a recess. He looked puzzled, but observing the excitement in her gaze, he nodded and turned to the judge.

"Your Honor, may we request a brief recess? My client needs a few moments to compose herself."

Thankfully, Mrs. Black's veils hid her surprise. Charles, puzzled, offered no objection. The judge nodded and rapped the gavel. "I will give you fifteen minutes."

"Thank you," Horace replied.

The crowd rumbled as Horace had the guard escort Mrs. Black outside. When Horace approached Winifred, she whispered to him excitedly.

"He's here. In the courtroom. Albright."

Horace turned to look and whistled softly. "Damned cheeky of him. Can you slip him a note, telling him to meet with us for lunch?"

"Yes, I will do that. Shall I tell him to meet us at the restaurant next door?"

"No, that will be too public," Horace said thoughtfully. "There is an old office behind the courtroom. I do not think it is being used. We can meet him there." His eyes met hers, and he smiled. "Good work, Miss Winifred."

She smiled, her heart feeling lighter.

IT TOOK a little doing to get her note into Albright's hands, but thankfully one of the newsboys managed to slip between the rows of people in the gallery and give it to him. Winifred watched his expression as he unfolded the slip of paper, then a grim look came to his face as he realized his identity was known.

The pit of her belly tightened as she saw him rise, then make his way to the rear of the courtroom. His gaze swept the room, as if trying to determine his betrayer, then his eyes fell on Mrs. Black. He sent her a reassuring look, as if promising that all would be well.

Winifred did not like it at all. There was something self-serving about the man, and she guessed that if it came down to his neck or Monica Black's, it wouldn't be his. She hoped she was wrong, but there was little about his appearance to indicate otherwise. With considerable trepidation, she followed him to the far end of the room and waited for court to break for lunch. If Mr. Albright decided to make a run for it, she wanted to make sure he was followed.

To her relief, he did not, but as soon as the court broke for lunch, he made his way to the vacant office. Winifred waited for Horace to join her, then together they walked into the room and quietly closed the door.

Mr. Albright looked up expectantly. "Hello, Mr. Shane. Miss Appleton. I believe you asked to see me?"

He was wonderfully alert, like an insect aware of a flyswatter. Horace sat on the edge of a desk, loosened his tie, and gave the man a friendly smile.

"I assume I am addressing Mr. Robert Albright?"

The man nodded nervously, seeming less than happy that Horace knew his name. "Good," Horace continued conversationally. "I will get straight to the point. Mr. Albright, we have reason to believe that Mrs. Black, the accused, was involved with another man. And that man is you."

The color drained from his face. He glanced at the door, as if considering bolting, then turned back to face Horace and brazen it out.

"Sir, you cannot accuse me! On what grounds—"

"Tut, tut, it won't do," Horace shook his head sadly. "There is no sense in bluffing. You see, my client has confessed your involvement with her."

Mr. Albright turned impossibly pale, then quickly recovered. "I must say I am surprised that she would say such a thing. I considered our relationship extremely private."

"I am certain you did." The older man's voice held a note of disgust. "Mr. Albright, you are in considerable peril here. My client has been accused of murder. It is likely that you will be called to the stand. Your involvement with my client will be questioned, and your relationship with her made public. I want you to be aware of all that, and I would suggest you obtain legal counsel. Am I making myself clear?"

"Yes." Albright looked miserable and raised a defeated face to Horace. "Is there any way we can avoid this? You see—"

"Am I right in suspecting that you, too, are involved elsewhere?"

Winifred's mouth dropped in shock as Horace questioned the man ruthlessly. Albright nodded. "I never meant for any of this to happen, never thought she would go so far—"

"Nothing has been proven yet. My client is presumed innocent. I would like to ask for your help in this case. You did, after all, seduce a married woman, and you promised her matrimony if she could rid herself of her husband, did you not?"

Some of the fear seemed to leave Albright, and he assumed a defensive posture. "I do not have to tolerate this. I will get my own legal counsel, as you suggested. In the meantime, unless someone issues a warrant, I do not have to talk to you at all. Good day, Mr. Shane. Miss A."

Albright rose, but then Shane put a hand on his shoulder. "You are right—you do not have to talk to us. But I think you will find it more agreeable than the police. I have to wonder what you have to hide. Perhaps there is more to this than meets the eye."

"What are you implying, sir?" Albright's eyes bulged.

"That murder may not have been Mrs. Black's idea after all. It would be convenient for you to be the consort of a wealthy widow in need of condolence, wouldn't it? Why, I ought to take a stick to you myself—"

Horace surveyed the room as if looking for a weapon. Albright dashed for the door, slamming it closed behind him.

Winifred and Horace exchanged glances. "Do you really think he was an accomplice?" she asked slowly.

Horace shrugged. "Women like Mrs. Black do not usually attempt murder unless they are desperate. I have no doubt that living with Mr. Black would have been enough to push her, but Albright was probably the deciding factor. Yet the man is a cad. I just feel sorry for Mrs. Black. When Charles puts him on the stand, she will really look bad."

"Maybe," Winifred said thoughtfully. A sudden

idea came to her. "But what if we take the offensive on this? Let us look into Albright's character. This time the reporters can help us by learning everything they can about Mr. Albright. What we find is not likely to be appealing. I have a feeling he is—"

"A despoiler of women, seducer out of wedlock, a wolf preying on the fairer sex." The thoughtful look on Horace's face changed to amusement. "I see what you are getting at. We can use their own prejudice against them and really pour on the sanctity of marriage, the weakness of a woman against an experienced seducer. He talked her into it. He's behind the murder plot. Damned good thinking, Miss Appleton. Damned good."

CHAPTER 19

THIS IS highly irregular, miss, but for a good story, I will make an exception. What have you got?"

"I want you to find out everything you can about Mr. Albright," Winifred said to the reporter, trying to hide her repugnance.

The little man peered up at her from beneath his derby with eager eyes like a ferret's, scribbling all the while. When he grinned, he displayed a golden row of tobacco-stained teeth. He was obviously enjoying himself. It wasn't often that a story sought him out, and Bert Ranney of *The New York Times* did not mind this turn of events at all.

"You say he's got something to do with the Black case?" He licked his lips in anticipation.

"Yes." Winifred mentally weighed how much to tell him. "Mr. Albright is a friend of the accused. I think he may have had an influence on her."

"Oh, I see, a playmate in the nest." The reporter's eyes narrowed into little slits.

Winifred nodded. "Mr. Albright, I fear, is a despoiler of women, a seducer of hearth and home. Mrs. Black is a woman in love, a woman who fell under the man's spell. I believe that when you look into Mr. Albright's past, you will certainly find more than one Mrs. Black. The scoundrel must be exposed for what he is. You will certainly set New York on its ear if you do. It's an angle no one else has."

This the reporter could easily understand. "Thanks for the tip, lady. I'll look into our good Mr. Albright right away."

"You may also want to look into Mr. William Black's activities," Winifred said, sighing as if the sordid tale troubled her greatly. "He may also have a few secrets he does not want exposed."

"I see. Is everyone in that household fooling around with somebody else? Maybe I should get to know the maid."

"Enough, Mr. Ranney," Winifred admonished. "I suggest you work quickly. This story will break anytime, and I would like to see you get the scoop."

The reporter nodded, avarice gleaming in his eyes, then scurried off like a rat down the street.

Watching him go, Winifred sighed deeply. What had she become, lowering herself to consort with the press in such a manner? Yet without her intervention, Mrs. Black would be labeled an adulteress as well as an attempted murderess, and everything would be lost.

A twinge of conscience pained her as she made her way back to the courthouse. Charles would never approve of her manipulation of the press. He would see it as yet another attempt to win an unfair advantage for Mrs. Black. But the deck was stacked against the defense. Even if the newspaper reported that both Blacks had partners outside of their marriage, the public would feel much more negatively about Mrs. Black's philandering.

Winifred could not stand by and watch Mrs. Black be thrown to the wolves because she succumbed to temptation. Passion, Winifred had learned only recently, was more mind-altering than any drug. Could passion be the real culprit in the Black case? Could passion have clouded the woman's judgment to the point of attempting murder?

It was an intriguing thought. As Winifred took her seat once more, Charles sent her a questioning glance. Another twinge pinched her, but she forced the feeling away. She had warned him that she would do anything she could to get Mrs. Black acquitted. Monica Black needed all the help she could get, especially now.

"BRIDGET FLYNN, to the stand."

The crowd rumbled as the Blacks' maid, a nononsense Irishwoman, marched up to the witness box. Holding up a well-scrubbed hand, she promised to tell the truth with a loud "That I do." Taking her seat, she smoothed her immaculate dress neatly and eyed Charles with an air of distaste.

"Now, Miss Flynn, could you describe for the court what you do for the Blacks?"

"I am their maid. Their only servant, really. Mr. Black could afford quite a few more, but he likes to keep his money to himself, he does. That is, unless he's spending it on showgirls and such."

Laughter broke out in the gallery, and Charles tapped his fingers impatiently. "Miss Flynn, please confine your answers to the question itself. Now, can you tell me something about your job? For example, is it customary for you to prepare the Blacks' food and drink?"

"Yes, that I normally do, as well as the washing, the cleaning, the dusting, and the sweeping. It's a big old house, and we certainly could use more help. Mrs.

Black pitches in once in a while, the poor dear, but it is a lot for one body."

"I see." Charles gazed at the woman sharply. "Can you tell the jury what happened on the night of March 8, leaving out your opinions?"

Bridget glanced sympathetically toward her mistress, then spoke with regret.

"Mr. Black had been out again. He'd been doing this regularly, going out for hours at night, the useless sot, only to come home late, demanding his tea. When I heard his steps in the foyer, I set the water to boil, expecting much of the same."

"And did he ask for tea?"

"Yes. He'd been drinking again, that much I could tell right away. Could smell the whiskey on him from across the room. The poor missus was up, pacing and worrying, wondering where he was, like she did every night. She deserves much better than him, that is for certain."

"Miss Flynn," the judge said sternly as the gallery erupted with laughter, "Mr. Howe has already warned you once. Please confine your answers to the question, or you'll be held in contempt."

"Yes, sir," Bridget answered glumly.

"Thank you," Charles said to the judge, then turned to the witness once more. "What happened next?"

Bridget turned up her nose as if he smelled bad. "He demanded his tea, and I prepared a meal for him."

"What did the meal consist of?"

"The usual. Some cold ham sandwiches, some seed cake, a few pieces of fruit, and the tea. Make it every night, and never so much as a thank you from his lordship. I put it all on the tray for him."

"Did you give him the tray yourself?"

Again Bridget glanced to her mistress. Almost imperceptibly, Monica Black nodded, and Bridget spoke softly.

"No, I did not."

Her answer was so soft, it was a struggle to hear her.

Charles spoke loudly. "What did you say? I am having trouble hearing you."

"I said no! What's the matter, boyo? Your hearing gone, along with your manners?"

Charles glared at the maid, who glared right back.

"Miss Flynn, I am losing my patience with you," the judge spoke harshly.

"I'm very sorry," Bridget replied unrepentantly.

"Who, then, gave the tea to Mr. Black?" Charles persisted.

Bridget didn't answer for a moment. Charles stopped pacing the courtroom and stopped before her.

"Did you understand my question?"

"I did."

"Would you mind answering?"

Bridget looked as if she wanted to murder him herself. "The missus," she answered reluctantly. "She gave it to him and stayed with him while he drank it. He never ate the food."

The crowd broke into outraged cries, and the gavel banged once more. Winifred covered her face with her hands. For all that Bridget loved her mistress, her testimony was damning.

"Was it customary for Mrs. Black to attend her husband in this manner?" Charles asked.

Bridget's glare would have shriveled the stockings from a less brave man. "No, she didn't. Normally, I took his tea to him."

"But on this night, she did it herself." Charles let

the statement sink in. "Why do you suppose that was?"

"Objection!" Horace shouted. "Calls for speculation."

Before the judge could sustain the objection, Bridget jumped to her feet in outrage.

"I know what you're trying to make me say, you scoundrel! You're all scoundrels, locking the sweet missus away! That cad she's wed to ain't worthy to wipe her boots! He's a no-good slug. If anyone tried to do him in, I say good riddance!"

The mob broke into chaos. Horace's eyes met Winifred's, and she shrugged with incredulity. The judge's gavel seemed like a soft tapping compared with the outbreak of noise. Reporters scrambled out the door, Charles stared at the maid, appalled, while the jury murmured to themselves. The judge finally rose, his face stern with outrage.

"Order! Order!" He turned to the witness, whose face was as red as her hair. She was glaring at Mr. Black as if she wanted to attack him personally. The bailiff approached her as the judge spoke harshly.

"Miss Flynn, I am holding you in contempt. This court will not tolerate such outbursts. Court is adjourned until Monday."

The maid was hauled off, still protesting and shaking her fist.

Charles collected his papers and met Jared outside. The other lawyer was still guffawing about what had taken place.

"Do you believe that maid? I thought for sure Culvert was going to lock her up!"

Charles joined in his laughter reluctantly, shaking his head wryly. "I can't remember ever dealing with a witness like that. But she helped us a great deal. It's too bad for the defense. On Monday Bridget will have to testify to the rest—that Mrs. Black was the only one who had access to Mr. Black's tea. It does not take a genius to figure out who tampered with it."

Jared nodded. "I know. For all Bridget's loyalty to her mistress, her testimony was very damaging to her. She even supplied the motive. Now we don't have to try to come up with one."

Charles nodded. "Then that's it. Winifred and Horace will be left picking up the crumbs by the end of next week. But then again, maybe it is for the best. Perhaps now she'll give up wanting to be a lawyer."

Charles felt no triumph. In truth, he did feel badly for Winifred. He would see her tonight, he resolved, and hold her, comfort her. It was the least he could do.

Suddenly Edgar Whitcomb rushed up to them, waving a newspaper. His face was red, and his eyes were bulging.

"Edgar! What's wrong?" Charles was concerned that the poor man might faint again.

"Did you see this? A boy is selling them on the steps of the courthouse."

Dread filled Charles. *She couldn't have.* Yet as he read the glaring print, a sinking feeling swept over him.

POOR MRS. BLACK, LOVE VICTIM!

According to the article, Mrs. Black, instead of being the perpetrator of an attempted murder, was a victim. A Mr. Albright, it appeared, had inveigled his way into her good graces, then seduced her into committing this despicable crime. Mr. Albright had a history of befriending rich married women, then living off their largess. Other well-to-do women—whose names made Charles's eyes go wide—had previously

been entangled with Mr. Albright. The article continued with quotes from Mrs. Stanton denouncing un-
scrupulous men who entrapped women in loveless
marriages. A statement from Mrs. Woodhull decried
the trial of an innocent woman and demanded that the
country adopt free love. Even the local reverend was
quoted declaring that women were helpless against
such libertines. Then came a statement from the mysterious Miss Appleton, finally identifying herself, that
"passion is the criminal here, not poor Mrs. Black."

The rest of the article described Miss Appleton's
legal work and her assistance to Horace Shane. "Miss
A." was undoubtedly part of the brains behind the
defense, the paper claimed. When questioned, Mr.
Shane heartily confirmed it.

Charles did not bother to read the rest. This was
too much, even for Winifred. Thrusting the newspaper
inside his coat, he started for the street.

"Where are you going?" Jared demanded.

Charles didn't stop to respond. There was one person behind all this, and he was determined to put a
stop to it, once and for all.

CHAPTER 20

I DEMAND to see Miss Winifred at once!"

Charles stood on the familiar steps of the Appleton household. It was not often that he shouted at servants, but today he was doing exactly that. The poor befuddled maid stared at him as if he were some kind of tyrant, then nodded, her eyes wide with fright.

"Yes, sir. Wait there, sir. I'll fetch her right down."

The woman disappeared with a flap of her apron, and Charles had the grim satisfaction of knowing he could still frighten someone. Winifred, for all the time he had spent with her, did not seem to give his feelings a second thought.

It was incredible that she would do such a thing. Charles looked again, amazed, at the newspaper article. Once again, after his repeated warnings, she had boldly manipulated the press. And this time he himself had supplied her with the story.

Aunt Eve appeared a moment later, delighted when she recognized him. "Charles! I did not know it was you. Our poor maid thought—" She shook her head, and Charles could very well imagine what she had said. "Do come in, I was just getting tea ready."

"No, thank you," Charles said firmly. "This is not a social call. I have something to say to Miss Winnie. I will wait outside."

"I see." The elderly woman's face grew concerned. "I will fetch her directly then. Are you certain you won't at least wait in the foyer?"

"No, I am perfectly comfortable here," Charles said stubbornly.

He would not allow them to do it to him again. He'd first met Winifred six months ago at an Appleton tea, warm and wonderful, with all the comforts of home, a ginger cat at his feet, the beautiful sisters attending to his every want, and the sweetest little old lady in the world adoring him. No, he knew where his Achilles' heel lay. Accepting even the smallest bit of Appleton hospitality would ruin his resolve.

Eve disappeared, and as he waited, he paced on the walk, muttering to himself, his outrage growing by the second. All of their differences—and Winifred's lack of gratitude, and her complete disregard for the law—came back to enrage him. She had taken a piece of information he had given her, information that he could have used against Mrs. Black, and had twisted it on behalf of the defense. Mrs. Black was not only a would-be murderess but an adulteress as well—yet Winifred had once again portrayed her as the victim! It wasn't to be borne! He could not wait to get his hands on her. When he did, she would never think to try such a thing again.

Finally Winifred appeared in the doorway. "Charles!" she said warily. "I was not expecting you."

Without preamble, he thrust the newspaper toward her. "Would you mind explaining this?" His fury made his words come slowly.

For a brief moment, as she glanced at the headline, Winifred lost her cool composure and shuddered.

"Charles, I can understand why you would be upset by this. But I have good reason—"

"There is no good reason!" he shouted, mindless of the neighbors, whose lace curtains had begun to twitch. "There is no excuse for this! How could you do such a thing? I told you about Albright in order to give you time to prepare. Instead, you turned it to your own advantage by ruthlessly manipulating the press!"

He took a step closer, immensely gratified that the cool assurance had left those incredible hazel eyes. She appeared far more uncertain than usual.

Taking a step backward, she spoke haltingly. "Try to understand, Charles. This woman has no other chance. The facts alone—"

"Should speak for themselves! The law is the law, and no one, not even you or your Mrs. Black, is above it!"

He was shouting loudly now, and the neighbors' curtains twitched violently. Somehow he had to get through to this woman, to make her understand that what she was doing was wrong. He took another step closer.

"Charles," Winifred tried, "why don't you come inside, and we can discuss this. I am sure you do not want to make a public spectacle of us both—"

Charles snapped at her incredulously. "Don't you think it is a little late to be worried about that? After all, *The New York Times* is your platform!" Then he lowered his voice and assumed a lecturing tone. "Winifred, I am very disappointed in you. I never tutored you for this end. No matter how you want to paint it, you and I both know that this woman tried to kill her husband!"

In his righteous wrath, he didn't notice that carriages were beginning to line the street. Nor did he see the derby-hatted reporters scrambling up to the wrought-iron gate, eager to catch his every word. Furious beyond measure, he advanced on Winifred until his face was mere inches from hers.

"Charles—" Winifred tried again, but he cut her off.

"Don't interrupt me! I am only getting started! I was teaching you the law, not some suffragette interpretation of it that happens to be convenient for your client!"

"Charles—"

"And how did Albright become the villain here? He is not even on trial! I suppose every man who consorts with a married woman is a murderer!"

"Charles—" Winifred gestured violently to the bushes behind him.

"I am outraged at your tactics, Miss Appleton! Outraged! You and Shane should both be ashamed of yourselves!"

He almost enjoyed a moment of satisfaction—until he noticed that Winifred was not looking at him at all. Instead, her eyes were fixated behind him, wide with warning and anxiety. Slowly he turned, and to his astonishment, he saw a throng of reporters scribbling frantically.

"That is what I was trying to tell you," she said softly.

Then the newsmen rushed him.

"Mr. Howe, do you often visit the defense?"

"What is the nature of your relationship with Miss Appleton?"

"Do you agree that Miss Appleton is the brains behind Mrs. Black's defense?"

"What is your position on the Albright angle? Will the prosecution call him as a witness?"

"Do you believe in women's rights and free love?"

Charles stared at them, aghast, then closed his eyes, wincing as he envisioned the story they would write about this. Winifred held out her hands, as if silently beseeching him, but he turned coldly on his heel and marched through the wall of reporters, tossing the newspaper to the ground. The newsmen were still shouting questions as he got into his carriage and the vehicle cleared the curb.

Some men, he thought, were born fools. Others became fools.

He hesitated to think which category contained himself.

WINIFRED CLOSED the door, refusing to give the reporters an interview. Charles was furious with her. Never had she seen him so angry. As she walked slowly toward the parlor, she sorted out her thoughts.

Had she been wrong to use the press that way? Her conscience stung her at Charles's scolding. But how else could she hope to get a fair trial for Mrs. Black, except by exposing the hypocrisy beneath society's double standards? Why was it so hard for Charles—or any man—to understand?

Mrs. Stanton didn't think men could understand. Neither did Miss Anthony. For every enlightened male who supported women's rights, a thousand, no maybe a million, wanted to keep the status quo. Men did not see women as equal partners, as people like themselves. Instead, they saw them as inferiors, as children, as pretty ornaments to wear on their arms or dolls to be adorned and admired but never taken seriously. Under these circumstances, how else could she help Mrs. Black?

Yet Charles was different, Winifred knew. Never once had he treated her with anything less than respect. His offer to let her apprentice with him clearly showed his appreciation for her brain, even if he didn't think she would stick to it. And even during their passionate moments, he always made her feel cherished. Why, then, was he being so stubborn?

"My, I have never seen Mr. Howe like that," Aunt Eve said solicitously, coming into the parlor with the tea tray. "He was in a fine passion, that is for certain."

Winifred turned quickly to her aunt. "What did you say?"

The older woman glanced up. "I said Mr. Howe got himself into a fine passion. Why, dear?"

"Nothing," Winifred replied. "It is an interesting choice of words."

For a long moment, staring into her teacup, Winifred absently stirred the brew. Passion. It really was the root of all disasters. Then, frustrated, she set down her spoon. "Oh, it's no use," she said to her aunt. "Why doesn't he understand? How can someone as intelligent as Charles fail to see the opposing side?"

"Is there another side?" Eve asked softly.

"Of course there is. There always is. Why, one only has to stand in the other fellow's shoes . . ." Winifred's voice trailed off as the impact of her own words struck her forcefully.

"Yes, dear?" Eve prodded gently.

Winifred turned to her aunt in dismay. "Oh, Auntie, I see now why Charles feels the way he does! He gave me the information about Mrs. Black's lover, and I gave it to the press, which he sees as a betrayal. But they would have found out anyway! He doesn't understand. He never will. He only sees things in black and white."

"Yet that is one reason you think so well of him," Eve reminded her. "Charles is a good man, and as such, he has strict moral values."

"True," Winifred agreed. "But he doesn't see that Mrs. Black is not being tried the same as, say, her husband would be. Somehow I have to make him understand that this case is not black and white, that there is gray—"

"Winnie." Aunt Eve took her niece's hand and held it within her own fragile grasp. "Consider what you are fighting here. You are doing everything you can to help this woman, and that is truly noble. But are you fighting something else too, beneath all this? What is making you push Mr. Howe away?"

"Whatever do you mean?"

"You deliberately outrage the one man you seem to admire above all others, a man who obviously has feelings for you."

"Why—that is ludicrous!" Winifred set her cup down firmly as if to punctuate her declaration. "Mr. Howe and I are . . . friends. That is all we can ever be. We disagree on how this case should be handled. Otherwise, I am perfectly happy with our friendship."

But how could they just be friends? They had made love. Overwhelming emotions had washed over her. Friends? Charles had offered her marriage, and she'd had a wonderful image of herself as his wife, with his children. . . . Winifred fought the constriction in her throat and quickly reached for more tea.

"I see." Eve smiled fondly at her. "You know, dear, it is not wrong to want a man. It does not mean you are betraying the women you are fighting for, or the fight for the society you long to change. And it is not weakness to admit that you need someone. That, my dear, is the beginning of real strength."

Winifred sipped her tea so quickly, she burned her tongue. "Auntie, I am not Penelope. I do not need gentlemen callers to feel complete."

"Is that why you lie awake late at night, unable to sleep? Or why you are most alive when arguing with Mr. Howe? Or perhaps the reason lies in your refusal to feel?" Eve's voice was filled with sympathy. "Dear, after my husband died in the war, I was frozen, unable to feel any emotion. I did not know it then, but the pain of his death was so intense that I had decided not to experience it at all. As a result, I no longer felt the pain, but I no longer knew great joy, either."

Winifred felt an intense interest in what her aunt was saying.

"What changed that?"

"You did. All of you." Eve smiled gently again, her eyes filled with tears. "When I took you and your sisters in, I did not know that loving you would re-open my heart, that Pandora's box of emotions. Yet I have never regretted it. Certainly, I felt the loss of my husband, and the pain was keen. But I also felt love, and nothing can replace that joy."

Winifred rose slowly, setting her teacup aside. There was truth in her aunt's words, and it struck her in a secret place that she had hidden for so long, she'd forgotten its existence. She was not sure even now she wanted to explore that secret place—to examine her aunt's wisdom and her own motives.

"I do not think—"

"I know how hard it was on all you girls when your parents died," Eve continued gently. "Penelope cried openly for days, and Jennifer was furious. But you, dear, never showed what you were feeling. Instead, you buried yourself in your books. I am not saying that is wrong. I just want you to realize that your anger at Mr. Howe may be coming from very different feelings, ones that you aren't letting yourself feel."

Winifred was not ready to talk about it, but her aunt's words had hit home.

"I will give your theory some thought, Auntie. But in truth, it may be too late. Charles is so angry, I don't know if he will ever forgive me."

"THE UNMITIGATED NERVE of Miss Appleton, using the press like that! We will never get you into the governor's mansion with that kind of publicity!"

Charles's father sat at the head of the table and carved the roast beef while he spoke. He speared a huge slice for his own plate and, chopping off a large piece, thrust it into his mouth.

"I told you I am not running for governor," Charles said in frustration. "After the Governor's Ball, there certainly is not much question of it anyway."

"Pshaw, my boy! That won't hurt you much. We have already spoken to the right people and made sure the correct story got around. No one thinks less of you for taking a swing at Mr. Marton. Where the hell is the gravy?"

"I will get it, dear." His mother called for the maid, who placed the gravy boat before his father, barely hiding a scowl. Charles laughed silently, recalling Bridget Flynn. Maybe the Blacks were not the only ones whose maid harbored resentments.

"In the long run, the story has only helped your image," his father continued, completely unaware of the servant's displeasure. "But this Black case is something else altogether. I don't like it. No one likes it. Can't Marton or one of the other lawyers handle it?"

"I have no choice but to prosecute it myself," Charles said firmly, helping himself to the potatoes. "No one else in the office is available. And besides, I have to finish what I've started. You should know that today's newspapers have shredded my reputation entirely. The press witnessed an argument between myself and Miss Appleton yesterday. The write-ups are simply horrendous."

They were even worse than he'd feared. The reporters had had a great time with his dressing-down of Miss Appleton. The *Times* suggested that Miss A. had bewitched him, while the *World* speculated that their relationship was intimate. *Harper's* even splashed a Nast cartoon of himself and Miss Appleton dressed as boxers on the front page, their gloves raised, prepared to do battle. It was incredibly humiliating, as was the story that followed. After reading the first few sentences, he'd simply tossed the papers away, unable to bear the rest.

"I told you to stay away from that woman!" his father thundered. "These suffragettes—Winifred Appleton in particular—are nothing but trouble! This case is ugly, no matter how you look at it. If you convict this woman, particularly after all the publicity, the women of New York will hate you. And if you don't, the men will be furious. There is no good outcome. There never is, when a petticoat is involved."

Charles glanced at his mother. Normally, she would have let such a stern lecture pass with merely a small flinch. But today, to Charles's surprise, she refilled her wineglass and spoke softly.

"It is so hard to believe that a woman could do such a thing. Attempt a murder, I mean." She shuddered, drinking deeply of her glass. "Women are life givers, not takers. Are you absolutely certain she's guilty?"

Charles gazed at his mother incredulously. "There is no doubt. I would not prosecute the case otherwise. The maid saw the woman give her husband his tea. He drank it and became ill with convulsions. The chemist confirmed poisoning. The woman even confessed—or said she did not remember if she did it, if you want to believe that nonsense."

"It's that damned Miss Appleton, distorting the facts, using the press as if it were her own personal vehicle!" Charles's father shouted, pounding the table. "That woman should be thrown in jail! Using the suffragettes, trying to turn this case into a ploy for women's rights, hiding Monica Black behind her skirts. It is despicable!"

Before Charles could defend Winifred, his mother surprised him again.

"Dear, what else has she?"

His father's head swung violently around to stare at his wife in disbelief. She shrugged, delicately picked up a piece of bread, and spoke softly once more.

"You blame Mrs. Black and Miss Appleton for hiding behind their skirts, but what else do they have? They have no voice in the courtroom. Not a single woman will sit on the jury and understand Mrs. Black's view. Nor will a female judge ever preside on the bench. Mrs. Black is shackled from the start, treated without respect or dignity. She is held to the same standards as men, but without any of their power or choice. If she and Miss Appleton hide behind their skirts, what other means have they?"

His father opened his mouth, closed it, then opened it once more. Instead of delivering another bellowing lecture, to Charles's amazement, the older man got up and stormed away from the table.

Charlotte Howe gazed at the empty place for a long moment, then picked up her fork and resumed eating as if nothing had happened. She gave Charles an apologetic smile.

"Sorry, dear. I know you did not come to dinner to hear this."

"I don't mind." Charles gazed at her in amazement. After all his father's bullying, his mother's calm opinion surprised him, particularly since it echoed Winifred's. Charles stared at her for a long moment, seeing her in a different light. She was dressed in a high-necked lace gown as always, her deportment was perfect, and her voice was properly soft and low. Had she ever been young? Had she ever laughed out loud? Had she had ever kissed his father, or any man, with the kind of passion he felt for Winifred?

He longed to ask her, but something in her manner forbade such intimacy. Instead, he changed the subject to something he had been wondering about for some time.

"How is Father's heart condition?"

A sparkle came into her eyes, and a smile tugged at the corners of her mouth. But instead of letting them escape, she picked up her wineglass, sipped from it, then gazed at her son with an expression he would never forget.

"Your father does not have a heart condition, dear. He just wants us all to think he does, so he can get his own way. I placate him because it makes him happy. Would you like more beef? I think it's getting cold."

CHAPTER 21

"BRIDGET FLYNN, please take the stand."

The woman strode to the witness box, much more subdued after a weekend in jail. As she gazed at Charles with defiance mingled with caution, he almost felt sorry for her. Picking up his notes, he attempted to concentrate. As he approached the witness box, he had to ignore how beautiful Winifred looked that morning, and how much he still wanted to throttle her. He could not blame her entirely for the newspaper stories, but her ruthless ambition had led up to it. And yet . . .

At that dinner with his parents, he'd been stunned to realize that his mother shared many of Winifred's opinions. Why did she bury her real thoughts? Was it because of his father's bullying, or society's expectations? He could not picture Winifred ever doing that, but perhaps the self-censorship was something that occurred over time, like a rock rubbed smooth in the ocean. Could there be more than a grain of truth in Winifred's assertions about women and marriage?

Charles glanced down at his notes, grateful that he had prepared carefully. "Now Miss Flynn, we left off with Mrs. Black serving her husband tea. Did you observe her add anything to his cup?"

The maid pressed her lips together tightly. Charles repeated the question, forcing her to respond.

"No."

"What happened next?"

"Mr. Black drank the tea. The missus stayed with him while he did. Soon after that, he got ill, and I fetched the doctor."

"Did anyone else, other than you and Mrs. Black, have access to that tea?"

Bridget glowered at Charles contemptuously. But the memory of her weekend in jail must have been still fresh in her mind, for she bit her tongue. "No. No one did. She alone gave him the drink."

The gallery erupted, and the judge banged the gavel. Bridget gave her mistress an apologetic glance, and Mrs. Black's veiled head nodded as if in understanding.

"No further questions, Your Honor," said Charles, satisfied.

"Mr. Shane?"

Horace strode up to the witness box and leaned comfortably against the rail. "Miss Flynn, do you enjoy working for the Blacks?"

"Yes. Her I do, anyway."

"By 'her,' do you mean Mrs. Black?"

The maid glanced once more at the veiled figure and smiled softly. "Yes, that's right."

"Would it be correct to say that you are fond of your mistress?" Horace asked.

"Yes, it would."

"Miss Flynn, could you describe Mrs. Black's character?"

The maid's face softened, and for the first time, she spoke freely. "The missus is the sweetest woman ever.

Helps me whenever she can and is never demanding of a thing. Unlike himself." She referred to Mr. Black as if he were a distasteful insect.

"Miss Flynn, how would you describe the relationship between Mr. and Mrs. Black?" When the maid looked puzzled, Horace attempted to clarify. "Would you say their relationship was cordial? Did they fight often? Were they friendly?"

"I wouldn't say friendly. I think Mrs. Black is a saint for putting up with the brute, what with his drinking and all . . ." She glanced quickly at the judge, then cut herself short. "What I mean is, the missus has always been very patient with him. A saint, she is."

"I see. A saint." Horace smiled. "Miss Flynn, you know Mrs. Black probably better than anyone else. You have seen her happy, sad, sick, and well. You have helped her dress, taken meals with her. Would you describe her as, say, a potential murderess?"

"No."

The gallery roared, and Charles leaped to his feet. "Objection!"

Charles knew Horace understood that such a question was not allowed. Yet the jury had heard his message loud and clear.

"Sustained. The jury will disregard that question. Mr. Shane, please keep your questions within the proper parameters."

"I apologize," Horace said, though his eyes twinkled. "No further questions, Your Honor."

There was no way the jury would disregard the question, yet Charles wasn't as annoyed as he should have been. Horace's tactics were standard in this kind of trial, and if Miss Flynn's opinion would help Monica Black, letting it in wouldn't ruin the prosecution's case.

Miss Flynn left the stand, giving her mistress a sympathetic pat as she passed. The gallery was amazingly quiet, apparently taking the judge's threats more seriously today. The crowd jammed the benches and filled the aisles, everyone from the curious working class to reporters to a few society folk. The Black scandal had become the talk of New York.

At Charles's nod, William Black rose and took the stand. Dressed in a dark coat with a striped vest covering his broad belly, he looked like a petty tyrant. After being sworn in, the man gazed around the courtroom with an air of injured belligerence. Charles wished the man had a more agreeable personality, for he was certainly an unsympathetic victim.

"Mr. Black, can you tell us what happened the night of March 8?" Charles asked. Better to cut to the heart of the matter and get the man off the stand as quickly as possible.

"She tried to do me in, Monica did!" The man glared at his wife, full of self-righteous outrage. "She put poison in my tea! Made me sick as a dog. Had my head in the bucket all damned night."

"Objection!" Horace leaped to his feet. "Mr. Black couldn't have known anything was wrong with his tea."

"Sustained." The judge glanced at Mr. Black sternly. "Please just give us the facts."

Mr. Black appeared even angrier at the reprimand, and he glared at his veiled wife with open hostility.

"Now Mr. Black, what happened that night when you came home?"

The man grumbled under his breath, then spoke begrudgingly. "I had been out for a few hours, having a few drinks. Married to a woman like that, who can blame me? When I came home, of course my tea wasn't ready. I had to ask for it, just like every night.

Bridget prepared the tea, but Monica brought it to me."

"What happened next?"

"Like I said, I got sick as a dog. Briddie fetched the doctor, who saved my life."

"I see." Charles paused for a moment. "Mr. Black, the charges against your wife are very serious. Is there anything you want to add?"

Mr. Black glanced at his wife again, and his scowl turned even uglier. "I hope she gets what's coming to her. How dare she try something like that! When I think of her sneaking poison into my tea—" Unconsciously, the man made a fist, causing a man in the jury to gasp. Realizing his mistake, Mr. Black quickly put his hands in his lap, but it was too late. Most of the jury had seen the gesture.

"No further questions." Charles strode back to his desk, while Winifred gazed at him in amazement. Charles, she knew, did nothing in court without reason. Could he have let the jury see Mr. Black for what he was deliberately? It was an interesting thought.

Horace approached Mr. Black in the witness box and smiled at him sympathetically. Mr. Black's eyes narrowed shrewdly, but Horace turned on the full blast of his charm.

"Mr. Black, you have been through a terrible ordeal. I don't think anyone can question that. You suffered a sickness, nearly expired, and your own wife is charged with poisoning. I think we all know how that must make you feel."

Mr. Black nodded, his face filling with self-pity. "A man works hard—and for what? This kind of end! This is terrible! These women have gone too far. I see the papers! All that marching, carrying banners— their husbands need to take control, now."

His face flamed, and he puffed out his chest even more. Horace nodded as if in total agreement.

"Very distressing, this state of affairs. Mr. Black, is there any reason you know of that Mrs. Black would want to kill you? Just hypothetically, of course."

Mr. Black's confidence vanished, and he stared at Horace suspiciously. "What do you mean?"

"Well, Mr. Black, you are, as you said, a good, hard-working man. I don't know many women who would want to—how did you put it?—do in such a husband. I am just asking you if you think she may have had reason. For us to believe your story, it is important that we know."

Winifred leaned closer, praying that Charles wouldn't object. Technically, the information Horace was after could be considered irrelevant, and the defense would have to cite cases in order to let the question stand. But for some reason, Charles let Horace spin this web around Mr. Black.

"I—cannot think of anything. Sure she complains that I go out and have a drink now and then, but that is not a crime, is it? A man has got to have his pleasures."

"And that is the only thing amiss in your marriage?"

Mr. Black shifted uncomfortably, then glanced at Charles as if pleading for help. But Charles was busy scribbling notes and did not seem at all concerned. Turning back to Horace, Mr. Black nodded.

"For the record, Mr. Black indicated a positive response to my last question," Horace said formally. Picking up his own notebook, Horace approached the bench, his voice rising. Gone was the shuffling, man-next-door best friend. Now Horace showed his years of training and went in for the kill.

"Mr. Black, I have witnesses who are willing to testify that your drinking consists of far more than one or two at night. Is it not true that you have lost several jobs in the past few years due to intoxication? And is it not true that you recently had to appear in a civil case for a carriage accident, caused by your drinking?"

"Objection!" Charles finally spoke.

"Sustained." The judge glanced at Horace. "Please stick to the present case, Mr. Shane."

"Withdrawn. I apologize." Horace said softly. "Mr. Black, have you ever struck your wife?"

The man shifted again in his seat, looking even more uncomfortable. He glanced at the jury, then at his wife, then finally at the judge. The older man looked at him expectantly, and Mr. Black's face heated.

"Just once! Then she popped me with a frying pan! I had a lump on my head the size of a grapefruit! It's still there!" He rubbed his head as if to demonstrate.

"Then your answer is yes. So Mr. Black, we have established that you drink and that you've hit your wife. Is there anything else we do not know about?" He stared at the witness, almost daring him not to admit the truth.

Mr. Black turned even redder. "I know what you're getting at—the girls! It isn't my fault my wife's not as pretty as she used to be! A man has to find his own comforts, that he does!"

"So you think marital infidelity is justified by— what did you say?—'She's not as pretty as she used to be?'" Horace let the statement sink in, turning toward the jury to make sure they understood. The jurors were looking at Mr. Black with expressions of disapproval.

"No further questions."

Horace walked back to the stand, giving Winifred a wink. Relief washed through her. While most men felt they had the right to chastise their wives, they frowned on abuse, and Horace had successfully portrayed Mr. Black as less than a model husband. Although the testimony did show motive on Mrs. Black's part, motive had already been established. Now Horace had painted Mr. Black as so unsympathetic, perhaps the jury would go easy on Mrs. Black based on pity.

"The court will adjourn for today," the judge said as Mr. Black got off the stand.

Horace signaled to Winifred, who joined him and the other defense attorneys. "Let's get some lunch, and we can talk about how to proceed."

"Nice job with Mr. Black," Winifred commented. "I think the jury sees what kind of man he is very clearly."

"Yes, but it is not enough." Horace sighed. "Unfortunately, too many men think infidelity, wife beating, and drinking are their unalienable rights. I know it is unfair, but that is what they think. No, we need something much more powerful if we are to help Mrs. Black. I will tell you right now, Miss Winifred, I am worried."

Winifred tried not to let her own worry show. But Horace was certainly right—somehow they had to broaden the picture. The newspaper stories about Albright would help, but they needed something else, something that would catapult the case to a new level.

THEY ENTERED the restaurant, and Horace accepted a table in the back, where the defense team could talk in private. As they passed the crowded tables, the male lawyers stared at them. One of them rose and approached Horace, slapping him jovially on the back.

"Well now, Shane. Didn't think you one for the suffragette crowd. I hear you are their latest darling."

Guffaws came from the nearby tables.

"I consider that a real compliment, Lufton, especially coming from you. Always been a believer in women's rights. Don't care at all if I am labeled in such a fashion."

Winifred gazed at him in amusement. Horace was enjoying himself and the ruckus this case generated.

Jacob Lufton, a young and brash lawyer, was not amused. "Well, you are making it harder for the rest of us. I daresay the bar will not think much of it, either. What is your next case? Bloomers on every woman?"

Horace shrugged and pulled on his long beard thoughtfully. "Not a bad idea. I have always thought stays were unhealthy for women. A few other enlightened men think the same thing. But I do not understand your concern in all this. Are you worried that one day the Miss Appletons of the world might take your job?"

The young man stiffened, obviously offended. "Not in the least," he spat.

"Good, then we are on the same side. I will see you in court next week."

The other lawyers chuckled, the tension broken.

As the defense lawyers took their table, Winifred began. "I am so sorry, Horace, that this case is causing you grief," but Horace stopped her immediately.

"Don't even think about it. I took the case knowing my fellow man was not going to appreciate it. I have to admit that I rather enjoy the commotion. Keeps my blood flowing. Now let us talk about Mrs. Black."

The other defense lawyers joined in, speculating

about the jury, the witnesses, and the rest of the evidence. As they talked, Winifred realized that their case was indeed weak, and they needed help.

Feeling a set of eyes on her, she was astonished to see Charles approaching their table.

"Mr. Shane, Miss Appleton. Gentlemen." Charles nodded and indicated for them to stay seated.

"Mr. Howe. I am surprised to see you," Horace said.

"I thought you might be here. I wanted to let you know that I plan to call Mr. Albright to the stand tomorrow. Normally I would have given you more notice, but after the newspaper stories, we are being forced to move more quickly."

Although he did not look at Winifred, she flinched.

"I have prepared a list of questions I will ask," he continued smoothly. "I thought this might help." He handed the document to Horace.

Horace glanced at it. "Thank you, Mr. Howe. I must say, I really appreciate the way you are conducting this case. You have given us a break in several areas, and I can only thank you again."

"Please understand, Mr. Shane, I am only doing my job. I, too, do not wish to see an innocent person sent to jail, so if there is information that the jury needs to hear in order to reach a true verdict, I will not keep it out. Good day."

Charles turned and walked out of the restaurant. Horace watched him leave, then said softly to Winifred, "That's a good man you've got there. One in a million. Remember that. You would be a fool to let him go."

Winifred's mouth dropped in surprise, but Horace returned to reading Charles's document.

CHAPTER 22

ARLY THE NEXT MORNING, Charles entered the courthouse hoping for a few hours of quiet in order to prepare for the day's testimony. He stood for a moment gazing at the polished fruitwood benches, the gilt ornamented desk, and the immense bronze chandelier overhead. In the center, like an altar, stood the judge's bench, an immense structure of French walnut, gleaming in the dim morning light. To the right was the witness box and the table for the court stenographers, and farther on, the jury box. In the corner was the desk of the high sheriff. It all looked like a stage, where the players would enact their story and their fate.

This room had always been home to him, a place where justice was done, where right prevailed over wrong. Yet to his amazement, he was now beginning to see it differently: it was a place where privileged men decided what was right, and what was law. His previous notions of solidity and fairness seemed contrived. Power reigned here, but it was the power of a few, select men.

Shaking off his thoughts, Charles smiled to himself. Winifred had really crept under his skin. If he wasn't careful, he would end up like Horace, donning the suffragette banner and marching in the streets. Still the notion was not as preposterous as it once might have seemed. Winifred might not be completely right, he thought, but he could see the truth in her position.

Taking up his papers, he retreated to an adjoining room where files and books were kept. Here he could get a few hours of work done without interference. Stepping into the room, he was surprised to find the gaslights already turned on—and the room occupied.

Winifred bent over the desk, yawning, her hair disheveled, books piled all around her. She wore the same dress as she had the previous day, and Charles guessed from her appearance and from the gutted candle at her sleeve that she had been up all night. Dark circles loomed under her eyes, and her shoulders sagged. Her notebook was open, and she scribbled furiously, glancing between it and an open book.

Charles observed her in silence. For all her inattention to her appearance, she looked adorable. A pencil was thrust behind one ear, her sleeves were stained with lead, and when she absently tossed back a stray lock from her forehead, she unwittingly smudged it. Yet her earnestness and sincerity shone in the elegant lines of her face, the intelligent sparkle of her hazel eyes, and the charming way she bit her lip in concentration.

In that moment, Charles knew how much he loved her. There was no other word for the overwhelming feeling that welled up inside of him as he studied her. It didn't matter that she was not his social equal, that she could not advance his career, that she brought to him no money, no connections, nor any of the other things more politically astute men sought in marriage. None of it mattered. All he knew was that Winifred intrigued him like no one else, challenged him, and brought out the very best and worst he had to offer. She would never leave his thoughts, nor could he ever extract her from his being. Somehow, with her ridiculous rhetoric, her Joan of Arc aspirations, and her utter defiance, she had wriggled her way into his heart.

With a start, she looked up, dropping her pen. "Charles! I did not hear you come in! How long have you been standing there?"

"Long enough," he answered, delighted to see the blush creep over her face. Self-consciously she tried to smooth her hair and grimaced in dismay at her shabby appearance. "What are you doing?"

Her eyes met his, and all thoughts of her looks disappeared. "I am trying to find something to help Mrs. Black." The fire left her, and to his amazement, tears welled up in her eyes. "You know how weak our case is. I have researched every possible angle I can think of and have come up short. We still do not have the tea tin, and we have no real evidence to help Mrs. Black, or even to introduce a reasonable doubt. I know, you told me so, but I still have to try."

His heart went out to her. Forcing his emotions under control, he came to her side and sat on the edge of the desk. As he lifted her downcast face to his, a teardrop rolled down her cheek. She brushed it away in embarrassment, but not before he felt a thick jolt of compassion.

"Winnie, you cannot honestly think I am happy about this, can you?" She shook her head, closing her eyes in mortification, and he continued softly. "Why don't you go home and get some rest? There is nothing more you can do right now. Mr. Albright's testimony will take up most of the day, and we both know what he will say. I am certain Horace has already prepared his questions, based on what I will ask."

"It was kind of you to help us." Winifred looked much more like a little girl lost than a tough attorney. "And Charles, I am sorry about the press. I did not intend for things to go so far—"

"I know," he cut her off smoothly. "I have thought about it and realized you used what you had at your disposal. I do not agree with your choice, but I understand it. Now go home. Get some rest."

"I cannot go home. There has to be something, something I am missing, something that would help. . . ." She gestured futilely at the open book, almost willing it to produce an answer.

"Darling, I have tried, and I cannot think of anything either." Charles knew he had to continue in his role but hated to see her pain. "Perhaps, I can go easier on some of the witnesses—"

"No!" Her eyes flew open in shock. "Charles, you cannot possibly think of such a thing! You have to do your job. Surely you are not implying that the only way the defense can win is if the prosecution backs down?"

"No, I didn't mean that. I think you and Horace are putting on a fine defense. I take my hat off to you both. You have managed to take an utterly unsympathetic woman and present her in a different light. I have not always approved of your tactics, but if I ever got into trouble, I would be very reassured to have Winifred Appleton on my side."

The tears came to her eyes again, and she self-consciously looked downward, folding her hands on the desk. Her voice came haltingly, filled with emotion.

"Charles, I think that is the nicest thing anyone has ever said to me."

"Well, I mean it." He smoothed her hair back

from her face and was rewarded when she looked up at him a moment later, an ink-smudged madonna, her face alight with happiness. Then the light dimmed as the futility of her efforts came to her once more.

"Still, we are going to lose, and this woman will go to prison. I have failed. I cannot help Mrs. Black. Oh, Charles, I have tried and tried, and I just cannot come up with anything! Maybe I should just give up."

She crumpled in exhaustion. Charles reached for her and took her into his arms. As she sobbed, he held her closely.

Once he would have been happy to hear such a confession. Once he would have encouraged her to quit. He'd anticipated that when Winifred saw how hard her ambition would be to achieve, she would give up and come to him. Yet now, feeling her breaking in his arms, he put his own selfish motivations aside.

"Winnie," he said in his harsh voice, "don't you dare quit now. You have to see this thing through to the end. A woman is depending on you. Horace is depending on you. He gave you a chance, and you owe it to him to perform. And you owe it to me." When her pretty lips parted in protest, he continued sharply. "I did not train you to run away when the going got tough."

"But"—Winifred stared at him in confusion—"I thought—"

"Well, think again," Charles said. "You know, Winnie, I never would have thought you a coward. I guess women just cannot cut it the way men can after all."

The fire blazed back into her eyes, all hazel fury. "What do you mean, women cannot do it? I am tired and upset, but that does not mean I am giving up!"

"It doesn't?" Charles asked innocently, struggling to keep his face straight.

"No, it doesn't! If you think just because things look, well, black right now, that I would just walk away from this, then you really do not know me after all!"

She was magnificent in her outrage, as always. Charles couldn't resist a laugh, and to her amazement, he leaned forward and kissed her soundly.

It was a wonderful kiss, full of passion, emotion, and suppressed desire. Charles groaned as he felt Winifred gasp, then soften into a mutual response. She felt exquisite in his arms, all soft and warm and womanly, and when she pressed herself against him, wanting more, he could not help but respond. He deepened the kiss, taking her to a higher level, gratified when she buried her fingers into his collar, forcing the buttons to pop open.

"Oh, Charles," she sighed helplessly, sliding her fingers beneath the stiff material of his white cotton shirt, tracing them over the bare muscled flesh beneath. Her innocent touch sent his senses roaring out of control, and he was filled with a fierce need to possess her. This was Winifred, his heroine, all fire and passion, and all woman.

"Winnie, I cannot believe what you do to me," he whispered, turning her face even more fully into his, feathering hot kisses along her cheeks, nose, and throat. Her laughter changed quickly to a frantic gasp for breath as he cupped her breast, stroking her, taking her into the wonderful white-hot world of desire.

It was only an awkward clearing of someone's throat that brought Charles back to reality. Struggling with his own reckless desires, he managed to look up and see the court stenographer standing awkwardly on the threshold of the room.

"I—ah, came to fetch my books." He indicated the filing cabinet. "I can come back."

"No, just give me a minute," Charles managed, grateful that the man just nodded, then disappeared. Winifred's eyes fluttered open, and she glanced toward the doorway as if in a dream state.

"What—who was that?"

"Just Edward, the stenographer. He wants his notes. I guess we have to get going. Court's probably ready to start."

A blush flooded Winifred's cheeks, and she sat up quickly, adjusting her clothing. "Oh my God . . ."

"Don't worry," Charles assured her. "I have known him for years and he will not say anything. Now take my advice and go home for the day. Get some sleep. I will even get a transcript for you, if you think that will help."

"No, I cannot do that. I will go home and freshen up a bit, however, before returning. Charles"—her swollen lips relaxed into a smile and her eyes glowed with warmth—"thank you."

"You are very welcome." He kissed the tip of her nose, then watched as she got to her feet and gathered up her belongings. She flashed him a smile, then turned and left, holding her books to her chest as if to shield it against the rest of the world.

Charles's chest tightened miserably. He knew what he had done: he had just helped her reaffirm her commitment to the law. Winifred was back on the case.

"MR. ALBRIGHT, would you mind telling the court what your relationship was to the defendant?"

Charles asked the question briskly, then turned away from the witness box. The court stenographer caught his attention. The thin, bespectacled man stopped transcribing and fixed his gaze on Charles's throat. Covertly, he gestured to his collar.

Charles touched his collar and realized his tie was undone and that three of his buttons were unfastened. Giving Edward a swift nod of gratitude, Charles turned his back to the jury and quickly redid his buttons. Thankfully, Mr. Albright took a moment to respond.

"I am a friend of Mrs. Black's."

"I see." Charles paused, adjusting his tie. When he was reassembled, he turned around and continued, ignoring the amused indulgence in the judge's eye. "How long have you been . . . her friend?"

The jury murmured disapprovingly. Mr. Albright coughed, then spoke firmly.

"I've known Mrs. Black for about six months. We met at a department store, where she was trying to select a trinket for her husband's birthday. I assisted her in that effort."

"Did you see her socially after that?" Charles persisted.

"Yes." A murmur rumbled from the gallery, cut short by the judge's threatening glance. "Mrs. Black and I discovered we had much in common. I remembered her from the days when she was on stage, and she seemed happy to talk about those memories. I did stop by her home upon occasion to visit her. She seemed very lonely to me."

The jury muttered among themselves. Mr. Black glowered at his wife as if mentally peeling away her veils, shocked at the woman he found beneath. Mrs. Black kept her face straight ahead.

"It was very kind of you to relieve her loneliness," Charles said sarcastically, prompting an eruption of laughter from the jury. "Mr. Albright, did you bring Mrs. Black any presents?"

"We exchanged a few tokens of friendship." Albright's face flushed, and he shifted uncomfortably in his chair.

"Can you tell the jury what they were?"

"I gave Mrs. Black a book of sonnets. At Christmastime, she presented me with a watch charm. I see nothing unusual about exchanging holiday gifts with a friend."

"You don't?" Charles was incredulous. "Mr. Albright, are you aware that Mrs. Black is a married woman, living with her husband?"

"Yes, I am." The witness flushed even deeper. "But that doesn't mean—"

"And would you not consider a book of sonnets a rather romantic present, and obviously inappropriate given Mrs. Black's marital state?"

"No, I do not!" Albright's voice rose in agitation. "Monica—I mean, Mrs. Black—enjoys poetry. I thought she would appreciate the book."

"I am sure she did," Charles said sharply. "I have here a copy of the book you gave her. Mr. Albright, would you mind reading aloud the first few lines of the poem on page one?"

Albright's face turned brilliant red. He glanced at the judge, as if to ask whether this was legal. He then looked to Horace, who was conveniently studying the ceiling. Having no other choice, he opened the book and read weakly.

" 'How do I love thee? Let me count the ways.
I love thee to the depth and breadth and height
My soul can reach . . .' "

The gallery burst into laughter at Elizabeth Barrett Browning's beautiful poem. Even the jury exchanged amused smiles. But Mr. Albright looked furious as he slammed the book closed. He stared at Charles with open animosity, as if contemplating his dismemberment.

"Very nice," Charles said. "Please note for the record that Mr. Albright presented Mrs. Black with a gift that was very romantic in nature. Now, Mr. Albright, did you ever escort Mrs. Black anywhere? Take any trips with her during your brief relationship?"

Albright was still so angry, he could barely speak. This time he refused to look up, but answered sullenly, "Yes. We took an excursion to Newport by steamer. Mrs. Black had always wanted to go there, and I had the means to take her, so I did."

"Anywhere else?"

"Just to lunch and occasionally dinner in town."

"I see. Where was Mr. Black during these outings?"

"He was away at a Masonic meeting when we went to Newport. Other than that, he could usually be found at the local tavern."

"That is a lie!" Mr. Black rose to his feet, shaking his fist at the dapper man in the witness box. The gavel banged soundly, and his own attorney rose to restrain him, forcing him back into his seat. The jurors glanced meaningfully at each other.

"Mr. Albright, did you ever express any physical intimacy with Mrs. Black? For example, did you ever kiss her? Embrace her? Caress her?"

Again Albright struggled. He glanced at Mrs. Black, at her husband, and then at the jury. Finally, as if all hope left him, he spoke softly.

"Yes."

The reporters raced from the room. The morning air would be rich with the scent of scandal.

Charles saw that Winifred had returned and positioned herself as close to the rail as possible, her hair neatly arranged once more, her dress fresh. Her eyes met his and he gave her a warm smile, then turned once more to the witness.

"Mr. Albright, did you ever promise Mrs. Black matrimony, or hint at such, if anything ever happened to her husband?"

The court fell quiet, as everyone waited in breathless anticipation for his response. Albright gazed about helplessly, and when he replied to Charles, it was as if someone had stripped off his mask.

"I admit I said that. I am in love with Mrs. Black, and I believe she cares for me. I know such an admission will cause my ruin, but that matters little to me now. The woman you are trying for murder is a good woman, sweet and kind. If she attempted to harm her husband, it was in self-defense. The man is a drunkard and a fool and does not deserve to kiss her boots."

WINIFRED'S HEART SANK as she watched Horace walk up to the witness stand for the cross-examination. No matter how talented he was, or how brilliantly he argued, there was little he could do now.

No one, after Albright's startling admission, would believe that he was a "despoiler of women." The emotion he described was too real, too honest, to be anything but true. The jury must have felt it, too. And Winifred realized something personal: the man was describing how she felt when Charles held her, kissed her. . . .

That was what had motivated Monica Black. With Albright, the woman had, for the first time, experienced real love. No wonder she'd been so desperate, so intoxicated with emotion, to think that poison was her only way out—if that was truly what she had done. . . . If only they could find that tea tin! Yet the police hadn't been able to find it, having scoured the house thoroughly.

The sad part, Winifred realized, was that the Blacks were miserable married to each other. Yet they were shackled together, unable to break free. If divorce had been more easily obtainable, Monica Black might never have come to this pass. Perhaps . . .

Winifred froze, a flash of brilliance coming to her. That was it! That is what she had to show them! She had to make the jury realize that Monica Black had been trapped and had had no other choice. And she knew just how to do that.

She hesitated for a moment as her conscience chided her. Charles wouldn't like this. Yet he himself had encouraged her to continue, practically forbade her to quit the case. Forcing aside her emotions, Winifred rationalized that Charles would understand. He had to.

Scribbling onto a piece of paper, she passed the note to the bailman. When Horace finished questioning Albright, he sat down at the defense table and read her missive carefully. The same silly grin spread across his face, and he turned to Winifred and gave her a thumbs up.

Court adjourned for the day, and Winifred rose, feeling ten times lighter than she had upon entering the courtroom. Whirling about, she stopped in surprise as Charles approached her.

"Feeling better?" he asked solicitously.

"Much." She gave him a soft smile. "Thank you again, Charles. You are so kind."

"I would like to be much more than kind," he said meaningfully. Winifred felt a flush of warmth. "Look, I know you are tired. Why don't we have an early supper together? I promise to tuck you in early."

The thought of Charles tucking her in anywhere

was almost too intoxicating. "I do not think that is a good idea," she began.

"Just dinner," he insisted. "Look, I know I should not be seeing you, either. I just thought you might need a friend to talk to tonight. That's all."

Friend. Somehow the word coming out of his mouth hit a discordant note. Winifred had to smile at her own fickle nature. Yet the thought of being with him was just too enticing, especially after that morning. "That sounds wonderful."

"Good." Then he turned cautious. "Would you mind terribly if we dined at my house? After the latest newspaper stories, it might be more discreet."

Winifred nodded, ignoring the little thrill that leaped in her veins. "You are right. It would be much better if no one saw us socializing."

"Wonderful. I will have your driver bring you directly." For a moment, Charles looked as if he would kiss her, then he remembered where he was. Winifred watched him go, feeling a delightful shiver of anticipation.

She and Charles dining alone, in his house. Whatever was she thinking?

CHAPTER 23

"YOU ARE SO BEAUTIFUL," Charles said softly, easing first one stocking from her leg, then the other. They had barely set foot in his townhouse before they were locked in a heated embrace, both of them starved for a taste of their familiar sensual pleasures. Charles wasted no time positioning Winifred on his brocade sofa. Arching beneath him, she pulled him frantically toward her, wanting everything his lean muscled body promised.

"Charles . . ."

"I know, sweet." He kissed her thoroughly, wantonly and at the same time, his hand moved beneath the layers of petticoats to her drawers. Finding the warmth he sought, he touched her there, where she ached for him, eliciting another gasp of sheer pleasure. His fingers lingered there, stroking her, arousing her to the point of utter forgetfulness.

"I don't know if I can stand this—"

"Just a little more. Trust me, darling."

His face left hers for a moment, but before she could protest the loss of his warmth, he knelt between her legs and drew her drawers down. Winifred felt his

breath, hot and arousing, close to her woman's flesh.
She started to rise up in shock, but Charles would have
none of her withdrawal. He held her down firmly, one
hand on each thigh, and kissed her intimately.

Winifred gasped, writhing on the sofa. A thousand
searing sensations tingled through her as he expertly
caressed her with his lips and tongue. "Ohhhhh . . ."
Arching against him, she cried out as the intensity
grew unbearable. "Oh, Charles, please stop. You
can't—I can't—oh, don't ever stop!"

The pleasure was incredible, more than anything
she had ever experienced. Within moments, the
sweetest climax she had ever had made her cry out
loud, clinging to him as she trembled violently. Her
body spasmed, the flooding pleasure throbbing
through her, washing her all the way to her toes with
fire, making her feel hot, vibrant, and alive.

Then Charles rose, rid himself of his trousers, and
entered her. It felt shockingly pleasurable and more
than a little naughty to make love like this, still
partially clothed. Then the throbbing pressure began
again, more deeply this time, and her hot, slick
warmth encased him eagerly. She lifted her hips
toward him, giving him everything and receiving so
much more in return. He feathered hot, sweet kisses
on her throat, stimulating her beyond control, and at
the same time, making her feel protected, cherished,
and . . . loved.

"Winnie, my beautiful, darling . . . I want to
see your face, I want to watch you—"

As he thrust deeply inside her, she convulsed,
bringing the tremendous pressure to a shattering climax once more. Her eyes flew open with astonishment,
then closed in rapture, letting all of the delicious feelings rush over her. He cried out her name, arching
against her and thrusting roughly inside her. His face

was wildly exciting, filled with passion, and even as he held her closely against him, he exploded in ultimate pleasure.

For a long moment, they simply enjoyed the aftermath. Winifred felt Charles's heart pounding in rhythm with her own. Then her fatigue overwhelmed her, and as soon as she rested her head on his chest, she fell asleep.

Charles smiled as he heard her unmistakable snoring. He'd have to tease her about that tomorrow, watch the indignant blush come to her face as she flatly denied any such thing. He could see her now, her head lifted like a noble heroine, her eyes flashing—she was everything he ever wanted, and more.

Having watched her during the trial, he was forced to admit something else: she would be a damned good lawyer. So how to reconcile her ambition with what he wanted from her—and with what, he was certain, underneath it all, she needed, too?

He had just received a letter from a colleague in Wisconsin. A Miss Lavinia Goodell had passed the bar examination. Yet when she applied for admission to the bar, she had been flatly denied. In response, she had authored an amendment to the state statute, an amendment that Charles's colleague intended to sponsor. The woman's work was brilliant, and perhaps they would succeed. Perhaps, with the right political support, the same thing could happen here. Such a law might not pass on the first attempt or even the second, but eventually public opinion could change.

As if hearing his thoughts, Winifred snuggled even closer into his arms.

"I WOULD LIKE to call Mr. Henry to the stand."

Winifred yawned, slightly bored. Mr. Henry, a

balding, portly man with chubby cheeks and a booming voice, took his place, lifting his hand earnestly. The druggist was Charles's last witness, and he would surely testify that he sold arsenic to Monica Black.

Listening idly as Charles raced through his questions, Winifred noticed how attractive the prosecutor looked that morning. When he caught her looking at him, he sent her a seductive wink that made her blush down to her toes.

All she could envision was Charles making love to her in the most intimate way possible, his face dark with desire. Embarrassment suffused her as she recalled falling asleep in his arms, only to awaken outside her aunt's home. Charles had dressed her, carried her to the carriage, and brought her to her doorstep. Their parting kiss had been so utterly tender that she had wanted to stay with him forever. Now she had to shake her head to force her thoughts back to the case at hand.

"So Mrs. Black bought the arsenic. Did she say what she intended to use it for?"

"Yes. She said she had a rat in the house that needed killing, and that she intended to take care of it."

The jurors shuffled in their seats, and Winifred rolled her eyes. The man was obviously in the prosecution's corner. Charles continued as murmurs rumbled in the gallery.

"Did Mrs. Black come into your establishment often?"

"Enough so I would recognize her. She bought a lot of powders for her husband. You know, medicinal mixtures like Parson's Potion, that sort of thing. Seems he had a lot of indigestion and headaches."

"I see. So you have no doubt as to Mrs. Black's identity."

"Nope. Would know her from across the street, that's for certain. Would stay there, too, if you get my meaning."

Horace objected, but the damage was done. The jurors looked highly unsympathetic. Desperation filled Winifred as the court recessed for a few minutes, to give Horace time to bring up the defense witnesses.

Yet even as Horace conferred with the stenographers, something was niggling in the back of Winifred's mind. There was something about Mr. Henry's testimony . . . quickly she ran through her notes. It had been simple and direct enough. But intuition told her that something here was not quite right, something that could hold real meaning if she could figure out what it was. . . .

"IS THE DEFENSE READY, counselor?"

"Yes." Horace took center stage in the courtroom and indicated the rear chamber. A small, elegant-looking woman with silver-blue hair and a lace dress stepped through the door and walked gracefully up the aisle, as if striding through a rose garden. When she placed her hand on the Bible, it seemed almost an insult for her to have to pledge to tell the truth.

"Let me present this witness as Mrs. Cecilia Weathermere, of Fifth Avenue in New York. Mrs. Weathermere, would you mind telling the jury how long you have been wed?"

The woman turned her face toward the jury box and spoke softly. "Fifty years."

The jurymen looked at one another in bewilderment.

"I see," Horace continued. "Now you are a noble woman of society, well known for your wealth and charitable work. Is that true?"

"Yes."

"And would you consider your marriage a good one?"

Suddenly the woman broke her elegant deportment. "No," she said softly. "I was forced to marry my husband because our families decreed that a match between a Chalfonte and a Weathermere would be advantageous to both."

"I see. And was it?"

The woman looked at the jury, and her eyes flashed blue fire. "For him it was. For me, it was hell on earth. I tried everything to make it work, but Mr. Weathermere was simply a domineering bully."

The crowds broke into a loud rumbling, while the jury stared at the society woman in astonishment. Charles rose indignantly to his feet.

"Objection! This entire testimony is irrelevant to the case."

"Mr. Shane?"

"Your Honor, if you can let me proceed, I will soon make its relevance apparent."

The judge gazed at Horace for a long moment, then glanced at the defendant. As if on cue, for the first time since the trial began, Monica Black lifted her veil. Her face was a little shopworn but still beautiful. She looked sadly at the judge, as if pleading. The elderly man nodded.

"Get to the point quickly. I, too, am losing patience."

"Certainly. Thank you, Your Honor," Horace said, then turned to the woman once again. "So Mrs. Weathermere, do you feel you can empathize with Mrs. Black's desperation?"

"I certainly can. While I do not approve of what she did, if she did it, I can understand completely.

More than once during my fifty years, the same thought crossed my mind about the old buzzard."

The crowd erupted into laughter, and the judge banged the gavel sharply. When the noise died, Horace continued.

"Mrs. Weathermere, you also have many friends in society. Would you describe your situation as unique?"

"Not at all," the elderly lady said with vigor. "Unfortunately, because of our ridiculous divorce laws, I know many women who are shackled to men much worse than my husband."

"Would you say a lot of women feel that way?"

"Objection!" Charles shouted.

"Would you say that these women, all pillars of society, support your view?"

At that, the doors swung open, and women began marching into the courtroom, one at a time. The "gray-haired battalion" as the papers would call them, paraded up the aisle, then stopped at the rail. The gallery burst into bedlam, the reporters scribbled frantically, and the judge pounded the gavel furiously.

"Counselor, what is the meaning of this?" the judge barked as ten elderly, well-to-do society women faced him calmly.

"Your Honor, these women are witnesses for Mrs. Black. They came here today of their own accord and of their own free will, to demonstrate that Monica Black's circumstances are not unique. All of them have stood where Mrs. Black stood. All of them have been miserable in their marriages but had little voice or recourse in the matter. Once a woman is wed, she is tied to a man for life and becomes in essence his property—an antiquated concept derived from English common law that is no longer appropriate today.

What is really on trial here is not Mrs. Black but the divorce laws in society as a whole."

"Mr. Shane"—the judge seemed about to explode—"you are turning this trial into a circus."

"On the contrary," Horace glanced at the saintly-looking ladies, all of whom smiled sweetly at him. "What is happening in marriages today is a circus, or rather a nightmare. Mrs. Black's life has been exactly that. She was not trying to take her husband's life. She was struggling to save her own."

In the gallery, some of the women applauded, while the men roared in outrage. The reporters scrambled out the door gleefully. The judge once more banged his gavel and gave Horace a meaningful look.

"Adjournment for the day. Counselors, I want to see you both in my chambers. Ladies, you can all leave. I do not think we need to hear Mrs. Weathermere's testimony repeated ten times."

The crowd rose to leave, arguing over Horace's tactics all the while. Winifred rose with them, delighted that he had made their point. But when she looked at Charles, all sense of triumph left her. He gave her a look of disgust. Then he turned swiftly to follow the judge, as if she were not worth a second glance.

Horrified, Winifred felt the people push past her, but she could not move. She had known Charles would not approve, but somehow that one look had made her feel physically ill. He obviously agreed with the judge, that their intention was to turn the trial into a circus. But if she examined her motivations, wasn't that pretty close to the mark?

With a sickening feeling, Winifred realized that this time she had gone too far. In her desperation to help her client, she had made a mockery of the judicial system, which to Charles bordered on sacrilege. Even as her clever mind thought up a thousand defensive rebuttals, she could not escape one clear thought—he was right.

As the crowd thinned, she walked slowly out of the courtroom. He would never forgive her this time, and she was not even sure she could blame him.

CHAPTER 24

NEVER IN ALL MY YEARS on the bench have I ever seen such foolishness! Good God, Horace, what the hell's gotten into you?"

Judge Culvert took a sip of water, then mopped his reddened face with a handkerchief, obviously in a spitting fury. Horace sat before him, appearing contrite, his hands lifted in the air as if unable to explain himself. Charles stopped pacing the room and turned to the judge.

"I think I can explain that part. Miss Appleton has been assisting Mr. Shane in the defense. I am certain this idea was hers."

"Is that right?" The judge turned to Shane, appalled.

"Yes," Horace admitted, giving Charles an interested look. "Miss Appleton has been a brilliant assistant. She has thought of a lot of angles that we more experienced old geezers would have never dreamed of."

"Shane, I have known you for a long time, and I never thought to see you taken in by a set of petticoats. Has your infatuation with Miss Appleton made you lose your mind? Whatever the intoxication has been, I order you to put it from your head or face charges of contempt."

Horace shrugged, then poured himself a tall glass of the judge's water. Lifting the cup as if in a toast, he smiled pleasantly.

"Here's to the ladies. They have finally had their day in court." He took a sip.

"What the hell does that mean?" Charles barked, suddenly wanting to strangle Horace. The judge, too, appeared even angrier than before.

Setting his glass aside calmly, Horace gazed at the judge and Charles with that same, benevolent look he always wore. "Gentlemen, I understand why you both are upset. I know this case has caused a lot of press, some of which hasn't been flattering to any of us. Charles, I know your feelings about this sort of thing, and Your Honor, I know you do not like to see the dignity of the courtroom mocked. Let me assure you that I agree one hundred percent."

"You do." The judge stared Horace down as if he were a witness. "Then why are you doing this?"

"Because the lady has a point," Horace said smoothly. "Look, we all know what Mrs. Black tried to do. As men, we are naturally appalled by that, and as humans, we feel we have to revenge ourselves upon the perpetrator. But gentlemen, consider this. If Mrs. Black were a man, and she and the defendant had been brawling in a bar, and one almost killed the other, would we look at it the same way?"

"But that is not the same at all!" Charles retorted. "This woman had an affair with another man and premeditated her husband's murder! It was only by luck that the man lived. Are you saying you support that?"

"No," Horace said flatly. "What I am saying is that we have to consider what it is like for a person to be in the power of someone stronger, someone who abuses that power. I know personally the feelings of helplessness and anger that Mrs. Black experienced every day. And I know if you live with despair long enough, eventually you do something desperate."

"Just how did you come to this enlightened understanding?" the judge asked mockingly.

Horace was silent for a long moment before answering. "I was adopted as a child and brutalized by the man who would be my father. Like Mr. Black, he drank, and like Mr. Black, he knew where to lay his fists. The courtroom was not there for me, either, nor were the police any help. You see, a father has a right to discipline his children in any way he chooses, just as a husband has the right to chastise his wife. And when he hit my adopted mother . . ." His voice trailed off, and he looked as if he were seeing again the horrible world he described. After a long sigh, Horace seemed to shake off the memory. "I ran away at age fourteen and lived on the streets. I knew that if I stayed, I would kill him. So you see, I have a different view of this case."

Something moved within Charles. Shane was always so moderate, so kind, so brilliant and amiable, no one would ever think he had such a painful past. Extending his hand to Horace, he spoke with deep emotion.

"I am terribly sorry. I had no idea—"

"Of course you didn't. How could you?" Horace smiled, accepting the handclasp. To the judge, who looked equally horrified, he said, "I was fortunate that a certain woman of wealth saw something in me. If it weren't for her, I would not be here today. Your Honor, Mrs. Black has the deck stacked against her. Like it or not, that is the way of our judicial system. And we men, gentlemen, have made the rules. We have the power to change them or to keep them as they are.

Because of that, I want her to have every possible
chance. Miss Appleton's tactics and my own may have
been questionable, but if they have succeeded in making the jury consider, even for a moment, the system's
inequity for women and the injustice of marriage and
divorce laws today, then we have been successful."

"You do understand that the facts will win out in
this case," Judge Culvert said, his voice low. "She will
lose."

"I know," Horace admitted. "But damn it, we
have to try. If this case, the newspapers, the parlor
discussions, and the silent evaluations make just one
person think about this, then our effort will not have
been in vain."

"All right." Culvert rose and put a fond hand on
Horace's back. "Shane, I have always admired the way
you manage to shake things up. But let's try to keep it
under control now. I want to wrap this case up
quickly, before it loses all semblance of dignity. If it's
any consolation, I too feel badly for Mrs. Black."

CHARLES LEFT the judge's chambers, deep in
thought. Horace's confession had moved him tremendously.

Dismissing his cab, he elected to walk home,
wanting the relief of physical exercise to help him sort
out the complexity of his feelings. How could he have
been so wrong? In his refusal to see anything except
that Monica Black had committed a crime, a heinous
crime at that, how could he have been so blind?

He thought about Mrs. Black, trapped in a marriage and unable to escape. He tried to imagine
himself in that situation, but it was nearly impossible.

Men had other means. They could travel, take a mistress, drink, carouse, all of which were socially acceptable, even encouraged. So even if he couldn't really empathize with Mrs. Black, he could sympathize with her situation.

Yet murder was murder, attempted or otherwise, and without laws against murder and other crimes, there would be chaos. It was all so damned confusing.

When Charles arrived home, he poured himself a good drink from his brandy flask and sat before the fire. His ideas of right and wrong, good and bad, had been profoundly shaken. He felt ashamed of his former ironclad convictions, his certainty that his way was the only way. He had been obstinate, refusing to see any other viewpoint but his own. Now Horace's confession had made him understand that the law, his precious law, really wasn't the same for everyone. And since it wasn't, could he honestly fault Winifred for turning the trial into a circus?

It was enough to make him reach for another glass of brandy.

"WINNIE! WHAT ON EARTH is the matter, dear? You look terrible!"

As Winifred entered the parlor, Penelope dropped her novel and raced to her sister. She put her hand on her forehead, but Winifred smiled, removing Penelope's cool fingers, and pressed her hand reassuringly within her own.

"I am not sick, dear. Not physically, anyway. I am just . . . upset."

Penelope was perplexed. Winifred was never upset, not even under the most provoking of circumstances. Even when their parents had died, Winifred had been a tower of strength. "What is wrong? It's this trial, isn't it? Oh, Winnie, don't be worried! You have done your best, after all!"

"It is not just that." Winifred sighed, lowering herself into the parlor sofa. Accepting a cup of Penelope's tea, she took a sip. "I am afraid I have really made Charles angry this time. I may have lost even his friendship."

"Oh." Penelope smiled, more sure of herself now. "Winnie, you could never lose that. Charles cares for you too much."

Winifred winced. "Yes, he once did. In fact"—she wanted desperately to confide in someone—"he asked to marry me."

"What!" Penelope exclaimed in excitement. "How wonderful! Oh, I knew this would happen! Why didn't you tell me?"

"I was uncertain of how to feel," Winifred said softly.

"So when is the wedding?" Penelope asked excitedly.

"There is not going to be one," Winifred said, smoothing Penelope's hair as her sister's face fell.

"Why not? I don't understand—"

"Charles would not be happy married to me. I would drive him insane with my need to practice the law. He needs a wife who can help him politically, who has connections, whose name is beyond reproach. The Appleton name can do nothing but hurt him."

"I see," Penelope mused. "Then you do love him."

Winifred started to object, but Penelope shrugged her off. "Why else would you care if marrying him hurt him? You love him."

It all seemed so simple coming from her sister's lips. Yet Winifred reminded herself that things were always simple where Penelope was concerned. Men came as easily to her as the law did to Winifred. "Yes, I suppose I do. But that does not change anything—"

"You are wrong," Penelope said authoritatively. "You are very wrong. It changes everything. Trust me, Winnie, I know."

Winifred gazed at her sister strangely. Of all people, Penelope would know. She'd had more suitors than any woman Winifred had ever seen, and she had always drawn men to her like bees to honey.

Penelope smiled fondly. "Instead of second-guessing what is right for Charles, why don't you just ask him? Maybe there is a way to compromise. Have you told him how you feel?"

"Sort of." Winifred felt something tighten within her. "But he wouldn't agree I am wrong for him—"

"Because maybe he knows you are very right for him," Penelope said. "Winnie, I don't think you are being fair either to Charles or to yourself. You love him; he loves you. You should at least give yourselves a chance. Oh Winnie, for once, let yourself be happy! Of all men, Charles can make you so. He has not held you back up until now, has he?"

"No," Winifred answered truthfully. "But when we are married, he will expect me to be a wife and mother. How can I do that and still attain what I want?"

"How can you not?" Penelope said, smiling sweetly. "You and Charles can work it out. You know you can. Charles would never have tutored you if he did not want to help you. Do not be afraid to love, Winnie."

Her words strangely echoed her aunt's and Winifred struggled with the realization that they were right. Fear was holding her back. An incredible joy welled up inside her. Could it work? Was it really all so simple? A moment later, she came back to reality and her bubble burst. "But Penny, that was all before. Now, after today, I don't know if he can forgive me. He thinks I made a mockery of the judicial system, and that is something I don't think he can forgive."

"Give him a chance," Penelope urged. "You do not give Charles enough credit. He knows how important this case is to you."

"But to Charles, the law is everything. In his eyes, what I did was almost blasphemy. Yet I had to try. If only I could find a way to win fairly, to prove to him I could do it. . . ."

Suddenly Winifred disengaged from Penelope's embrace and dug out her notes. Quickly she scanned the day's testimony. "There was something I heard the druggist say earlier, something important . . ."

Penelope crept back to her seat. She wasn't insulted; she knew that her sister wasn't being rude. She watched as Winifred buried herself in her notes, her brow furrowed, her lips tight with concentration. After a good half hour, she looked up, and an expression of suppressed excitement lit up her face.

"Penny, do we have a bottle of Parson's Potion here in the house?" Winifred's eyes sparkled.

"Why, yes," Penelope answered in surprise. "Aunt Eve takes it for her arthritis. I will get it for you. Vile stuff. Why, do you have a headache?"

"No, nothing like that. Can you fetch it, please?" Winifred could barely contain herself.

Penelope went to do her bidding, then returned with the amber-colored bottle and handed it to her sister.

Winifred studied the bottle intently, then a huge grin broke out across her face. "I have to go out for a while. I'll be back. Tell Auntie not to worry."

"But Winnie!" Penelope stared after her sister in confusion as Winifred threw on her cloak and raced out the door, taking the bottle with her. Giving up, she sat back down, gazing at her sister's full teacup. She had heard that sometimes genius bordered on madness. Penelope was grateful that she wasn't either.

"WHO IN BLAZES is that?"

Horace Shane sat up in bed, hearing a slight tapping at the door below. His wife murmured something in the next bed, then fell blissfully back to sleep. Grumbling, fighting a yawn, he got to his feet and reached for his robe.

Stumbling down the stairs, Horace swore to himself as the knocking persisted. Glancing at the grandfather clock, he cringed at the lateness of the hour, wondering what drunken sot had landed on his doorstep.

"Damned intruder—" Flinging open the door, he was amazed to discover his beautiful assistant on the marble steps.

"Miss Appleton! What on earth are you doing here at this hour? Has someone died?" He glanced down the gaslit street and saw only Winifred's carriage waiting at the curb in the warm spring night.

"No, sir, nothing like that. I am sorry, but I felt this just could not wait. May I come in?"

"Of course."

Winifred stepped gratefully inside the lawyer's plush home, then strode purposefully to the table and turned up the lamp. Horace waited expectantly while Winifred told him her thoughts. Skepticism was quickly replaced by interest, then finally, astonishment as Winifred handed him a sheaf of beautifully prepared legal documents.

"Are you positive about this?" Horace gave her a penetrating look. "We have to be absolutely certain."

"I could not be more certain." Winifred fought to keep the excitement out of her voice. "I double-checked everything. Do you think it will work?"

Horace's bushy-white brows rose a good inch. "Not only do I think it will work, but this is the best damned bit of investigating I have ever seen in all my years as a lawyer. Good God, woman, do you know what this means?"

Winifred giggled. "I think so. Can you bring Mr. Henry back to the stand?"

"Absolutely." Horace read the paperwork, then looked at Winifred again with amazement. "I knew Howe must have seen something in you to tutor you himself. I only suspected the obvious, a romantic interest, which is certainly there." At the heightened color on Winifred's face, he continued more gently. "But now I understand it even better. You were born with a gift, child, a God-given gift, and in spite of all your circumstances, you have chosen to use it. We need you. Mrs. Black needs you. God bless you."

Tears started in Winifred's eyes, and she wiped them quickly away. "Thank you, sir. I daresay, I have often questioned myself, but I really believed I could make a difference. Still—"

"No buts. Someday all women will make choices such as you have, and no one will think anything of it. Our society will only benefit as a result, for it desperately needs the talents of the other half of our civilization. But it will take time, and the heroines, the ones who lead the way, will unfortunately struggle the hardest. Remember dear, you can be anything you want and do anything you want. You are breaking the rules now; continue to break them. You and that man of yours can work this out. Nothing is impossible with love."

Winifred gazed at Horace, whose opinion meant

so much to her. She wasn't sure she knew what he was hinting at, yet it gave her tremendous peace. When he reached out and gently touched her cheek, she smiled at him in tearful gratitude.

"There now, don't get mushy on me. We have a case to win. Leave this paperwork with me, and be in that courtroom bright and early. You want to see Mrs. Black freed, do you not?" At her nod, he continued with a smile. "Good. Now go home and get some sleep. That is an order."

"Yes, sir," Winifred replied.

CHAPTER 25

YOUR HONOR, the defense would like to recall Mr. Henry to the stand."

The crowd murmured at Horace's statement, the jurors looked surprised, and Charles glanced up, perplexed. Mr. Henry, the druggist, had not been at all friendly to the defense. No one could imagine why Horace would want any more of the man's damning testimony.

But the druggist rose and took the stand, glancing curiously at Horace. The elderly attorney picked up a sheaf of papers and a brightly labeled bottle of medicine.

"Mr. Henry, are you familiar with this preparation?" Horace asked, placing the bottle before the druggist, in full view of the jury.

"Yes, I am. That is Parson's Potion."

"I see. Is this the same medicine you referred to in your earlier testimony?"

"Yes, it is." The druggist shrugged.

"Will the court please note that Mr. Henry identified a bottle of Parson's Potion for the jury? Thank you." Horace set his documents aside, then indicated the bottle. "Mr. Henry, as I recall, you mentioned that you knew Mrs. Black so well because she frequently purchased this preparation for her husband. Is that correct?"

"Quite correct." There was a note of annoyance in the man's voice. "But I do not see—"

"How often would you say Mrs. Black purchased this medicine?"

The druggist shrugged once more. "I do not know for sure. About two or three times a month, I guess. Mr. Black frequently had headaches, or so she said."

"Two or three times a month. For how long?"

"I would say at least a few months. He—Mr. Black, I mean—used to take another preparation that is no longer available, so he switched to Parson's. I recommend it to all my patrons."

"I am sure you do." The amused note in Horace's voice made Charles sit up straighter, and his pencil stopped scribbling. "Now Mr. Henry," Horace continued. "Would you mind reading the list of ingredients in the potion for the jury?"

The judge was beginning to look annoyed, but Charles nodded, as if signaling the man to admit the testimony.

Mr. Henry dutifully picked up the bottle and began to read out loud.

" 'Water, sugar syrup, cherry flavor, root of licorice, sarsaparilla, alcohol, and—' "

Horace prompted the man. "And? Speak up, Mr. Henry, the jury cannot hear you."

" 'Arsenic,' " The man finished. "It says arsenic."

The gallery exploded, and the jurors stared, slack jawed. Charles, in amazement, turned to Winifred and gave her a look of such glowing admiration that it warmed her to her toes. The judge looked positively stunned, then he slammed down the gavel, ordering silence in the courtroom. When the noise finally died down, Horace continued conversationally.

"Just to make sure there is no mistake, my assistant, Miss Appleton, yesterday had Professor Caldwell test Parson's Potion himself. I submit to the court the result of those tests, which indicate that the potion contains, among other things, arsenic." Horace handed the paperwork to the judge.

Turning back to the witness stand, Horace continued, "Is it not true, Mr. Henry, that arsenic can accumulate in the system over time, and could ultimately lead to an accidental self-poisoning?"

"Yes," the druggist said glumly, "I suppose it could."

"So, Mr. Henry, it appears that even if Mrs. Black put arsenic in her husband's tea, she was not solely responsible for his poisoning. Indeed, factually, you are as responsible as she is, and Mr. Black himself is equally responsible."

The druggist rose up in outrage. "That is not true! Why I—" he sputtered furiously, while the people in the gallery rolled with laughter. Mr. Black gazed at his wife in bemusement, while Mrs. Black stared at the druggist in disbelief.

Horace picked up another sheaf of papers and deposited them on the judge's bench. "Your Honor, I ask for a dismissal. We have clearly demonstrated that Mrs. Black cannot be blamed for Mr. Black's ingestion of arsenic."

"Case dismissed," the judge said solemnly. The gallery broke into a cheer, the working-class men and women standing up and thrusting fists into the air. Mrs. Weathermere and her brigade stood and applauded. Mr. Albright raised his eyes to the heavens, as if thanking a higher authority. Mrs. Black leaped up, hugging Horace as the man strode back to the defense table. Even Charles rounded his desk and approached Shane, giving the man a hearty handshake. Both of them looked toward the gallery. When Charles's eyes met Winifred's, his look went straight to her heart. Reporters swarmed Monica Black. Only Mr. Black sat alone, as if wondering how the tables had been turned so completely.

Charles smiled to himself, watching Winifred disappear into a mob of admirers. It was all happening for her: the attention, the respect, the acknowledgment of her talents. In spite of her sex, in spite of male prejudice, in spite of incredible odds, she had done something that very few women even dreamed about. She had challenged the system and won. She had saved a woman from death. Her methods, he had to admit, had been brilliant. By showing that the man had been ingesting poison all along, she had proven that Mrs. Black alone was not responsible for her husband's near-death.

Yes, Winifred had shown her ability. Chances were that she would still be seen as an oddity, but she would be taken much more seriously. Offers would come her way, discreetly. Winifred Appleton had made her mark.

And he had helped her to do it. Charles rose, feeling a welter of conflicting emotions in his heart. He was enormously proud of her and glad, for she was incredibly talented, and the world needed her passion, her fire, and her refusal to quit. When she passed the bar, as he was certain she would, she would no longer blush unseen. Every moment of triumph, every thrill of victory, deserved to be hers.

As he picked up his case to leave, he realized something else: Winifred was farther than ever from his reach. How could he possibly convince her to become his wife and the mother of his children? Unless . . .

A broad smile crossed his face. Winifred might be the brains behind the defense, but he was the star prosecutor. He would have to use his talents to convince her, and to come up with a suitable compromise. The thought was not at all discouraging. It was, after all, what he did best.

"MISS APPLETON, what made you think to examine the potion?"

"Was it your strategy all along to disclose this at the last minute?"

"Was your tutor really Mr. Howe, or would you credit Mr. Shane with your brilliance?"

"When will you take the bar exam?"

Winifred beamed as the reporters gathered around her. A heady sense of triumph filled her, and she nearly giggled with joy. She had won.

"I credit Mr. Shane, of course, but Mr. Howe was responsible for much of my training. Yes, I plan to take the bar examination, and I eventually want to practice. I am very happy for Mrs. Black, and I hope all women everywhere know that the law can be on their side."

The reporters scribbled furiously, but only came back with more questions. Smiling and waving, Winifred turned away from them, seeing Horace at the center of one mob, and Mrs. Black in yet another. Her eyes searched the crowd, looking for one face, one man whose presence always made the difference.

An odd sense of depression suddenly came over her. Had Charles left the building? The memory of his approval, that look he had sent her upon hearing the druggist's testimony, had filled her heart with gladness. Now she wanted nothing more than to share the moment with him, the limelight. Yet he was nowhere to be seen.

Her moment of triumph seemed all at once to mean little without Charles. Like it or not, she needed him. Wanted him. Loved him.

It was as simple and as complicated as that. Pushing her way through the reporters, Winifred hastened toward her carriage. Why had it taken so long for her to see the simple truth? Without Charles, the rest was meaningless. Although she did not have the first idea of how to combine a life with him and pursue the law as well, she knew she had to try. Otherwise, she would regret it for the rest of her life.

"Home, Egbert!" Winifred called to the driver, who awoke with a start. Grumbling, he whipped the horse into a trot. As crowds of curious people waved and shouted outside her window, she settled back into the coach, grateful for the quiet. Somehow she had to make Charles understand, had to find a way to make it all work.

"Penelope!" Winifred shouted, yanking off her gloves as she entered the parlor. Penelope raced down the steps, pausing at the bottom.

"I heard what happened," Penelope said breathlessly. "You won! Oh, Winnie, you won!"

Winifred allowed herself to be enveloped in Penelope's sweet embrace. Her sister smelled of fresh roses and lilacs.

"Yes, we did win. Oh, Penny, I'm so happy! But I realized something else. You were right, Auntie was right. I have to find Charles, I have to tell him—"

A strange light twinkled in Penelope's eyes. "So you have finally come to your senses! But you cannot go to Charles looking like that! You look like a vagabond!"

Winifred smoothed her hair, then glanced down at her dress. "Is it that bad?"

"Worse," Penelope said flatly. "Let's go upstairs, and I will help you. Jennifer can help, too. I was just having a bath drawn, but you need it more than I do. We will pick out something nice for you to wear, get some perfume—Charles will be dazzled!"

"Jennifer's here?"

"Yes. Gabriel is out of town for a few days, and with the baby due, Aunt Eve insisted she stay with us. I think my crystal earrings will be perfect, don't you?"

Winifred fought the impulse to run right back out of the house. If she knew the law, Penelope knew men, and there could be no harm in taking her advice.

Penelope led her upstairs, giggling all the while. "What is going on?" Winifred questioned, but her sister merely shrugged innocently.

"Nothing at all, we just want you to look your best."

Jennifer looked very round and very, very happy. She tossed several gowns onto the bed and gave her sister an appraising look. "Penelope was right. That dress will never do."

"What are you talking about? 'Do' for what? I just want to see Charles——"

"Patience, dear," Eve said cheerfully. "A woman owes it to a man to always appear at her best. A curl here, a dab of perfume there makes all the difference."

Winifred saw quite clearly that she would not escape until they had satisfied themselves. An hour later, having been pinched, prodded, powdered, and perfumed, she thought she would scream. Penelope only laughed all the more, while Aunt Eve fussed over her hair.

"Now dear, just a few more pins. You have such lovely hair—and such a pretty color. Burnished gold!

What a shame that you usually just knot it at the back of your head."

"Are we finally ready?" Winifred tried to keep the restlessness out of her voice.

"You look lovely," Jennifer declared, standing back and nodding with approval.

Turning to the mirror, Winifred had to look twice to be certain it was indeed her own reflection. The woman who stared back at her was frankly beautiful. Her hair, drawn up from her face in a smooth chignon, looked elegant, while small crystal drops dangled from her ears. Her eyes seemed even larger than usual, and their hazel color more stunning, especially with the dress Penelope had chosen for her. It was a deep gold taffeta, high-necked but with very few ruffles. The dress clung to her slender figure and swept simply to the floor in a lovely flow of fabric.

"You do look wonderful," Aunt Eve said, standing back as if this golden goddess were her own creation.

"Charles will not be able to take his eyes from you," Penelope said with the air of an expert.

"You look ready to face anything." Giving her a hug, Jennifer smiled joyfully. "Be happy, Winnie. I love you."

"I love you all, too." Winifred hugged them back, until all four women were laughing and sniffling.

"Gracious!" Winifred said, reaching for her handkerchief. "One would think Mrs. Black had lost today, the way everyone is carrying on."

Jennifer blew her nose loudly, startling everyone into laughter. Winifred dabbed at her eyes, then stepped gracefully down the stairs. Halfway down, she stopped abruptly. Roses, golden yellow roses, were everywhere. Vases of them lined the staircase, baskets stood at the door, and bouquets filled the tables. The room was filled with luscious, wonderfully smelling blossoms.

And at the foot of the stairs, dressed in an elegant suit, was Charles. Winifred clasped the handrail in astonishment.

"Charles! I was coming to see you. Whatever are you doing here?"

The rustle of gowns sounded upstairs again, followed by a suspicious giggle. Winifred looked around just in time to see the door slam. When she turned back, Charles was still waiting for her at the bottom of the staircase, his hand outstretched. Winifred descended in confusion, her heart pounding. Then he took her hand and sank down on one knee before her.

"Winnie, I came here today to formally ask you to marry me."

An understanding finally penetrated. All of the emotions she had been holding back bubbled up inside her, along with an incredible joy. He meant it—he was here, and this was real. Then Winifred, cool, logical Winifred, burst into tears and flung herself into his arms.

"Charles! Do you really think it will work? I was coming to see you, to tell you the same thing . . ." She fumbled for her handkerchief, remembering belatedly that she had given it to Jennifer. Charles handed her his own, and she laughed, crying at the same time.

"Winnie, my sweet girl—"

"I realized a lot of things today, Charles," Winifred said when she could speak. "It was wonderful to win, to see Mrs. Black freed. But I need you as much as I need the law. Charles, do you really think you could be content living with me, knowing what I need to do? I want so desperately to make you happy, I just don't know—"

Charles laughed softly and placed a finger on her lips caressing her.

"Winifred, dear, you do not have to make my argument for me. You see, not only am I certain you will make me happy, I intend to do the same for you. As your husband and as a prosecutor for the State of New York, I will find a way for you to practice law. I just received a letter from an associate in Wisconsin, who is sponsoring an amendment to the state statute that will admit women to the bar. I plan to do the same thing here. As you so clearly demonstrated in the courtroom today, the country needs your talent. I need it. And until you get your license, I can think of no better assistant to work with me. I would be honored to have your help. What I am offering you is a partnership, in the fullest sense of the word. Will you accept?"

"Oh, Charles! Yes, of course, I will."

A cheer rose upstairs as he handed her a black velvet box. Her hand was shaking as she opened it and found a beautiful diamond band sparkling inside. Withdrawing the ring from its soft depths, Charles turned back to Winifred and slipped it on her finger. Smoothing the tears from her face, he kissed her gently. Lifting her face, he gazed into her eyes, heedless of the audience upstairs.

"Do you mean it, Winnie?" Charles asked urgently. "Can you make this kind of commitment to me? I promise we will work something out so you can practice. If my amendment does not pass here, we can always move west."

"I know you will," Winifred said, smiling through her tears. "Oh, Charles, I will try very hard to be a good wife, to make you happy. I promise not to use the press again, to make a mockery of the court—"

Charles groaned. "Please, Winnie. Do not make promises you cannot keep. I do not want you to change anything about yourself, dear. As I told you before, your passion for the law is sorely needed. Yes, some of your tactics need fine-tuning, but as your husband, I do not imagine you would object to some of my help in that area."

"No! Not at all," Winifred declared. "But Charles, are you sure—"

"I can honestly say I have never been as certain of anything in my life. I never wanted anything except what I have here. I love you, Winifred. We belong together. We always have."

Winifred smiled, tears in her eyes. "I love you, too, Charles. Now and always. And if you are truly certain, I would be proud to be called your wife."

Charles kissed her, amid applause from the well-wishers upstairs. The maddening Winifred Appleton was his. Nothing, he was certain, would ever be the same. She would torment him, make exquisite love to him, and practice the law with him, and they would raise their children together. Somehow they would make it all work. Of that he was certain.

MRS. BLACK LEFT the courtroom amid a crowd of well-wishers. Returning home, she let herself into the house, then softly walked up the steps to her room.

She was free. The fear and torment had left her soul, and she closed her eyes in gratitude. Her hands shook when she thought of how narrowly she had escaped imprisonment. If it were not for one remarkable woman, she would be seeing those bars close even now.

Now her life would have to start over. She would have to leave this place, maybe move out west. A dance hall girl could make good money there, she'd heard. Maybe she would work a few years, save her coins, find a little place that she could call her own, and live out her days in peace. . . .

When she opened the door to her room, Bridget was waiting for her. The maid jumped up, as if she had been dozing, then rushed into her arms.

"Oh, miss, I am so glad you are free! I was so worried about you."

"I know, Briddie," Monica soothed her. "Thank you for your help in court. I know that must have been hard. But why are you waiting for me? Is something wrong?"

"No." Bridget wiped the tears from her eyes. "I just . . . There was something I had to give you before you go." Reaching beneath the bed, the maid pulled out a duffel bag and handed it to her mistress. "I kept this hidden in the attic, inside the old trunk. I figured they'd never look there, and they never did. I am so glad you were set free, that justice was done!"

Monica Black peered into the dark interior of the bag. Deep inside was the tea tin.

ABOUT THE AUTHOR

KATIE ROSE is thrilled to be a part of Bantam's FanFare program. Her first book, *A Hint of Mischief*, won Colorado Romance Writer's Award of Excellence, and *RomCom*'s Reviewer's Choice Award. Her newest release, *A Case for Romance*, was called "A delightful love story that successfully blends mystery, humor, and a steamy romance into a western style adventure!" by *Publishers Weekly*, and was a Romantic Times Top Pick for March, 1999. A lifetime resident of New Jersey, Katie lives with her daughter in Marlton and spends her time horseback riding and researching American history. Katie has a degree in journalism from Temple University, and has been published in newspaper, book, and magazine form. Katie's web site is located at www.tlt.com/authors/krose.htm. She loves to hear from readers.

Don't miss any of these breathtaking
Historical Romances by

Elizabeth Elliott

Betrothed ___57566-X $5.50/$7.50 Can.

"An exciting Wnd for romance readers everywhere!"
—Amanda Quick, *New York Times* bestselling author

Scoundrel ___56911-2 $5.99/$8.99 Can.

"Sparkling, fast-paced...Elliott has crafted an exciting
story Wlled with dramatic tension and sexual Wre-
works."
—*Publishers Weekly*

The Warlord ___56910-4 $5.99/$7.99 Can.

"Elizabeth Elliott...weaves a wondrous
love story guaranteed to please."
—*Romantic Times*

From one of romance's brightest new talents comes five breathtaking medieval epics of danger, temptation, and forbidden desire

JULIANA GARNETT

*T*HE QUEST

___56861-2 $5.50/$6.99 Canada

*T*HE MAGIC

___56826-0 $5.99/$7.99

*T*HE VOW

___57626-7 $5.99/$7.99

*T*HE SCOTSMAN

___57627-5 $5.99/$7.99

*T*HE BARON

___57628-3 $5.99/$8.99